She Took My Arm

As If She Loved Me

Herbert Gold

St. Martin's Griffin ☙ New York

THOMAS DUNNE BOOKS
An imprint of St. Martin's Press

Library of Congress Cataloging-in-Publication Data

Gold, Herbert,
     She took my arm as if she loved me / Herbert Gold.
          p. cm.
     "A Thomas Dunne book."
     ISBN 0-312-19525-7
     I. Title.
PS3557.034S48   1997
813'.54—dc21   96-53663
                                                                 CIP

First St. Martin's Griffin Edition: November 1998

10 9 8 7 6 5 4 3 2 1

For Nina, Ari, and Ethan—

on your own voyages now

She Took My Arm
As If She
Loved Me

Part One

Chapter 1

I stood on the wooden plank in front of Poorman's Cottage on Potrero Hill and stared at the raccoon that had knocked over my garbage can. Probably it was a daddy, like me, and standing up for its rights against this recent arrival with a coffee mug in one hand and a piece of paper in the other.

Alfonso had just demanded that I meet him at once. I was going to take the time to brush my teeth and stare down the raccoon and then I'd be on my way. I didn't have to jump because Alfonso said jump.

There had been a complaint. My friend Alfonso, police detective, sometimes covered for me, but in this case he was trying to get me to cover for myself. I might have to deal with it despite my inclination to wait for it to go away, like the swelling and scuff marks on the knuckles of my right hand, and continue spending my morning hours blinking in the sun and studying the rampaging Potrero Hill raccoon clans.

"You got to stop solving your problems by making bigger ones—" Alfonso told me by phone.

"Why?" I asked.

"—and here's where I want to see you."

"Why there?" I asked, but he had already hung up. Probably this was a duty shift for Alfonso and he was squeezing me in.

Alfonso liked to show me things, get me out of myself. Not being enough out of myself was the reason I had these hurt knuckles, this swollen hand, which was not sore enough to keep me from driving down to Ellis Street in the Tenderloin. I thought I had a picture in my head of Smiling Janey's Medal of Honor Tavern, but driving slowly up the street I couldn't find it. Then I remembered it was on Eddy, not Ellis, which meant I wasn't thinking at top form. I cruised like that, the street noticed, the transvestites yelled, the kids at the corner whispered and peeked. I stopped for a drunk in a motorized wheelchair; no legs below the knees and all caution to the winds. "Smoke? Smoke?" demanded a black seventeen-year-old running alongside my Honda; he then tried to make the sale more nicely, showing large square teeth that strangely reminded me of Priscilla's as he drawled, "Smo-oke, brother?"

Everyone's got aches in this life. My hand and heart would be eased by a purchase from the saleslad, but I was at a different place on the analgesia chain. I parked and hoped the dope dealers would keep the break-in folks away from my car.

In front of Smiling Janey's Medal of Honor Tavern a haggard giant with a tentlike dress and matching plugs of wax in her ears said, "I'm an old RN with five degrees, you got to treat me with respect."

"I do, I do," I said, edging past her, not wanting to keep Alfonso waiting while I discussed self-esteem with this person.

"Just because I used to be a man but now I'm a certified, registered woman is no reason to dis a person. My driver's license says female. All my new records. I'm a female woman."

"Right, right, right," I said.

"So fuck my birth certificate, hey?" she asked. "I'm an unfairly terminated RN with five degrees, so can't you spare a little time to hear how it happened?"

"Can't do that," I said. "Busy." But the person stood squarely in the doorway. I hoped to avoid shoving.

"Gave the kiss of life to save many a soul . . . no matter what sex it happened to be, even brown or black, the kiss of life is one of the low-tech ways we still have to use if we take the Sacred Oath of Florence Nightingale, so let me tell you one thing, mister—"

"Out of here," I muttered.

The voice kept after me. "You may get tireder, older, and uglier, but make sure you guard your precious memories and, above all, your precious eyebrows—"

Further explanation surely would have come, had I waited for it.

Smiling Janey's was an old-fashioned gay bar that did not invite peering in from the street. There may have been tavern windows at another stage of its gender journey. In their place were redwood shingles, so that Smiling Janey's Medal of Honor resembled a woodsy cottage outpost here among the junkies, transvestites, Tenderloin cowboy ramblers, and General Assistance mumblers; among patrolling squads of Guardian Angels in their maroon berets and carrying their walkie-talkies; among the corner boys working their all-day, all-night hustle shifts; among the unarmed response teenage hookers who were careful to keep AIDS at bay with regular injections of crank or inhalations of crack; among the sifting of small, harried, busy East Asian immigrants between the unbusy, floating, abandoned souls of the 'Loin. Mutant kids off the Greyhound looked over the territory, saw it was different from San Antonio, found it to their liking. Somehow laundries, video rental shops, and palm readers made the rent. Next door to Smiling Janey's a gypsy who knew the future and the past had lettered on a box that stood at her doorway:

THE ONE WHO PISSES HERE
AGAIN, ON HIM I WILL PUT A
VERY BAD MALEDICTION

A sexist assumption; reading the past and future, she believed the perpetrator was a man. Probably he did do the deed and in due course would receive a very bad malediction, deservedly so.

The retired RN was watching me decide to enter the Medal

of Honor. I had to take my medicine. The doorway was painted in glowing Cantonese headache pink, but there were no ferns or shiny-leafed plants as in a new Chinese business. I pushed through.

The bartender, who wore a row of earrings not just in the lobes but up and down the cartilage of his ears, smiled and didn't wince when he drew me a beer. I winced because the rings in the bartender's pierced nipples were catching in his T-shirt. The T-shirt said SMILING JANEY'S MEDDLE OF HONOR.

"Medal," I said, inadvertently correcting the spelling.

"Don't I know that?" asked the bartender. "Quench up first and then Janey's out of the can—used to call the head." I lifted the draft brew, which was evidently on the house. "Ronnie's my name, like the former president," said the bartender, introducing himself. "Not that many things I got in common with that certain former president, other than hair color. Used to be Janey's, oh, ward, now I work for her. When she was in the navy, she won the Muddle d'Honneur, you heard that? Ask her to show it to you. There's a photograph, she got it laminated, she'll show it to you if she kind of likes you. Standing in front of Harry Truman, he was a previous president, too, a little fellow, you can see him pinning it on her. Janey was a beautiful guy before she became this terrific person. 'Nother splash?"

I shook my head. "Waiting for someone."

"Alfonso? The dick?"

Like a good bartender, he tended to sympathetic understanding.

"That explains it—you like African chubbies, am I right?" But he didn't pry. He spread his arms, announcing, "And I give you . . . *Janey!*"

She made her entrance out of the back room. She was indeed smiling, a six-foot-tall woman, careless of her weight problem, in fifties housewife dress. Janey had not been in the can; she had been watching for an audience to gather. She swayed, she sashayed, but not on her own feet. The bartender, Ronnie, had put quarters in the Wurlitzer and mariachi music squealed. The feet on which Janey sashayed were a pony's. It was a dancing pony, and Janey's feet almost touched the floor.

The pony seemed to wear a beard, a little fringe around the muzzle. I didn't know ponies grew these, even an exceptional Tenderloin pony. It pranced and its tiny hooves clicked to the mariachi sounds. The fringe of beard made the pony look a little like a nineteenth-century president, perhaps from south of the border. The music brought that thought to mind.

As a Medal of Honor winner, World War II or maybe the Korean War, and probably the only woman in the Tenderloin with this credential, or at least the only woman who was formerly a man and presently a naval cavalry heroine, Janey loomed closer on her steed with plump assurance, shedding strong smells of lilac and soap. She leaned down upon me. She had a right to smile. "How about that Alfonso?" she asked.

The pony reared its bearded head. Alfonso, also overweight, was lumbering through the door but not moving smoothly as usual, just concentrating on moving fast. "Son of a bitch!" he said.

The bartender with the rows of earrings said, "Don't believe I know how to pour that one, but I can do you a Brandy Alexander, big boy."

"Stopped by a goddamn fire," Alfonso said. "Couldn't get through the street, had to dump my vehicle and walk—shit, man, you are a burden."

Janey reined up and away. She was clip-clopping back through the door into her office.

"You can't do like that, Dan, I can't let you do like that. Shit, man, that a horse under her? From her garden back there?"

Maybe pony stables weren't legal in the middle of the city anymore.

Alfonso's eyes were red-rimmed and enraged. He didn't

have emphysema, yet he was wheezing. Compressed rage is worse than a lifelong cigar habit.

"Asshole! You think I'm going to let you do like this?"

What came out of my mouth wasn't what I meant to say. "You don't have a son!"

"Hey, I'd like to meet her," the bartender said. "I bet she's adorable." He was picked up by the early-afternoon action. Normally he wiped the bar, stood there sweating in his nylon panties, waiting for something to do, an occasional mixed drink to compose, a little gossip. Now the gossip was happening right before his eyes. When he said *her*, he meant Jeff, my son.

Alfonso kept his squeezed, red-rimmed eyes fixed on me. "I got a boy in Newark ain't seen in six years," he said. "No need to tell you why, no need to 'splain. I know when it hurts. But you're not going on like this, pal, without you get yourself up on charges. Criminal you might like, but civil? And your license?"

"He made a complaint?"

"I'm not going to let you do like this, hear me?"

I thought I heard Janey in the back room, punching a telephone and murmuring in a low angry alto, singing to a beer distributor or a feed store a barkeeper's song of missed deliveries.

"So you might ask," Alfonso said, "then what are we going to do, since you can't go beating up on the public no more?"

"He isn't the public."

"Far as I'm concerned, he's a citizen. You got a sore hand there, pal. Come on now, a little hike to your vehicle, man, let's go."

I followed him out into the flat white midday Tenderloin sunlight. Anger was still turbulent in him, the flesh heaving and sweating under the shabby plainclothes suit he wore on duty, and he didn't want to yell at me indoors. He couldn't even punch me up a little because he was my closest friend, whatever I was to him; and although I could tell it would be a pleasure for him to apply a touch of legitimate and necessary police brutality in order to emphasize his points, somehow it wouldn't be right. "You got to stop waltzing around with Karim—make up your mind, man. You got to learn that cute Xavier ain't your real problem and lay off. About your lady there, all I need to say is, get a life."

"What a help, buddy."

"Shit." He was softening a little and he hated that tendency of his character. "Look, I ain't perfect either. About my kid in Newark or Trenton, not even sure anymore where she took him. I'd prefer to be a better daddy. You got a chance to do so with your own kid."

"Thanks." We watched the former RN pissing on the gypsy's antipissing sign. Evidently she wasn't superstitious.

"What I'm saying," Alfonso said, "is straighten up, is that clear?"

"Couldn't hardly be more so."

"Don't fuck with me. Don't fuck with yourself more than normal. Don't show me that no-sleep old dogface no more—do it, will you, man?" Then, as if the question just happened to occur to him, Alfonso suddenly grinned and asked, "Hey, what made you think you'd get away with a dumbshit performance like that one?"

"Didn't think about it. Just decided."

"Why?"

"I gave you the reason—wasn't thinking. Anyway, one punch—felt good."

Alfonso sighed and, with his softest caramel rumbling voice, said, "Nice satisfying sore hand, and that'd be the end of it. Thought you'd get away with it?"

"Might."

One more time: "What made you think . . . Okay, I know now. Wasn't thinking. It was the limbic system."

"Pardon?"

Alfonso worked his heavy shoulders. "Now's not the time to educate you, pal—"

"I so stipulate, Alfons."

"But if you listen carefully for a change, you know I'm saying 'pal' and you not my pal just now. You a dumbshit asshole put himself in trouble and don't know how to get himself out of trouble he put himself in." Thought, seemed to be humming to himself, rumbled. "Not properly you don't."

I would stipulate to that, too.

"You in trouble now and heading for worser trouble."

He went into his cornerboy talk to let me know he was less my friend than a cop who smelled a perp in the making.

From a boarded-up storefront that hadn't been occupied for years—a sign said STARSHINE KARMA, so it must have been a late flower-child vegetarian restaurant or giveaway center—came the same three notes of an amplified chord, shaking the timbers nailed across the broken glass. A growth of outdoor lint, cobwebs, and city dirt that had taken hold on the two-by-fours vibrated with the sound from within. A band was rehearsing. They stopped, they started; the same three notes of a strung-out C-major chord. The musicians were apparently adjusting the dials to louder, in case they made a mistake, and then even louder, scaring away the street person trying to take a relaxing pee in the doorway—he scurried off, dropping droplets on his knees, addled by years of heavily sugared Thunderbird plus three amplified notes of a C-major chord. Another victory for gypsy-lady clairvoyance.

The arts were thriving again in the Tenderloin. Alfonso was singing something under his breath and I said, "Huh?" Since I asked, Alfonso sang in the key of C major: "Teenage tragedy, lotsa kids are dead . . . It's about getting stalled on a railway track in daddy's car. Like you stalled, asshole."

A friend could be mean sometimes. Meant he thought I was stupid sometimes.

"I guess when you see them in the clubs they thrash around, wear them geek leathers, studs, swastikas, cut-out crotches, everybody's stoned on uppers and Ecstasy combined . . . You know these nonmusicians, pal? In our day at least they looked good and you wanted to make it with the, ah, female members." He asked slowly: "Still . . . do . . . don't you?"

"Got to deal with priority now. Plus goddamn you, Alfonso."

He didn't take offense. He had experience handling inefficient behavior, his own and others'.

"He made like a complaint, asked about a court order, that type of shit. I said I'd talk to you."

"You just did."

"I still am. Now don't go hitting your wife's boyfriend no more."

"Just one little punch now and then?"

"I *said* don't go around exaggerating. Get drunk like a man. Or is there someone here on the street might offer a touch of companionship?" He pursed his lips and surveyed the terrain. "No more spirit of adventure in your present state of mind, seems like?"

I was tuckered out, fit for nothing but swatting mosquitoes and pretty people and repeating my regrets to myself with the usual result in close concentration on the sounds of three A.M. on Potrero Hill. Now that mouthy person who had spent most of her life as a male and was beginning the adventure into her inner lady, with the aid of hormones, depilatory creams, Clairol, makeup, and one heck of a lot of optimism had swept up again and was listening to us. I caught her shaking her head and saying, "Some folks. I'm an RN, yet they hes-i-tate."

Alfonso didn't mind my secrets getting told, plus a transsexual perspective on judgment. We're together in the world, see, and it may be unpleasant, but acts have consequences. Alfonso lived by that. I was a slow learner despite his efforts to educate me.

"Give it up," Alfonso was saying. "Did you hear me? Give her up."

"You don't know."

Alfonso stood curbside at my vehicle. "Already told you maybe I don't know. I got a boy someplace too. I had a lady I liked. A lunge just get you in deeper shit."

Alfonso helped me find police records, histories, little details a man in my career needed, but our friendship wasn't built on that. I had similar help from the DMV, the Social Security Administration, a supervisor at the IRS; we thought of each other as clients, small business part-timers. I remembered them at Christmas and they remembered me all the year round when I was curious about a few details concerning someone's goings and comings in the world. But record keepers didn't necessarily become friends like Alfonso.

"Let's get moving," he said. "You ready now?"

"I guess."

The lengthened skin of a road-killed rat lay stretched in the gutter, just ahead of the plumper corpse of a cat with bits of fur looking like trampled slush. "Must have been a truck took them both out at once," Alfonso said. "Died doing what they suppose to do—rat running, cat after him."

"What makes you think it's a him?" I asked.

"Don't plan to look any closer, my man. Hey, you notice Janey's horse—"

"Pony."

"—was a boy or a girl?"

Chapter 2

I protect. People may say I go around losing my temper, but in general I do not, and I'll break the knees of anyone I catch saying it. I watch out for wives, kids, offshore accounts; folks bring me in to save their goods. I don't do hubcaps.

Heart and clients bedeviled by loss and regret is where I intervene.

At present I don't know what's going to happen to me or anyone. Dan Kasdan doesn't tell fortunes. Dan Kasdan preserves them.

And how I love my wife and kid.

Close-cropped salt-and-pepper hair, pink cheekbones, tired pink-and-yellow eyes—these things make me look like a healthy, aging philosophy professor from a pretty good university; or maybe, if only I knew how to dress, like the vice president of a socially aware insurance company based in San Francisco. The look is not too far off. I'm a private investigator in the Bay Area, which includes Berkeley, Oakland, parts of Marin, even as far south as San Jose if you're willing to pay travel time. I use Murine, but it doesn't help the pink, and I forget to take my doc's advice to wash the eyelids with baby shampoo, scrubbing with Q-tips, because, oh, conjunctivitis isn't all that bad. And I hate to stare at my face in the mirror, which you have to do in that Q-tip deal or else you're going to jab a place that shouldn't be jabbed. It's tender in there.

With women, their business with mascara and Q-tips,

they know how. I don't. I have sad eyes because I still love, am in love with, my former wife. This is an appetite that does not nourish.

Divorce carried all sorts of unexpected problems into my life. For example, I knew all about the famous San Francisco house fleas, but the mosquitoes surprised me. I left a couple of beer cans outside. The drought ended, it rained and rained, it dripped some more, which gave meteorology an idea—the clouds opened up, rainwater slopping into the beer cans left outside Poorman's Cottage on Potrero Hill. I doubt if there was much remaining flavor to the beer, but then the sun came back and—what do you know?—in those beer cans, unbeknownst to their proprietor, swam squiggles of anxious life, invisible mosquito larvae. And then what do you further know? The anxious squiggles ripened into humming, buzzing nocturnal biters. And just when I had finally accepted the high-pitched, nearly inaudible fleas, which after all can be controlled by regular vacuuming (Hispanic old lady, silent but mechanically adept except for changing the dust bag).

No fun to be bereft and hurt in the soul, plus itching lumps on the knuckles that clutch the sheet over the head in desperation insomnia.

To manage the mosquitoes I had to empty the yard of beer cans so that future mosquito generations would have no place to brood and breed, swim and prosper, before taking off on their whining nighttime missions around my ears and knuckles. Otherwise my cottage on Potrero Hill might turn into New Jersey, the Garden State, where I had recently pursued a father to remind him of his responsibilities concerning child support. (I told him I had friends whose names ended in vowels and we would always know where he slept. He told me to buzz off, like a mosquito. But then he thought seriously about the trouble I was taking with him, noticed the broken capillaries in my eyes, and wrote a check that cleared.)

"I come better with my chocolate bunny when I don't

have to pay for the kids I left behind," said the depressed deadbeat.

"Whyncha learn to come without you need foreplay involving the cash flow or afterthoughts?" suggested Dan Kasdan.

"Say what?"

"You said chocolate bunny," I said. I wanted to put him at his ease by letting him know I listened. "That's cute."

He seemed to recognize me not only as a person with close personal ties with the driver's license bureau and Social Security Administration, so I could always track him down, but also as a fellow sufferer, a kindred spirit, a human being. "I need money," he said. "My chocolate bunny craves security. You and me, if we're not good-looking, we got to offer the ladies something."

"Try getting rich and famous," I suggested. "How about tall and handsome?"

He considered those possibilities, decided it was too much trouble and he wasn't cut out to be a star, all that public exposure, *People* magazine, the adulation of the multitudes—not for him. "My chocolate bunny likes presents," he said.

"Your chocolate bunny?" When people keep repeating something, I've learned they want to be taken up on it. "So she's a black girl."

The deadbeat beamed triumphantly, as if I weren't cut out to understand anything important, never would, only getting my way in business with reddened eyes and threats of violence. "It's a cute saying between us," he explained. "I met her on Easter at the parade, she was wearing like a bonnet, have you heard of romance, Mr. Kasdan?"

"I'm more into tangible when I'm on the job."

"Nothing more tangible than Linda, let me tell you."

I just stared. I don't mind sarcasm or correction from the mark, so long as the check clears for the client and myself, and the future checks keep coming. "I'm a frequent flier," I said. "You and your chocolate bunny don't work out an arrangement brings pleasure into your lives without taking essentials out of the mouths of your kiddies, I'll definitely be back. I like Jersey, the parkways. Trenton's a beautiful town. I enjoy my trade."

The deadbeat father thought I'd be a little Jew with felt pens staining the pocket and a plan to graduate from private eye to CPA. Instead he saw a skinny fellow with grayish hair, pink eyelids, and a sad way of saying, "Pay up or you're a fugitive gets his hand caught in a car door. His knees. His neck. The worst kind, mister. And as a divorced dad myself, I have no sympathy."

The deadbeat sighed. Obviously I didn't understand anything about the importance of Easter. "She should've married one of your kind. They love their kids. I guess it's because of all the persecution they brought on their own heads due to nagging, nagging, nagging."

"Sorry if I repeat myself, asshole. But you're a little slow. Pretend you're a loving dad."

Out of his stingy emotions he broke his deadbeat wind, yesterday's farts saved for my arrival. The deadbeat gave up.

This was the Resurrection and the Life. "From now on I'm Mosaic," he said.

I looked at him and he looked at me. His expression was one I knew from other deadbeat husband/fathers. *You a pimp for my ex and I can't even say it?* Yup, that's what I was, pimping food, schoolbooks, and doctor bills out of this nice person who just wanted to live in peace with the world and his chocolate bunny, plus not pay his dues. That's how it was.

While he was staring at me, trying to kill me as best he could while unable to do so, I passed the time by not humming or cleaning my fingernails or consulting my travel itinerary. It was time to go, but I wanted to make sure he would remember me. It was part of the deal, making sure the client wouldn't need to send me back to Jersey. So I looked at him as if he were an invisible clot of bugs in the air. I could sit on him in a chair and not even notice, just scratching my butt a little.

The deadbeat seemed a little slow. I could either rev myself up by admiring his general insufficiency as a human dad being or pretend I was revved up, which would save time and spare me from tapping into my reserve stock of adrenaline. I wiggled my fingers into and out of a fist. Needed to be limber in case he surprised me. I didn't want to get totally dreamy and out of focus, and I didn't want to miss my flight, and I guess I was losing patience in general, another fault that comes with the irritations of age.

"Hey?" I inquired.

He raised his left eyebrow. I don't put up with that kind of elegance in a stupid deadbeat dad, so then both his eyebrows suddenly shot up in a much more satisfying kind of surprised inquiry as I grabbed him by the collar, taking fistfuls of cloth and neck, and lifted him forward so I could conveniently yell into his nose: "Far-staysh, Mr. Asshole? Far-staysh?" Suddenly I was transformed into a crazy individual shouting something that made no sense to him.

"Hey, watch it, watch it, don't, I'm sorry." He was mumbling and white faced.

"Far-staysh means do you fucking understand?"

"I do." It was like a wedding. "Hey, let go." He wriggled, he struggled. For some reason I seemed to have lifted him slightly off the floor, a trick of deadbeat levitation. "Hey, come on, please."

"Do you plan to write a check for your wife and kid—" I released his collar and wiped my hands on my pants. I hate getting deadbeat slobber on my hands. "Okay, calm down. Write the check right now, while we're both thinking about it, okay?"

"Okay, okay, watch it, Mr. Kasdan."

"I know you're a man of honor, so I won't ask for certified paper, but somehow I just know you're gonna have the check covered by the time I hand it over to your wife. Am I right in that? I trust you, asshole. 'Cause you just know in your heart of hearts it's the decent thing to do and if the check bounces I'll be back." I grabbed him again. "So you say you far-staysh." Grabbed him tightly.

"Far . . ." (Strangled.) ". . . staysh."

"Now write. I'll just run a little clean water on my hands while I'm waiting."

I wash my hands before peeing, because it's a precious object I'm about to handle, a sacramental gift of God, and also after grabbing a deadbeat's neck, because it's a dirty, dirty thing at best. Also helps to cool down.

"Thanks for your consideration, asshole."

He was fingering the red blotches on his neck, which looked a little like monkeybites from his chocolate bunny. I wondered how he would explain them to her. He caught me looking at him. What else should I do? He pulled a check and started writing.

"Hey, asshole?"

"What?"

"I said thanks, so say you're welcome. You hardly know me and already I'm helping you take care of your kid back in San Francisco."

He wrote. I pocketed.

"Mr. Kasdan, you didn't need to do that."

I shrugged and turned out my palms in my Jewishest way. "Maybe not, but in my business a person has to make judgment calls. Time is money and none of us is getting rich off this. You were a case of judgment call, so what can we do?"

"You could have . . ." It trailed off.

"But I'm sorry if I called you a deadbeat, and for that I apologize, asshole." I sincerely wanted him to remember me.

I flew home to San Francisco and said to the client: "You married him, but I'm also wed to him now. He accepted my offer not to have him hurt."

"How much do I owe you, Mr. Kasdan?"

There's the airfare, the Budget rent-a-car, the Motel 6. There's the per diem.

"Mr. Kasdan?"

I was thinking of Priscilla and Jeff; my wife, ex-wife, former wife, love; my son. I answered something.

Chapter 3

When a man breaks up with a ladyfriend or grows older, which seems to happen all the time—and to other folks besides me, and even, I understand, to women—it's probably best to fill the idle hours with a complete physical checkup. One of those things you do when you've got nothing to do. I definitely needed tangible in my life.

My pal Doctor Weinberg, Fred, asked me to blow hard. I blew into some kind of puffer-fish ballooning device. I did this proudly because I don't smoke. I imagined carefree scuba diving off some lovely tropical reef.

Fred frowned. "Do it again."

I concentrated and this time imagined thrashing against flinty coral, bleeding, gasping, and drowning. Fred performed snapping, putting-away motions. "Okay." He looked gloomy and depressed.

"Okay? Just okay?"

"Better'n I do."

I had to be content with doing better than my gray, overweight doctor who was born the same year as I was. It wasn't a whole lot of praise; he wasn't offering gratuitous comfort. I wasn't going to tell him about my hearing (the tintinnabulation of the bells, bells, bells) because I didn't want any useless sympathy or useful suggestions about audiologists.

He took blood. They would run the complete set on me; insurance pays for most of it. "I don't have AIDS," I told him.

He grunted. He and the lab would be the judge of that.

Now he sighed and tried to pretend it was just ordinary breathing he was undergoing. "Bend over, please."

Hey, pal. But I knew this part all too well. My pants were down at my ankles. (What if there was an earthquake and I had to run?) The snapping sound was not that patriotic one of Old Glory in the breeze; Fred was slipping on his mayonnaise-colored disposable rubber gloves.

"Oh no," I said.

"Oh yes," he said.

"It makes me seasick," I said.

I clutched the edge of the table while my innards objected to the whole interlude. His finger was reaching through my butt toward my prostate. I was wondering what he did when folks were constipated. Oh, I didn't like this; a world that allows such procedures on a totally healthy person is all askew. I lurched in sympathy with myself.

He mumbled explanations. "Smooth is okay. Rough is not so okay. The PSA test is conclusive, plus margin of error."

"I don't, uh, uh, uh, understand."

He withdrew. I felt better. Some sort of lubricant was tickling my butt. Next hour, the same finger up a different patient.

"Feels just fine," he said. "Slightly enlarged is normal. How many times you pee at night?"

"I drink lots of water."

"How many times?"

"I drink coffee, too."

"How many times?"

This guy, my pal, my doc, was uncivilized. He demanded the truth. "Well, one time. But then maybe a couple hours later, another time, And if I sleep seven–eight hours, just before my last dawn nap, oh—"

"Yes?"

"Not usually."

"Sometimes?"

"One more time."

He was writing. I was repeating myself about drinking one hell of a lot of water and coffee, or soda, beer, other liquids, or diuretic substances, maybe spices in my Mexican food, terrific digestion, eat out almost every night, always thirsty . . . tried the lite beers but don't really prefer them . . .

"Any diabetes in your family?" he asked.

"None! Never! Not!"

So I seemed to be getting away without telling him about my hearing loss, probably from an old war wound, too much rock and roll during my ten-year-long summer of love, and my occasional narcolepsy, falling asleep almost without warning when I was depressed, sometimes taking two naps a day—that isn't narcolepsy, it's escapism—and my lack of joy in my love arrangements; and then my wife, my former wife. Some things are none of a person's doctor-and-friend's goddamn business.

He was looking me straight in the eyes. "Have any problems with anhedonia?"

The question exasperated me. "Some people say 'prostrate.' I get it right. I leave out the *r*. But what the fuck is anhedonia?"

"Inability," he began gloomily, sighing, "or difficulty . . . in feeling pleasure."

"I come okay."

"I mean pleasure in general. The deliciousness of the morning chill, the smile of a baby next door, the smell of the dew on the flower . . ."

"So why didn't you say? Yeah, sometimes I wonder if it's all worthwhile. Actually, there are other things I like better, Fred. The smile of a baby next door? Where I live it's more like raccoon doo-doo on the flowers."

We sat looking at each other in silence, two men of a certain age, divorced, our children escaping into their own lives, the years inexorable. I doubted the entire world-historical import of the smell of morning dew. It was a good thing Fred stuck with medicine because his career as a lyric poet would have been a nonstarter. But I felt certain he too knew what it was like to have history buzzing in his ears, keeping him awake, giving him a bat's nighttime alertness, along with sudden hibernations during the day. Our distant cousins, the bears and bats; my immediate neighbors, the raccoons, fleas, and feral kids from the Projects.

"Old days, when I started out, we used to try thyroid or speed with vitamins, that turned out to be not so good an idea, or advice, the talking cure . . ."

"Yeah."

"Now I say: Enjoy your naps. That's not narcolepsy."

"And enjoy my anhedonia?"

He walked me to the door and made one of those growling Japanesey sighs. "How about a movie and the Early Bird dinner?" he asked. "You name the night, I got nothing on, either."

We'd have to sit halfway down the aisle at the movies. He was farsighted, liked the rear, but I needed all the help I could get to pick up the sound track. A lot of healthy young folks prefer to sit forward, folks who can sort it all out in their heads, process the music when a Korean cutie is saying "Cling?" but means to ask "Drink?"

Getting old was a full-time occupation. I wasn't sure I still had the time for it.

Chapter 4

"Cling?"

High-energy Susie in her black tights and micro-mini, dictator of Korean pots and barbecue, supreme regulator of fermented cabbage for the masses, bounced impatiently on her toes and shouted her question over the counter of Hann's Hibachi, *cling! cling! cling!* tolling at me on Polk Street in San Francisco like a happy, high-pitched bell while I realized I was still growing older.

"Cling?"

I didn't understand her. I didn't speak Korean, but she looked as if I were supposed to. "Cling! Cling! Cling!"

"Pardon?" I asked, feeling desperate, wanting my garlicked shrimp, rice, tofu, and kimchee, wanting to be in tune with the world's doings.

She too was desperate. She tossed her head back and called out, gargling, "Glug-glug-glug," and then I knew she had been asking me "Drink?"

"Tea," I said.

And so over my late-afternoon seafood snack, including shrimp and mixed fish, mostly shrimp and oily sprouts, I faced the fact that my hearing was less acute than it used to be; also my brain processed information at a slower pace; and I didn't finish my plate, either.

The program for today was fuller than usual. This morning I had watched Jeff play indoor field hockey, along with the mothers and a few distracted fathers—he darted like a fish, which should have made me feel good and sort of did. Now I was scheduled for Korean barbecue and a visit with Alfonso; then a serious scrub of teeth with the toothbrush I kept in my pocket (bachelor hygiene); then a visit with Carol.

Alfonso had said not to hold my order for him. He had stupid paperwork down at the station house and you know how the stupid paperwork goes. I was temporarily alone with fermented pickled cabbage and faulty ears, waiting for my friend who was also my police-force resource, personal assault and battery counselor, and fellow bachelor. We didn't play on a level playing field. I was older, less wise, and more discouraged, but he carried the extra weight around his ass and middle.

"For I am the voice of your conscience," Alfonso was saying, slopping into his chair and reaching for a shrimp from my plate. I hadn't seen or heard him coming, though I would no longer say my buddy moved like a cat.

I greeted him with characteristic enthusiasm: "You're getting fat, Alfons."

"A healthy conscience knows no limitations to size."

"Now you've got some kind of barbecue sauce on your face."

He swiped fastidiously across his mouth with his wrist and then transferred the gunk to a paper napkin. "But a good conscience does keep clear, agendawise," he said. "You sleeping any better?"

"Lots."

"But better?"

I shrugged. I was a partisan of grief and complaint but hadn't determined when I crossed the border into maudlin and fanatic. I preferred not to be denounced by my old pal.

I tried a defensive action. "I been seeing this Carol," I said.

He breathed heavily through his nose. He was struggling and failing to pick up a piece of my leftover tofu with his fingers. It kept mooshing apart, falling to the plate. I handed him a fork; he didn't say thanks. "Lonely nights, cheap grass, and lots of self-pity—hey, you got it made."

"I don't need you to tell me this."

He was licking his fingers. He was signaling to Susie for a cling of beer. He said to me, "It's gratuitous. It's a gift, pal, no extra charge. You're my early-warning system, so it's only right I offer you something in return. Someday maybe me, too, I'll gonna be old, skinny, and sorry for myself. And white." He was grinning and oozing his caramel good nature at me. "Fat chance."

"This Carol, you'd like her—"

"Good. Good. Stick up for yourself, my man. But I bet she ain't got any meat on her, right? Not anorexic, just a workout lady, right? I'll bet she's a natural-foods, sushi, ethnic-folk-health-munchies person, am I right there? Purple sweats? Runs every morning? Am I right?"

"Wrong," I said. "Only part right."

He gazed with longing eyes at my plate. There was a little rice left, one shrimp, a mound of Alfonso-fingered and abandoned tofu, that great spicy kimchee, which meant I had to do a lot of tooth brushing before I went to meet Carol. On a chlorophyll or Binaca scale my breath would still be at the low end of acceptability in contemporary San Francisco. "Didn't leave much for me, did you?" Alfonso asked. "And it's too early to buy dinner, so I'll just finish what you left. So you can tell me about this Carol."

I wished I could brag a little. "Nothing much to tell," I said.

"She know that song? I bet she don't—'Stick out you can, here come de garbage man'?"

"Never thought to ask her."

"Don't pay no mind to the essentials, brother?" He peered into my face. "I notice you're still not having such a good time." He tugged at his tight nap and then looked at his fingers. The hair didn't come off. "Well, I don't know. You got a friend. You ought to get your respeck back—"

"That's not what I'm missing."

"Whatever."

The friend I had was Alfonso and he knew that. We both knew a good pal wasn't enough.

"Uh, what I gotta say. Been seeing Karim?" Alfonso asked.

"Not really."

"Not really? Sort of? Negotiating?"

"Shit, he calls. He's got ideas for me. Priscilla thinks I'm slacking off, got to accept my responsibilities."

"What gives her that idea?" Alfonso inquired. "But Karim ain't the way to go."

"Maybe one good score would make people happy."

"Don't. I said *don't*. The reason you even thinking about a score is not a good reason to be thinking about it. Okay? And been beating up any lovers since last we discussed?"

"No," I said carefully. "Not Xavier." Just the thought of him gave me a stomachache, for which the thought of punching him out was a temporary remedy.

"Don't that either," said Alfonso. "Don't Karim, don't the loverboy. Don't get yourself arrested for assault, don't get your license suspended, don't go to jail."

So what to do? I sighed, he sighed.

"Hey, not so bad, have a good time," Alfonso said. "You got kimchee on your breath, but maybe she likes . . . Carol? . . . the stink of pepper, cabbage, and garlic on a fella, if that's what it is. I don't know about this shit you eat, man."

He waved goodbye through the window as I glanced at him from the sidewalk. I was on my way. He was calling to Susie and ordering his own plate of something.

I was on my way to my early-evening workout with an account executive in advertising who had a dinner meeting coming up but could use some exercise first. Carol enjoyed a recreational spasm in the late afternoon, Carol and Kasdan, together or more likely separately. It crossed my mind that she was slightly more plump than I ordinarily liked, but this was not a moral flaw. Not to worry at the present time.

Worry about the opportunity Karim was offering to change my life. Worry about the choice between breaking out or giving up. No, take an hour to worry about nothing.

As Carol was dressing for her meeting, she remarked, "When you go, after your little postcoital nap, please remove my keys from your keychain and leave them on the desk. I know I can trust you to do no damage. Just pull the door shut."

"You mean it's all over?"

"For me, too," she said.

She must have read my mind. I was somewhat skinnier than she liked. But she had confidence I wouldn't tear the place up or steal anything or even take what might be considered mine, of which there was hardly a trace. She credited me with decency, like a responsible sublet; my toothbrush would go straight into the wastebasket. I would try to live up to that.

She looked clean, sweet, and a little too plump as she swept toward her dinner meeting, on time as usual. I sighed, didn't doze, departed. How could I sleep in peace when her goodbye words were "And your breath smelled like shit."

"It's the kimchee," I said. "Or maybe the garlic. Whatever."

But she was gone.

Gradually it was beginning to sink in that I was no longer a promising young man. I was a promised older guy—promised to heaven. That was the optimistic way of looking at it.

Part Two

Chapter 5

Now let's go back a few years to when I was a former philosophy instructor who had gone into the groovier trade of private investigator. (Person imagines his future teaching philosophy at Hayward State until retirement and finds a message of nausea waiting in his belly; person during beatnik overture to the Age of Aquarius notices there's more to life than he ever dreamed of, including under-the-table income; person takes an internship with Hal Lipset, pioneer of the sneaky mike hidden in a martini olive out there in the real world.) It was that time long, long ago when adult males sewed embroidered strips, or astrological symbols, or peace signs on their shirts; young women ironed their hair straight and practiced inner voyages, sticking mandala decals on their hair irons; it was so long ago, in the misty reaches of the sixties, that chalk-faced street mimes were not yet obsolete—back, back we go.

The days when I was the youngest person in the room were already gone and I pretended not to miss them. I was settling into bachelor middle age, except that I called it *early* middle age, hoping for a merry twinkle in my wise old eyes. And just about the time I began to get used to what is unavoidable, letting the sweet seasons of San Francisco wash over me, the world changed—and not only drugs, rock and roll, the Vietnam War, and Bob Dylan songs full of nasal lists and ambiguous inventories, those external delights that entertained the late sixties in the hundred-year-long operetta of San Francisco. Something abruptly disappeared—my comfortable loneliness, dailiness, beer drinking, grass smoking, hanging out with Alfonso. The years were silting up and then suddenly they were flooded away.

Comfort was taken from my grasp. I consented. It was a case of complete surrender. Alfonso looked at me and said: "The full catastrophe, you're gone now."

It had nothing to do with hormones or the solitude I had come to enjoy. Love was crackling in the sky and wings unfolded across my back; it can happen to almost anyone, even to me, even at the blandest, most unlikely occasion. Such as dinner offered by the nervy, twitchy, recently divorced Lillian to whom I found myself appointed companion. Young Priscilla was the friend of a friend, recently arrived in San Francisco, teaching kids at the Museum of Modern Art, and my sociable companion believed a sweet thing, a friend of a friend, should have something to do on a Saturday night. "Let's be helpful, shall we?" Lillian asked.

"I don't mind," I said.

Priscilla was willing to take what came along, at least this once. When she needed a ride home, I offered it, although our hostess was planning for me to spend the night, and I drove Priscilla past my flat, pointing at the dark windows. "That's where I live. Not that you'll ever need to know."

Later, she said she took this as a challenge. She would not only come to know where I lived but also would make me forget that any other woman had left traces in my middle-aged lair. On her first visit she reached into a closet and held a raincoat between her fingers like a dead rat, commanding: "Get this thing out of here."

It was a blue Pan Am Airways raincoat.

"Out!"

We were both laughing and falling all over each other.

Tall, bony, and reddish, with a careless insulation of extra flesh that would soon melt off, since it was unneeded by a fast-moving athlete; yellowish square teeth which got brightness from their intensity of use in grinning; hugely amused avid— that's *hungry*—blue eyes; a look of turbulent health for which youth was only partly to blame.

The style was not cute; I had seen enough cuteness in California. It was beauty. Her stride was long, she threw a ball long; she took a long view of things while accepting the day on its conditions, at least until she decided not to. I didn't understand her at all.

Before I could proceed to the vital business of not understanding this woman, exploring the lack of understanding, entering the mystery between us, the full catastrophe, I had to settle things with Lillian. It was embarrassing to go crazy for the guest she so kindly, tolerantly, with a sigh, felt obliged to feed one Saturday night, but I could live with embarrassment. Lillian might be the nervous, noisy, angry kind of person in a procedure of parting ways; it was her right. I took earnest thought to the matter. I asked Alfonso, who managed to live with a weight problem, women problems, the problem of being a black cop, plus all the other normal problems.

"In public," he said. "Won't want to screw up the place screaming if she knows the waiters. Put her in a little jail where she'll try to behave if she can."

"Jail?"

"Take her to Enrico's, it's not exactly lockup, but figure it out for yourself, my man."

"Maybe."

"It's your hope. Worst thing can happen, she breaks a bottle over your dumb head."

There are many wise men in the world, of whom I am not one; I've learned to take plausible advice. The trouble is that it's usually plausible without being comforting, but Alfonso made sense. In a public place, Lillian's good manners might prevail and she would not create a noisy, destructive, glassware-breaking scene. Such was my prayer.

I invited Lillian to Enrico's Coffee House for a bit of wine and to tell her I had fallen in love with her last-minute guest at dinner. I ordered the bottle, a chardonnay. I started my tale. She drank the wine in long gulps (the California whites have really taken hold) as I kept refilling her glass.

I talked about the mystery.

She stared at her empty glass.

I poured.

I explained.

She dabbed at her lips and gazed accusingly at the few drops left alone on the rim of the glass. I repoured.

Lillian seemed unable to speak. She was inhibited by the presence of familiar faces in this neighborhood hangout. Her head was thrown slightly back, tendons standing out on her neck, as if she were ready to sing an aria from *Manon* (I pick that opera at random), but paralysis stopped the music.

She began to cry. She began to squirm in her chair and cry and make little farting noises—*farts,* she made, not noticing that she was doing so—and at the same time sipped the wine without clear explication of her emotions, only those squeaking sounds as she shifted in her chair and nodded at me to replenish the supply. "Chardonnay from Napa," she said, "sweeter than the French, but a lovely bouquet."

It was unnerving. I wanted something more.

"Hey, I never really liked you that much anyway," Lillian said. "You were an interim solution."

Alfonso had turned out to be correct in his analysis of the Lillian situation; and if so much care and wine hadn't been necessary, I'd never have known, would I? Alfonso wasn't perfect, either. He thought she might break a bottle; she only broke wind.

The air was cleared. I was free to pursue Priscilla, the lady who felt irritated when I said she'd never need to know where I lived. She liked challenges. I called to invite her to dinner; she offered a counterinvitation—a picnic among the flowers on the springtime mountainside just outside town; Mount Tamalpais, where the Tamalpais Indians once hunted game and hid from the Miwoks, who specialized in fishing but sometimes wandered up to kill a Tamalpais.

"Great," I said, rushing, "there's the Mountain Home Inn, they have a nice view, it's a pretty place."

"No. Stop."

"Stop? No?"

"I have something else in mind."

"Pardon?"

"Picnic—listen, will you?" She explained about her straw basket and how she liked a certain kind of eggs, I'd see, and she had some wine in stock, and would I mind too much if she just put together a little lunch for us?

Graciously I did not object. I don't take offense easily.

She drove a red TR-3, battered but clean, smelling of sun-baked leather. The top was down and her hair flew in the wind. Freckles and need for shampoo result from the sun, she said. I sort of knew what she meant. I felt a silly grin on my face that I couldn't erase. We shambled up a hillside, holding the straw basket between us. When she opened the basket and everything was nicely lined up, stacked inside, I noticed there were cloth napkins, pale blue ones, rolled into napkin rings.

"You could have brought paper napkins."

"We'll use these again next time," she said. She had written my name on one of the napkin rings.

The sun pure and dry, dappled shadows from the redwoods overhead shading us, flickering heat and coolness in the air, we allowed ourselves to answer the questions that lovers who plan ahead, or plan to plan ahead, allow themselves to ask. What did I want for the rest of my life? (Her, but I wasn't ready to say that aloud.) I liked looking for and finding people who needed to be found, I liked collecting money for people who were owed it, I liked the edge of improvisation and even the bit of risk when a reluctant debtor or adolescent speed freak got pissed off. I enjoyed runaways, credit violators, and deadbeat fathers.

"You're serious about your job?" she asked.

"I have to admit it."

"That could be good, depending on how serious. I'm serious, too."

"About what?"

"How do you feel about real ambition? How about real money?"

"Never been a huge priority. Maybe been in California too long."

She was playing with a twig. "Hey, there are lots of Californias—think LA, think San Jose."

She poked at my palm with the twig. I closed my hand around hers. "Together," I said, "my seriousness, your restlessness, we make a good team."

"Probably we might." She grinned. She liked keeping things a little out of balance. But then she added in her formal way, very politely: "Dear man."

She peeled the foil off a dish of caviar from Marcel and Henri; a picnic needs surprises. Our promises should be taken fresh, like caviar, and enjoyed for what they are right now, on a mountain day in the sun and shade, with sharp and salty tastes and no doubts.

The next times lasted eight years and a son. On that secluded mountain slope in the spring green and brightness, she uplifted her thighs to me hilariously, her pale eyes defying the sunlight flooding down upon us, going dreamy and wide and dissolving into the vision of the two of us alone in the world, on a mountainside, forever.

Then she was laughing, laughing, and asking, "Hope there wasn't any poison oak, don't you?"

A toadstool grew in the shade nearby, a giant prick with a shiny carapace, and Priscilla blew a kiss toward it, saying, "I'll be right there." Her nostrils moved with a little fishlike oscillation as the deep after-pleasure breath went in and out, in and out, easing down and continuing oh please God forever. It was the full catastrophe.

The afternoon shadows were lengthening. We stretched and stared at each other. Then we straightened this hollow on Mount Tamalpais where we had lived for a time. I hooked the lightened picnic basket under one arm; she took the other. I felt her long fingers on my elbow; her hand sliding up to find a place; hand holding and resting. She took my arm as if she loved me. This is the most beautiful sentence of my life. She took my arm as if she loved me. This was the happiest sentence of my life.

"When we get back," she said, "I want to get the twigs out of my hair, I want a good bath."

"Not a bad idea for me, too."

"And then," she said, "I want to do all that again."

She touched me as if she loved me. She looked at me as if she loved me. She took my arm. I surrendered to the full catastrophe.

How her eyes faded blue to black and then to pale blue again when we made love, the dreamy distance of her gaze. The headband around her forehead when her hair was sunlit and we were pedaling our bicycles in Golden Gate Park. At Ocean Beach, she stared out at the sea, leaning on her bike, and I thought she had forgotten I was there until she suddenly touched my arm. "Save water, take a bath with a friend," she said. "Let's go now, it's time to start saving water. We'll be an example to future generations."

She was like one of those shiny new several-plex movie operations—different shows going at different times, but the facilities shared by folks whose dreams could only be guessed at. We stretched out; water lapped against the edges of people and sometimes over the edge of an antique deep-bellied tub with clawed feet. I hoped, as we bathed together, we were scheduling ourselves for the same program.

Priscilla's legs were a long and very interesting evolutionary event, slim at the ankles, widening, bunches of smooth musculature up to the complex juncture at the knee, sockets, and joints (try sorting these things out through the medium of kisses at the surprisingly warm backs of knees); and then after a brief reprise of slimness the event turned full and muscled again on the way up to oceanic mysteries. The better to grip you with, dearest; the better to hold you, my love; the better to walk speedily away, if necessary.

The message up at Brain Central, a galaxy removed from the moist warmth of the oasis at the joining of her legs, the estuary, the slow warm heading out to sea—the message up there in the control panel seemed to be: Not only do I want you to want me but also I personally, on my own, choose to want you. I select you from the hazards and accidents of millions.

How rare and wondrous this conjunction of ideas. I'll take this happiness above all others.

Just, please God, don't let me lose the memory of good luck. We saved water together. She put on Bob Dylan's *Blonde on Blonde* to dance to. She didn't mean dance. Whoever would think of dancing to "Sad-Eyed Lady of the Lowlands"? Well, folks can, lovers can, moving with that lazy beat under the nasal thrumming of a voice that seemed to drift over the walls of the madhouse of the sixties. But she didn't really mean dance. Dance was only in the heart and soul. She meant climb into each other, sing into each other, keep humming and keep it on forever.

Chapter 6

It's a well-known fact that aging persons, even persons with a pronounced tendency to grow older, are sometimes allowed to fall in love. God winked. I was such a person.

General metabolic luck helps when God looks the other way, slyly averting His eye. I was lucky enough to meet Priscilla before I sprouted hairs in irregular patterns all over my nose, or perhaps unlucky, because those hairs might have protected me, armored me into peaceful recreations with Alfonso and Lillian or Lillian's successors, especially if the nose hairs betrayed a coarse tangled rug growth on the back and chest—kept Priscilla from liking, teasing, loving me in the blithe, abandoned style of a gifted young woman whose metabolism, so far as she can tell, is only going one way, upward, toward more beauty, more sweet smells and emanations, more liveliness and yearning appetite.

Of course, even nose hairs might not have saved us, especially since they are rigorously plucked in most cases, men aiming for that bald-nose look so much in demand these days in the higher social circles. My vanity: probably I would have stood spraddle-legged and squinting at a mirror, plucking away, so that even in the sunlight of that picnic on Mount Tamalpais, silver gleaming out of her straw basket, wine chilled, her eyes blue as heaven and her hair the brightest thing on the mountain, no telltale specks could have been discovered on my nose as cartilage invisibly thickened. And the rocks churned upward through the mountain in the continual tectonic shifts of California geology. By this time boulders are exposed that were buried in soil then, and the descendants of the bees and other humming insects that attended our picnic have evolved in ways some researching genius might care about . . . the humming confusion and harmony of the air that day.

Priscilla might even have enjoyed the maturity and sage majesty of a wise hairy nose, busily sniffing samples of life in her crevices. She said my nose tickled her. We were so busy falling in love that even the bee-humming world distracted us only a sigh's worth, then our mouths distracted us with wine and toy food, and then our bodies continued their business. Joy. What a business.

Fate. Dire destiny. Nothing to be done for it or against it. Happened. She, I, we loved making love, more every time it seemed, though now I can't be sure. I praised her, she praised me, we praised each other. I guess the thing I didn't know was how much I would love her forever and how she might have been a victim of the concept "forever." Only the day was endless, it seemed.

And then we went home. She said she liked the darkness and smells of my bedroom. She asked if I kept memories of other women there and I said none that I could recall and she said, Hello, Hello, you're not making any sense, and I said, Why bother?

"Right. Right. Okay. Now," she said.

"Are you thinking something?" I asked one day after we made love and I was watching the dim ghostly motes spinning in the afternoon air. Brown burlap curtains were stirring. The summer evening fog was sweeping through the Golden Gate.

"If someone else walked in," she said, "they'd find it stuffy. Why don't you open the window wide."

No one was going to walk in. We didn't have to consider

the fresh-air needs of late-afternoon burglars preparing for their nightly drug intake.

"So why don't you? Or should I?"

I opened the window. I did so. She stirred, moving her hips delicately.

"Anything else?" I asked, but it wasn't sarcastic, just inquiring.

"No, that's good. Good."

"Do you love me?"

There was no answer. This wasn't rudeness on her part. She was asleep. A breeze from the window unfurled the burlap like a sail, cooled my thighs and my thoughts, washed over any burglars who entered while we slept.

She tried to tell me she was an ordinary person, but she didn't succeed in convincing me. She was once just a child with childish ways, she said. I didn't believe her. She looked exasperated. She told me she started spelling her name with a *y*, with two *y*s, when she was a silly little girl . . . Pryscylla? . . . and even that couldn't change my mind. I was hopelessly in love, and she noted fairly: "Hopeless, Dan, hopeless. But nice. That's n-y-c-e."

I understood her perfectly, but not the way you or others understand her and not how she understood herself. That is, I understood her how I needed her to be. That is, I didn't understand her at all.

Beauty is generally distressing; in particular, both scary and inciting. The genes are jumping and the hormones are hopping. Men and women, wary of the unknown, can also be tempted to seek the adventure of . . . *We're Made for Each Other! We Are!* The distressing beauty chooses to confuse the confusion by organizing a picnic and taking the suitor for a stroll in her garden. Priscilla leans against him. These are my flowers, these are my tomatoes. This is you and me. She takes his arm. She offers to mend the favorite red flannel shirt from L. L. Bean; come on, strip it off, it's warm out here, I'll have it back for you later. Then she refuses to return the shirt. "I want to keep it in my bed when you're not here. It has your smell in it."

Priscilla took my arm, sewed my sleeve. She does light sewing and charm; she does laughter; she does kindness. He will change everything in his life, including his faulty character. He is captivated. The world is a miracle on the plus side; it's a marvel. The universe belongs exactly where it is. He is captured.

Men like me, which means all men, almost all men—well, the foolish ones—welcome this funny idea where we think a woman's pleasure is something we should credit ourselves for. Mark one up for me, please, on the lighted billboard, the way burgers might be counted by a monster universal franchise operation from God. Priscilla did fine when we made love. I felt like a hero striding triumphantly at the head of her parade. It didn't come to mind that she could do fine whenever she wanted such a result. If she chose to have one joyous convulsion and then sleep, one it was. Or two. Or three. Or a caffé latté afterward, plus philosophical conversation and then to bed. Depending on how deeply burrowing into the body, how loftily flying from it, the spirit chose. Whatever. It was Priscilla's Thanksgiving Day parade.

The event didn't have too much to do with the chosen man's exertions, although I was certain she felt a special indulgence for my chatter and enthusiasms. I worked on the puzzles of life, I rambled about the private eye's career . . . "When a fellow sees me circling his house with a flashlight at three in the morning, digging in his trash, he begins to wonder."

She laughed, although I'd said this before.

She got off on laughing, therefore chose to laugh.

What turned into a bewilderment and confusion to her was that the solitary middle-aged private investigator with one good friend, a black cop, ended up enchanted by a person who seemed to fall out of the sky. To herself, she hadn't fallen out of the sky. She was there all the time, present in her world, and didn't require miracles or meteor showers.

"You ever have any awful unsolvable problems?" I asked her.

"What's that? You mean like 'God is dead' or alcoholism, that type of thing? Twelve-step kinds of problems? No. No, I don't think so."

"You'd know if you did," I said.

Her laughter pealed forth. "If I remembered," she said. "Generally I don't dwell on the bad stuff. No, I don't think there's been much. At least not yet." With a slight shrug of modesty, she added, "Probably yet to come, don't you think? I'm not impatient. I can wait."

I lay there with my head cradled between her thighs, gazing at her legs, wondrous immense structures close up like this, filling the known universe, although from other angles they were just a handsome woman's long legs; and like someone hiking in a forest, fresh from the city, in awe of what he sees— redwoods! butterflies! look at the vines!—I found myself compelled to name the present miracle aloud, saying, "Your legs."

She moved slightly. This naming habit might be irritating to some people. My head slid off and I slid it back. "Your smells. Good."

Drowsily she reached her hand down and put it over my mouth, but otherwise she scarcely moved. Through her body, transported by vibration to her legs, to the damp forest place where I rested, I could feel the regular breathing; and pretty soon my own; and both of us were sleeping. I dreamed I was falling through a mirror, Kasdan in Wonderland. I'm not sure about Priscilla's REM or non-REM dreams. I think she just slept. In the middle of the journey of our lives, in the dark wood where we dwelled.

We also liked the out-of-doors. We made our own

weather in a meadow, scrambling about on a hillside slant, scraping our knees; and then another day under arching and bending eucalyptus trees, in air made pungent by damp and sun on the leaves; and then—a habit of picnicking—in the cathedral shade of a giant pine in Muir Woods. She needed to stay out of the sun; I didn't mind. Afterward we sat up to pluck out of the picnic basket the good surprises she had concocted; I brought fresh fruit salad and cakes from a shop called Best Karma run by a young woman in a granny dress. It was that time of the Aquarian Age when businesses used the word "Karma" and Priscilla and I surprised each other, our legs waving hello to the California sky like heliotropic filaments.

Once we spent Saturday afternoon listening to the impromptu bongo orchestras that gathered at Aquatic Park on San Francisco Bay, joined by guitars and stoned groupies shaking tambourines or cans filled with pebbles. Alfonso joined us, shaking his head, saying, "You guys. Next time, man, I got to bring some company for me." Later we walked back up Russian Hill in the dark and watched the winking lights of Marin and the searchlight that still turned in the bay. We held hands up Hyde Street. Someone waved from a cable car. We waved back in case it was a tourist who deserved a friendly wave.

We turned ourselves inside out; we were children again. I showed her mine and she showed me hers. It was all good news to us. We marched with picketers at the Federal Building because this was the time of the Vietnam War; we visited the Free Store in the Haight with our leftover clothes, on our way to dance in Golden Gate Park because that was how San Francisco stopped the freeways, tore down the high-rises, brought racial justice to America; how selfish we were. I did pro bono work for CORE, tracking possible Tac Squad infiltrators. She served breakfast to Tenderloin teenagers at Glide Memorial Church. We passed a dreamy year of turmoil.

The wet-ashes smell of my contented middle age was gone. I told myself in wonderment, in disbelieving, incredulous total conviction: Forever! This is forever! After a long history of floating on the sweet surfaces of San Francisco, working enough to get by, killing time, occasionally killing some brews with Alfonso—now I thought, Forever with this lady, just because little songs come out of her eyes when she smiles? I answered the question: Yes.

We kept talking to each other as if we had found endless marvels to tell. I brought her the stones I had collected in a longer life than hers. She wrapped in ribbons the delights and pains of her growing up. We sat laughing and breathing into each other. We ate all the time and grew thin. We were in a state. We were too happy. Our friends hated us. I noticed her secret pre-pregnancy sleepy smile. Probably I walked with a strut. I knew we would have children. Envy is as legitimate and human as any other enjoyment. Alfonso was right to dislike so much happiness. He also forgave us. That's the job assignment for friends who have to deal with lovers.

About that time, probably due to the confidence shed down upon my life, the swagger of a happy lover, I finally had the chance to get rich. An offer came my way. Karim Abdullah was a friendly person of enterprise, hefty across the chest and in the thighs, wearing semitropical clothes that emphasized his heft. He kind of liked heft; he also kind of appreciated a skinny, different sort of person like me. Despite his body's tendency to weight, his spirit was delicate and precise. He kept his eyebrows carefully sculpted into widely separated bunches of dense hair, clean outlines, with antlike dots of plucked growth between the clumps. He liked a lot of things about doing business in San Francisco, including his own eyes, and reminded himself and others of his pleasure by wearing a touch of eyeliner.

The sex shows he ran in a former movie theater in the Tenderloin were the legal, tax-paying part of his enterprise.

I used to notice Karim looking at me, nodding, nodding, smiling, building up our acquaintance on the sidewalk terrace of Enrico's, where we both took lunch. When he saw me there with Priscilla, he made the beer-ad approval sign with his hand, circle of thumb and forefinger, three thick fingers upraised, meaning, Hey! She's okay!

"That man likes me," Priscilla said. "Funny eyes."

"I think he likes *me*." I said. "He's a local business guy who thinks . . . Here he comes."

There came Karim, smiling, snug, warm, advancing his ample vibes, carrying a bottle of champagne in an ice bucket; explaining that he could have sent it over with a waiter, which would be the normal way to do it, he fully understood the etiquette of such gestures, but this was far more than a mere gesture; rather, it was a tribute to a remarkable couple whom he admired from afar but with whom he now sought to build a personal association; explaining that he desired to save the time that is lost in the practice of ordinary courtesy; explaining that he admired the lady and also deeply, deeply respected my reputation in my chosen field of endeavor and why hadn't I returned his calls?

"Pretty busy these days," I said. "No sort of office staff. I'm a solo practitioner."

"Like that, like that. Solo practitioner," he repeated, rolling the words juicily. "You sing alone, Mr. Kasdan."

Perhaps I smiled. Priscilla kicked me in the universal language of stand up and be polite. I stood. "Look, I promise to return your call," I said. "Just now I'm having a day off with . . . This is Priscilla."

"I know, I know, I know." He beamed. "Today is not the first time I have seen you two together, deserving so many good things in your life. And so now I leave you, please drink in your own honor, celebrate your good fortune."

He bowed—he wore his wide, inappropriate, white linen suit with pride—he backed away, he knew I would call. I had made an oral contract. From his table he smiled and bowed again, and then turned away, meaning that I could talk freely.

He knew I would be talking about him. His own companion was a young woman wearing a black-and-white cowl and nun's habit although Halloween was still a few weeks away.

Priscilla smiled at him across the crowded lunchtime terrace, raised her glass and held it there. The nun told him to look and he looked. He raised his glass and both Priscilla and Karim drank, and the nun also drank. I didn't.

I held Priscilla's wrist while I explained that we were getting to know each other these days, she and I, and now she knew there was some work I didn't do, some folks I didn't want to know, and Karim fitted the category. In fact, he just about filled it for me.

"But he wants to know you."

"It's nice to be loved, isn't it?"

"I kind of like him. He seems confident."

"Wants professional services," I said. "Collections, or traveling with cash, or maybe better or worse. There seems to be a fair amount of money circulating around him."

She liked the sound of this. "Is it illegal? Am I so innocent you can't explain it in detail?"

I didn't know in detail. In North Beach and the Tenderloin it wasn't always helpful to know in detail. That was Alfonso's business, not mine. I didn't have to build a case to know as much as I needed. I explained about how a lack of knowledge can be a helpful thing in my trade. She wanted to learn. Also at times she didn't mind teaching as it came to her. "He'll be back," she said.

"You don't get prophecy points for that."

"He really wants to persuade you."

I didn't enjoy this. She was longing for adventures and I was longing for limits on them. "Not persuadable," I said.

"He'll be back, lover."

People can join a parade and dance along with the band, giddy with the joy of sunlight on their bodies—a class action of merriment and mystic oneness in community—while the band, which is the source of all this terrific rhythm, is paying strict attention to its own music.

Sometimes Priscilla and Dan stayed joined, kept their bodies locked into folds and membranes, not moving, breathing, hardly moving at all—a mutuality of decision, both of us deciding, nobody's idea—lying there and desperately still at first, then calmly still, whispering, telling all the things we loved, admitting freely that the first among these things was each other (I think it was more Dan, my tongue set free by the blessedness of bodies breaking the boundaries of bodies, who spoke these things) until the light started to seep under the shade, in the edges around the shade, and there were morning noises outside. The paperboy's footsteps. A whistler.

"Is it okay if I come now?"

"Whatever. Yes. Yes."

I could feel a bone at her middle rising and falling with her breath as she said yes.

"Now?"

"Yes!"

That cry we all make, smart or dumb, sex-drunk or just human, agreeing, assenting, convening, calling up the spirits of past and future and now, just the two of us here on earth together. Sometimes adding, as a kind of afterthought, "God, God, God," though God isn't really what we are believing in. The prayer just pours from some history of love and belief in the joining of souls, the prayer cannot be shut out, as the dawn light and the day cannot be shut out. Priscilla and Dan Kasdan.

Like many who marry, we married to learn who and what else we could be. "Let's," I said.

She asked: "I was wondering. Do we need to see the other side of the mountain?" That was what she called transforming this courtship into marriage and permanence.

"How do you feel about it?"

"I'm curious. We could drive to Big Sur and find a Universal Life minister."

But we passed a courthouse in Monterey first and decided to stop for lunch, a flower, and a wedding. The judge took time out from a drunk-driving trial and kept the culprit waiting while he asked if we thought the poor jerk—one prior alcohol-related accident—should go to jail and wished us a long happy life together and please drive carefully on Route 1, the winding narrow road to Ditjen's Big Sur Inn. Congratulations, you are man and wife, don't drink your wine till you get there.

The cabins were nestled into the hollow of a steep, sun-dappled slope of alluvial granite which poured down through the pine and poppies, bush monkey flowers and wild mustard, ending abruptly in a jigsaw of rocky beaches, eddying tide pools, the Pacific Ocean. A Norwegian settler had built these rooms with Hansel and Gretel as his architects. There were hawks overhead, hummingbirds nearer by. Priscilla claimed to see a whale just this side of the fog bank and I didn't argue the point.

She was still holding the rose I had bought when we entered the courthouse. I asked why.

"Because I like it. Don't cross me," she said.

When it was dark, we didn't mind bringing our first day as man and wife to an early close. We built a fire. The bed smelled of mustiness and wood smoke. "Well, it's been a long drive, no one'll judge us if we don't look for trouble in downtown Big Sur."

"Not that long a drive," I said.

"Let me be the judge of that. Long enough."

Her hands were on my shirt. Mine were on hers. The bed smelled of wood smoke and Priscilla and Dan.

"Wait. Wait," she said. And then: "Stop waiting."

She came undone; it was a way she had, fainting with terrible sighs, seeming to scatter under me like a puzzle or break over me like a cloud, Priscilla fragments raining down. And then, after a moment when time stopped, the pieces came back together and she was ready to make jokes, sit up and hold her knees, look for something to eat. It took me longer to come together again and remember who I was. Her eager smile and fading freckled flush were already there to welcome me. "Hey! Let's change the music, okay?"

This was the other side of the mountain. It wasn't the only other side.

I dozed through furniture-buying expeditions. In my sleep I mumbled, "If you like it, sure." The coffee table. The new plug-in appliances. A toaster that also baked—did it whistle "Abbey Road"? All I really cared about was the bed and a kitchen table for late-night snacking. Nevertheless, a house occurred, with closets, nothing not inside the closets that belonged inside the closets. In progress was an extreme late-sixties, early-seventies effort to be normal human beings despite San Francisco and an abnormally spirited woman.

On the other side of the mountain lurked a creature no one truly anticipates until it suddenly makes its claim and the universe is filled.

After we moved into the proper Marina flat, pregnant Priscilla, a garage for the pregnant Priscilla's automobile, a new life for the beatnik private eye on the other side of the mountain, it seemed important to share my blessings, each other, with my two best people, Alfonso and my wife. I said to Alfonso, "Just you for dinner, not a party."

"I'm bringing my dog."

"You don't have a dog, Alfonso."

"My new puppy. I need a social life just like you."

"Alfonso, I don't want a new puppy shitting on my new Marina hardwood floors."

He shook his head with wonderment at what Dan Kasdan, the married man, had become. "First place, Mingus wouldn't do that. Second place, this is true love, too. I'm committed to this equal-opportunity puppy. Where I go, he goes."

"Mingus?" I asked. "A cute name?"

"Loves that modern jazz, man. And he wouldn't do what you said on your hardwood floors."

Priscilla agreed that my law-enforcement backup would never bring a non-housebroken animal into our flat. She said, "A Boy and His Dog, what a cute story."

"Don't call him 'boy' to his face," I said.

Probably she was continually aware that he was black, as white folks usually are about black folks. He was heavy, smart, smiley, the officer who helped me in my chosen career, and my all-time buddy; we would try to love his dog, too. It so behooved us in our state of grace.

I think both Alfonso and I liked showing off for Priscilla as we sat over drinks and continued our tales of semilegal behavior in defense of the public against illegal behavior. She laughed at the right places and had the proper response to analysis of the one-joint rule for minors. The profit motive also came under discussion as I described staying out of money laundering and narcotics transport, although someone once paid me in airline tickets that turned out to be stolen; tainted, as the prosecutor delicately pointed out when he decided not to prosecute; Alfonso had vouched for me there. That's what friends are for. When Priscilla asked what he knew about Karim Abdullah, Alfonso said he was a smart hustler, medium bigtime so far, who might even manage to keep free of the criminal justice system, and then Priscilla inquired if that would be true for those who worked for him too. Alfonso said maybe, depends, and raised his eyebrows at me. "Smart woman," he said. "But don't think too far ahead, it's dangerous."

"I'm not averse," Priscilla said, although the eyebrows had been lifted at me.

I could feel Alfonso relaxing and happy as he tickled the nose of Mingus and told him not to bother the nice folks or eat their furniture. Mingus chewed a little at his socks, but that seemed to be permitted in this sudden romance. Alfonso mentioned his son living with the mother in Newark or Trenton, one of those places, she didn't even like to tell him her address. It was hard on him but he was patient and would wait it out because he really didn't have a choice. He didn't. Someday the kid would make up his own mind about his father. Priscilla listened and said nothing and that was the right thing to do. There was a space of silence and then we filled our plates.

"Kids need a dad," Alfonso said. "I'll be there."

Just before dessert—I was sure she was making some sort of flan, bronzed crust and burnt cream, something domestic and sweet like that—I was discussing how Mingus tended to yip and yap a lot around our legs. "Tole you he love the jazz," said Alfonso.

Priscilla was in the kitchen. "You like her?" I whispered.

"You already asked me that about every time I see her. Look, you're the guy's in love. I'm only the guy who sees what you see in her."

"Thanks."

"The rest is your own business, pal." He didn't believe in keeping his voice down. "Yeah, I like her."

She was in the kitchen a long time. Mingus was with her, and quiet. I headed for the kitchen to help with whatever she was doing.

Priscilla was on her knees, head down, lovely tail up, arms flailing with a dishcloth. Mingus was very quiet, whimpering guiltily. Priscilla was wiping at wettish dog doo on the floor. "Damn!" I said. "Let me get him in here to do that—the goddamn mutt—he said he'd be housebroken."

She looked up, her face purple, and said, "No! No! He'll be so embarrassed."

"Ought to be, come in and clean it up—"

"No! He's your friend—"

I stared. I was so amazed I didn't take the wet dishcloth

away from her to scrub the floor myself. Something in me may not have wanted to scrub dogshit after a good meal, dessert on its way but delayed by puppy circumstances. But cleaning up wasn't what I thought of first; seemed to be an instinct I lacked. I was still thinking Alfonso should do it. "You're gonna be pissed with me—"

She looked up again. "Later maybe," she said, "not now." And then she thought it through. "Yes. Later."

Maybe this was the evening when romance began to turn domestic. Maybe marriage, that's what it is or comes to be, complications of who cleans up what and why. Priscilla should have said what she wanted. Dan should have known what she wanted. If Alfonso wasn't doing the cleaning, I should have done the cleaning. The sure thing, surest of all, was that Priscilla should not have been down on her hands and knees wiping away at a yipping puppy's wet and runny plumbing error.

In a dream later I grabbed Alfonso's dear face, rubbed his nose in Mingus shit. A person can rethink history in dreams, but that doesn't do anything about it. Alfonso never knew how he once stood at the turning point.

When Mingus and Alfonso left, after he said her flan was sure different from any previous custard in his life, Priscilla started to put things away, I washed the dishes, we shut down the lights and double-locked the door. She was pregnant. Sometimes nowadays we didn't have sex but just went to bed, went to sleep, snuggled a little and grunted, turned over. But always the lovemaking was at least present in our bed. This time it wasn't.

It'll be there tomorrow, I thought.

In fact, it was there tomorrow and I could forget about a little domestic nonoccurrence. But something was started, there was a precedent. It could be said our marriage was becoming normalized.

"Hey, whyncha at least say goodnight?"

"I said goodnight."

"Kiss?"

Long wait. Slow breath. Stranger sleeping alongside.

When Jeff was born, he wasn't just our baby, our son, the hyphen between us forever. A new world had been created. We were discovering a world others had explored before us—even the greedy vanity of new parents could admit that—but I was Columbus in that delivery room in Children's Hospital, and as I watched a knee appear between Priscilla's legs—it was actually a dear bald head, with a few stringy wet black hairs—the nurse faded to my left in a clever delivery-room maneuver, ready to catch me if I fainted.

I didn't. Priscilla, wan, face and hair drenched, defenseless it seemed, said, "We did it."

"Thank you, thank you," I said, sobbing. Even in the turmoil of childbirth she remembered good manners and said "we." And maybe it wasn't only good manners; she meant that *we* had done it together, were doing it, would do it. Oh welcome to the world, sweet son. And to parents who love each other.

Not even then forgetting that the world is a place crisscrossed with nerves meant to be tickled, Priscilla asked sweetly, eyelashes still wet with tears, "Darling . . . now say—"

"What?"

"Dan. Now say, Thank you, ma'am."

Welcome to your family forever, Jeff.

Chapter 7

I watched her from our bed. Maybe she thought I was sleeping. She stood before the full-length mirror, briskly drying herself after a morning shower, no nonsense about it, humming under her breath in the new day, bidding pearly droplets of water to be gone. Then she stopped and stared. She liked what she saw in the mirror. She eased off in her scrubbing, she slowed down. It was a pleasantness to continue the work of probing crannies for moisture that came from outside the universe of her body. She noted herself with interest, worthwhile changes after childbirth, worthwhile resilience. She was at peace with the mirror and in life.

I admired her ass as she bent to dry between her toes. I admired it partly because she also loved it; blessed soul, free of doubt; blessed lady, ass in the air.

Then she straightened up and saw me watching. She smiled into the mirror. "Jeff's still asleep," she said. "Second time he slept through three nights in a row."

"What a considerate lad."

"Knows the worn-out parents need their rest." And she wriggled back into bed, careful in so doing to awaken me thoroughly.

I may have seen more clearly before early cataracts began to bathe everyday matters in mist and glow. Calcified shell hasn't yet blacked out the lens, no clogged duct or glaucoma, but that common disease of age, call it pernicious memory, slides a series of tinted postcards into the collector's album. Nostalgia sneaks into daydream like a preview of deteriorating eyes. Vitamin E capsules, yellow fish oil, are supposed to eat up the impurities, oozing off with their cargo of calcification. They can't sweep away the past.

No ripened cataracts yet, no glaucoma—it's a case of Retroactive Clairvoyance.

There's Dan Kasdan on the bus heading down Columbus to a dental checkup when he sees long-legged Priscilla, hair reddish golden in the sparkly North Beach midday sun, striding along with Jeff bobbing up and down in the baby pack on her back. Jeff is a few months old, still a bald young person, but already my brilliant son has learned to laugh when he is jiggled. Priscilla's walk jiggles this fine upstanding little fellow, his paws clinging like a monkey's, his hair getting ready to sprout through his scalp, the future on its way.

"Hey!" I cry out, too loud, an emergency appeal to the bus driver. "Let me out! That's my wife and kid!"

The driver says, "Man, this ain't a family unification service."

"That's my wife."

"Not doubting your word, man. This ain't the stop."

Everyone on the bus is laughing except the Chinese passengers, but then one man says something in Cantonese. White ghost begs to leave in violation of transit system regulation orders because of wish to share rice plate with his wife—probably not the precise translation from the Cantonese here—and now the Chinese travelers are also shrilly laughing and poking each other. We are in the middle of an all-American new-father city bus melee.

"Man, this ain't the rules, but I'll tell you what I'm gonna do—"

He has done it already. He stopped the bus. The passengers are enjoying an urban laughter break as the husband and father is running—getting jostled by a blue VW but pushing against the fender as the stoned motorist shouts, "Groovy end run, asshole"—and yelling, "Priscilla! Priscilla!" because she disappears pretty fast when she is striding along like this, even with a baby on her back. And she hears me and we kiss ungainly (the pack, the straps, the baby).

The bus stops again alongside us. The passengers are applauding. A black guy yells, "Gimme back my wallet!" The driver has violated the rules, but a Muni inspector might determine that he has demonstrated empathy for the potential for the blues in marriage and parenthood. Priscilla asks: "Where did you come from?"

Just more blessed luck. It was an accident. Wasn't intruding on her maternal bonding time—no, no, not this paternal dad. I kiss our son and he comments filially, "Urrggh," a most melodious moist blending of vowels and consonants.

The smells of bus, baby, and Priscilla surrounded me. Life is good, life is the very best. Here is what I felt: Love, love, love. So I lack all proportion and cry aloud, "I love you! I love you!"

Priscilla slips me a sidelong glance of smile-suppressed forgiveness for uttering such language on the street, on Columbus in North Beach, in the full brisk light of midday and well outside the normal and appropriate marital context. But what was I doing here, performing vocabulary stretches, interfering with her sandwich at noon with her baby? The business of motherhood was a woman's earnest, dreamy hormonal work. The father's business at that hour happened to be getting his teeth cleaned.

Fuck dental hygiene.

"You'll have to pay for the appointment if you don't show up," she says.

"I floss, I floss! I love you so much!" I answer.

"Thanks. Me too."

As we stand on the street, then turn to go to the sandwich shop, the Minimum Daily Requirement—hippies, beatniks, newspaper readers with shreds and stems of green stuff hanging from their mouths, sprouts, lettuce, meat, avocado; Jeff still bobbling on Priscilla's back, half asleep, half giggling from the motion—she forgets to remind me again to call the dentist's office. That would be nagging repetition, the enemy of marriage—one of them. In twenty years, when her stride may be a bit slower, her hips heavier, Jeff in college and doing well, we might take a senior tea in the afternoon instead of a fast and noisy sandwich amid folks who could be defined as "denizens." She was saying something over the noise of the shop, which didn't disturb Jeff, who was trying to get his mother hopping again. "I have an idea," she is saying. "Dan? You want to?"

I like the sound of that.

"After we eat, because I'm real hungry," she says.

I assent to that.

"Hey, I'd like a roast beef on rye—no mustard for me because it upsets Jeff's tummy—"

"But I can have mustard."

"True enough, you don't make the mother's milk, you only make the father's milk—"

Where is this heading? To reproach because a woman's work is never done, even in the automated factory of lactation?

"So then I'll feed Jeff and he'll stop that bouncing, get some sleep, sack time you used to call it, World War II, didn't you? But if you come home with us, okay, I know it's the afternoon, Dan—"

Her hand is creeping from location seven to location ten, from my knee to my crotch, where the mother's fingers give a clarifying squeeze to what she finds there. A simple explanation always works.

Her voice is softer now, with the delighted energy laughter tuned all the way down. "I know it's afternoon and you've got to do the work of the world, and you always get sleepy afterward too, just like Jeff after a feeding, but—"

"I'll call the dentist," I say.

"So let's go home and fuck, dear man," she answers.

The sun is high. Jeff is gurgling and jumping a little, wanting the pleasure of that long stride rocking him. My roast beef has mustard and too bad hers can't have. My happiness takes a pedantic turn, bound to correct her formulation of the program for the rest of the day: "Let's make love."

"Sometimes I have trouble expressing myself. You've got to learn my WASP style."

She expresses herself well enough. Under the table, well beneath the roast beef sandwich, she was squeezing what she found there. I guess I'll settle for what she gave.

In his high chair, propped on a telephone book for greater height, Jeff leaned forward with his little neck and his now downy head of hair, mouth open, eyes wide, as I extended the spoon of cereal, saying, "Here comes the airplane," me buzzing like an ancient prop cropduster, and his hangar snapped it down with a fake look of surprise and we both laughed and then I did it again. Why does every father with every child play airplane with spoonfuls of mush, and why does every child gurgle happily at the father's idiot crooning? Jeff and I didn't mind sharing everyone else's family pastimes; playing airplane during the child dining procedure is part of the great chain of being. Sneakily I hoped Priscilla noticed that father and son were essential to her housekeeping arrangements.

"Jeff," said Priscilla, "now why don't you give your father an airplane ride?"—getting it wrong deliberately—and he extended the dripping spoon and I ended with a face of Pablum.

The Kasdan Family, Open for Business. This firm under new management, Jeff's mom and Jeff's dad accepting clerical and cleanup duties as experienced, sleep-deprived partners in the merged enterprise. Jeff busy eating, drinking, shitting, and sleeping on a twenty-four-hour schedule, not excluding Sundays and holidays. The new CEO, Mr. Jeff, doesn't bother to wonder how he got into this. The father accepts conditions he had not anticipated. The unearned perfect intimacy of family, like sunlight, doesn't need discussion. Pride happens. Contentment happens. The years happen. The mother begins to wonder if this is what her life was supposed to be.

And here is what I feel now: Love, love, love, horrible desolation and regret, love.

We make love and say to each other, "Yes . . . Yes . . . Oh yes . . . Yes," and then the baby is crying when we get out of the bath together.

"Yes, yes, yes," she says to Jeff as she picks him up, holds him to her breast, and he subsides into happy feeding sucks. I lie near the other breast, dozing, loving the Chinese on the bus, loving the bus driver, loving Jeff, loving Priscilla. Even daring to say yes to myself as I pick up clothes blown hurricane-style around the bedroom, one of my socks miraculously planted inside one of the legs of her silken panties. Pale sweet silk, smelling of her sweet strong stride. Yes for sure, forever and ever.

So much affirmation to come to naught in its doomed due course.

And here is what I feel now: Love, love, love, horrible desolation and regret, love.

Yes anyway, yes, because it was.

Chapter 8

We painted our walls white, did it ourselves because Priscilla liked climbing on ladders, wielding rollers, dripping thick paint on drop cloths, then breaking to go at turkey sandwiches on sourdough bread held in speckled hands. We hung Fillmore Auditorium posters, psychedelic works by Mouse, Rick Griffin, Moscoso, Wilfred Satty, gazing at them with fond irony, and then we suspended stained-glass mandalas and zodiac images from the vendors on Haight Street to improve the Aquarian Age sunlight through our windows. In the bathroom we mounted a sepia-tinted photograh entitled "Chocolate George's Funeral," which showed the memorial motorcycle cortège of Hell's Angels commemorating the life and tragic end of a colleague who had collided with a black-and-white van full of pigs at an intersection where the right-of-way belonged to the survivors. Priscilla had once joined me in a summit conference I scheduled with George, who got his name from lounging about with a trademark container of chocolate milk propped against the hairy gap in his jeans. I needed to ask about a meth factory allegedly run by an alleged chief of a motorcycle sport club. We met at the corner of Page and Ashbury, near the detox unit of the Free Clinic. George graciously offered Priscilla a swig of his well-browned, well-muzzled milk; she, of course, accepted the Chocolate Milk of Peace. About the methedrine sulphate factory, whatever that might be, C. George declared he didn't know nothing, but he sure thought the world of my old lady.

"She's a mama I could even have a go at myself," he roguishly hinted. So the sepia commemoration print was meaningful to us.

Around this time the Native American separatist movement launched its war canoes to occupy Alcatraz Island, first installment on the rest of Amerikkka—important to include all those *ks*—and Alfonso suggested I put up a Free Hawkfeather St. James poster on my nice new white walls (how about the kid's room, buddy, next to the seesaw mobile?) but not get otherwise involved. Some rough stuff going down, he said. Alfonso gave me these hints now and then, because what else are friends for, especially if they're on the police force?

I asked Priscilla to stay away from this cause. She had already cooked up the buffalo stew but agreed to send it out under cover of darkness with an expedition of feral English rock and roll journalists. But then, bang, I was hired by a grieving father to look into the death of a Native girl who fell/jumped/was pushed down a flight of stairs, so I got involved anyway. And Priscilla asked if it was cool if she wore a headband. "You'd look cute in it," I said. So she didn't wear it.

Even when it wasn't the sixties anymore, it still was. We had entered these times from different doors, at different stages in our lives. We kept rolled joints in a cup in the fridge, wrapped in Baggies so they wouldn't dry out, but I preferred brownies because my whole life could be reexamined if that happened to be the program, unrolling with stoned concentration in super-meta-magnavision, without having to contend afterward with a scratchy throat. It was normal for me to move from spectator to chorus in the Aquarian operetta. Secretly, in my heart of hearts, soul of souls, ball of balls, I too was a runaway child. Those questers on Hippie Hill in Golden Gate Park, strumming their guitars, blowing their dreams at each other—well, maybe their parents hired me to find them, my brothers and sisters, but I tracked them down in the encampments of the Haight warmly, compassionately, cordially. Heaven and Siddhartha, patchouli and Isolde could be found in every crash pad.

One girl, Tanya Tangiers (born Terry Templemeyer), explained that she couldn't go home to her parents because (a) she was now married and had been for a very long time, and (b) she was no longer sixteen years old. She was living in the Kerista commune and married to thirteen husbands. (How long? Since last Thursday.) And since Thursday she was two thousand years old.

I arranged for her father, an admiral in the U.S. Navy, to have a little talk with her and bring her home. I was not only Tanya's spiritual brother but also her father's.

Priscilla, my bride during these zigzag voyages, tripped and smiled triumphantly from her twenties into her thirties. She was willing to contribute small miracles as part of the whole-earth acceptance deal. She invented adding roast potatoes, carrots, onions, and leftover chicken from a sandwich to a can of Campbell's Whatever Kind of Soup, cooking it with her secret, recycled ingredients so that eventually it actually tasted good, yummy, the best; as she did, too; and maybe a trickster brownie for dessert or maybe not. These were times when tremendous doings were afoot all over, and even kitchen life could be magnified, become tremendous.

Lots of LSD Jesuses seemed to be shipped to San Francisco by my personal guardian angels in order to provide employment opportunities. The father and mother of a freshly anointed Jesus would come on a referral from another PI search service, or just telephone from Frantic, Indiana, or the upper peninsula of Michigan, saying that their lovely son, Dennis, was heading west on a mission to be Savior of the World and would I please ask him to take the bus home because Mom was worried sick. Mom was often too distraught to come on the extension line with more than "Filthy drug addicts got ahold of him on a trip to Dee-troit. You'll recognize him—grew his hair long and whiskers."

The pokier Jesuses headed toward the Jerusalem of Marin County; the freak Jesuses liked the Haight because of ample free parking—in doorways, in the Panhandle, in Golden Gate Park—plus crash-pad wise men for company and potential discipleship, plus the best music. They turned on, tuned in, and bought tickets; rock and roll was here to save.

A Jews-for-Jesus kid sang his hit single in front of the Haight Straight Theater—"*I Knew Jesus Before He Was a Gentile*"—whomping and wailing, until I put my hand on his guitar and led him off for a heart-to-heart discussion about the Last Supper. This one turned out to be somebody else, a second-generation Jew for Jesus, and later a star of the San Francisco Sound, with a record that landed up there with "By the Dock of the Bay," "Hello, Hello," and the one about if you come to San Francisco, wear flowers in your hair. "The Last Supper," he explained, "was really the first free feed, like the Diggers, man. Now if you ask if He means for all the folks to join Him in the Big Auditorium—"

I didn't ask. I was looking for Dennis. When I found him, inquiring at the Psychedelic Shop or the Drog Store, checking on Haight or in the Panhandle or on Hippie Hill in the Park—Lords of the Universe tended to stand out in crowds—sometimes all it took was a kind word: "Your mom misses you, Dennis. Your dad says you can drive the Trans Am on Saturday nights." It got cold sleeping outside, because San Francisco doesn't have the California weather people imagine, and the doorways were crowded with competition: L. Ron Hubbards, Paul Bunyans, Strangers in a Strange Land (symptom of an apolitical bent—never met a Napoleon around here). One Jesus got suspicious about the weekend driving privilege: "Where you get that Trans Am shit? My old man drives a '64 Buick Skylark."

I snapped my finger and scuffed my boots, eyes modestly downcast. If you try to carry your office in your head, you sometimes get the file on runaways jangled. "I meant that, son—Buick Skylark, right, right—just slipped out wrong. Hey, how about a little breakfast—two pork chops and some mashed potatoes sound good to you?"

"You can call me Joshua," he said. "They got fries?"

The non-exalted runaways were harder to find, secretive, depressed, and sometimes in trouble. The girls were in danger. They would turn up pregnant if I didn't hurry and sometimes if I did. Often I had to contend with a boyfriend or a pimp and a lot of sadness. I would go from squat to commune to group dwelling, generally within a mile or two of Haight Street—those free spirits tended to huddle together—and then find Valerie or Sharon suffering from malnutrition, venereal disease, and bad habits. "Can't go home. They don't want me." "They want you, they love you." "If they did, why'd they treat me like that?" "They're going to do better now." "Promise?" "Promise. Hey, come on, I've got a hotel for you, a suite, nice warm bath, the shampoo and conditioner kit, and listen in on the phone while you talk to them." "What'll I tell Luther?" (Luther or Dwayne or Terrence would be the boyfriend-pimp-guardian they had found to improve on their parents.) "Don't you worry about Luther. I'll handle Luther. Just pick up your kip, honey, and here's a nice taxi."

If Luther came bopping around on his cork heels, he would notice my mean eyes and think, Plainclothes cop, chick underage, and usually let go okay. Sometimes I'd help him: "I'm gonna watch you walk down that block to Page Street, Luther, and then you turn right without looking back. 'Cause if you do . . . I bet you've met Officer Jones over to Park Station—Alfonso Jones?"

Luther was less trouble than the girls. No tears, no snot in his nose, no turning back.

Priscilla called me "Finder of Souls." I said I was only the shepherd dog barking after a little flock of Jesuses and Mary Magdalenes—was that disrespectful or sacrilegious? She worked her lips, checked her Sunday school memories. "I'll have to see."

While a sitter watched Jeff for a few hours a week, she was back to teaching at the Museum of Modern Art, running tour groups and lecturing on French Impressionism to high school visitors, some of whom wanted to know about American Impressionism. Opportunities for art history graduates were narrow if they couldn't type, no matter how sweet their scalps smelled, how salty they tasted. The advantage of her job was that sometimes she could take time off to help in a difficult Jesus treasure hunt.

This one was Jesus Christ Satan, a solo practitioner of good and evil, spangled and caped over a red satin dress, iridescent, clumping along with his crooked staff, his puppy, his cat on a string, and occasionally a follower. His hair was put up in pink ribbons under a tin helmet with Viking horns on it. People tended to notice, even during those special times; maybe it was the red dress, non-natural fiber. I already knew him, but darned if he didn't give me the slip for a week once he heard I was looking. Sometimes he lugged around clay tablets under his cape. People feared he might use them to sock sinners, but I sensed a middle name—Jesus Christ *Moses* Satan—and these were merely his ten commandments. Thou shalt end the war in Vietnam, thou shalt daily dose on acid, thou shalt not fuck with me, and so on. I asked for him up and down Haight and Page, down the Panhandle, on Cole, Stanyan, and Central, deep into Golden Gate Park. Everywhere his congregation cried out: "Dug him yesterday, looked kind of uptight, man."

His shoes clumped; he believed in sandals, but these hiking boots happened to be more practical for a wandering freelance prophet and savior in the San Francisco Gomorrah. In the case of Jesus Christ M. Satan, it wasn't parents. He stood apart, beyond family. He had been the art director of an advertising agency in New York and there was an urgent query about missing funds. His art director training accounted for his attractive decor (sometimes battery-powered Christmas lights flashing under the black-and-red cape); LSD accounted for his new role as King Messiah of both Heaven and Hell; he owed his taste for embezzlement to innate character.

It was frustrating. I knew him, but now I couldn't locate him. He was wriggling out of view like a magician out of a cage. Jesus C. Moses *Houdini* Satan. In a shiny red dress, slippery.

And then Priscilla spotted him on Polk Street, hastening along with his animals doing their best to keep up behind the billows of cape. He was noticeable, but I was looking at Priscilla and Priscilla was looking at the world, saw him first, and ran up, inquiring with her happiest smile, "Mr. Satan, that's such a cute couple of God's creatures, I wonder if you got them at the pound or a pet store—"

"Not talking to womenfolks this week," he said.

By that time I had him by the elbow, cornered him in the crowd at Travel Agency for Trips, had my own questions and statements, had a firm grip on the arm of the Ruler of the Here Below and Beneath. "Jerry," I said, "since I'm not a womenfolk, I'm sure you and I can have a nice conversation."

The folks lined up at the Travel Agency for Trips at Polk and Vallejo weren't buying many plane tickets to LA, Denver, or Disneyland. They were buying tablets to take them farther than far out as they sat in the front row of movies and watched *2001*, grokking and grooving, or *Reefer Madness* at midnight, hooting and hollering, their fingers in the crotches of the neighbors in the seats on both sides. J. C. M. Satan also sold high-test dynaflow acid from a pocket of his embroidered, button-loaded cape. As the Savior of the World, he embraced what came to hand, occasionally changing acid into sugar and the other way around.

"Begone," he commanded me; he should have commanded Priscilla, since she was the one who had picked him out of the crowd, but because he wasn't talking to womenfolks this week, I would have to do. I introduced myself cautiously— his middle name might also be Attila or Jack the Ripper—but he turned out to be a part-time sweetie.

His name used to be Jerry. Depositions were not his bag anymore. Besides, the tithe from the ad agency had all been spent in his unique combo of good and evil works. His mission on earth and in San Francisco required new sources of income. Expenses—grade A tunafish for the puppy and kittens was only the beginning—seemed to be the result of having an optional added spare middle name: St. Francis. This guy in the red dress kept a lot of arrows in his quiver.

I gave him my business card. He put on his glasses to examine it. Office Depot, nothing fancy. "Come to my pagoda," said Mr. Satan. "I think you'll find it dissolute but attractive. Lava lamps, I've got your basic Esalen pillow situation, I've got ample closets . . ."

"Jerry, you're wanted."

"And I want *you*, Mr. Kasdan. This card represents you correctly? Have you investigated the Path?"

"Jerry, if you want to settle this matter amicably, it can be handled. Otherwise, you know Sergeant Alfonso, he can cut a warrant and he's no farther than a phone call away."

"I know Alfonso, love that schwartzer, for even the Nubian shall find the Path. Doesn't a warrant need a judge?"

"Jerry, come off it. I'll give you a day to find a good home for the lava lamps and the pillows, but you may have to send the pets to the pound."

"Eeek, sir," he said. From a distance he had dramatic eyes, those of a silent film siren, darkened and intensified with soot; up close, as the mascara peeled off in the heat, they were bright little mouse eyes, darting here and there under the cosmetic burden he put on them. They wished Priscilla had never brought endarkenment unto this day. "I may have to pronounce a Malediction and summon the powers of Night. You wouldn't like that."

"I may have to summon the powers of the police. If I ask Alfonso to pick you up—"

"Eeek! Interstate warrant on what they're trying to nail

me won't hold up, Mr. Kasdan. It was petty cash. It was discretionary funds at the art director's disposal."

"Hey Jerry, I'm not your lawyer. That's why I say go back and settle."

"Eeek! Sanctuary!" He held his fingers up to my face in the shape of a secular, authority-defying cross. The cape flopped. The puppy started yipping. The cat withdrew, yellow eyes incommunicado. "I'll ask for sanctuary down at Anton LeVey's Temple of Holy Satan Mark II. They got goats, they got chickens, they got a direct line to the ACLU, buster."

"Ah, Jerry, no need to get abusive. Call off your terrier, okay? Let's discuss this like gentlemen."

But Jesus Christ Satan doesn't have to be a gentleman. We stood there arguing and eeking about legal matters on a windswept corner of Polk Street, surrounded by gray wolves, runaway boys from San Antonio, chicken queens, and, carrying the new plastic shopping bags, your normal middle-class shoppers from Russian Hill, for whom the sixties were just another time when the kids had to be fed, clothed, and sent off to school. I asked Mr. Satan what I could do to persuade him to go back and deal with his problems. He asked me what could persuade me to stay here and let him help me deal with mine. Standoff time at the Polk Corral.

Ultimately I failed with this one, made the call to Alfonso, and another Savior of the World ended up in Vacaville. The ad agency in New York got zilch. Mr. J. C. Satan's ultimate line of defense at his hearing was that maybe he belonged in Napa, a resort for the normal insane, but certainly not in Vacaville, which was reserved for the criminally insane. He was productively, creatively mad, an art director and bringer of miracles down from Twin Peaks.

The judge begged to disagree. Alfonso and I felt a sense of both relief and failure. Priscilla said she learned her lesson and it was the last time she would be party to a crucifixion.

"Just doin' my job, ma'am," I said.

"Come here then"—crooking her finger—"I've got another job for you."

Happiness was my lot. Happiness was our lot. Alfonso said, "You guys. Let me take you down to Third Street for some barbecue, that sound okay?" We were so easy with things we could even digest Sam Jordan's fried fish and ribs with sauce at the Primitive Bar-B-Que, 4004 Third.

And then there was the Pomona College boy I had to find. He thought he was Antonin Artaud, the French poet and actor who was also Joan of Arc. When he raised his cane, every woman in Paris peed her pants. So I was looking for a fresh-faced kid, blond, about five eight, freckles, carrying some kind of cane or staff and suddenly lifting it cloudways and darting glances at the passing girls, giggling, giggling.

It seemed that life in San Francisco just then was a carnival, and a festival for Priscilla and Dan. But not everybody was licensed to be happy on this planet earth, even during the Age of Aquarius.

An older man with hair beginning to gray—"gradual blonding," I called it, "from all the chlorine in the YMCA pool downtown"—I lay alongside my wife and love and wondered if we should just go ahead and have another child. Then, as she moved her butt in a particular way, and grinned and squinted sideways at me, and that flush came over her face, I forgot that lovemaking had anything to do with child-making. Her butt made enough sense all by its lonesome, flying and twitching and rosy pink; she wasn't afraid of Chocolate George's slobber or of mine.

A newscaster on the "all the news, all the goddamn twenty-four-hours" station—much of the news being urgent bulletins about discount appliance sales—gave us unending joy. "Turn on KCBS, spouse, I need some giggle time," and here was a flash flash flash about a cable car tragedy: "Several people are injured not up to the point of being considered dead."

"Now I can rest in what some might call peace," said Priscilla.

We wondered if it was correct to laugh about the report of a serious accident. We decided it was funny, we could share the guilt, silliness was an American birthright. "Not up to the point!" cried Priscilla, choking. "Not up to the point of being considered dead! . . . It's brutal," she said, frowning at a thought that troubled her for a millisecond. "People laugh. They can be so awful."

"That's how people are."

"It just amounts to awful, doesn't it?"

She switched off the radio. We listened to the ticking and creaking of household events. There was marital risk among our family accumulations of objects and histories. We aimed for the love of slow. San Francisco in those years also sent us other offers, but we steered our three-wheeled vehicle, Jeff, Dan, and Priscilla, down the highway into a shady tunnel of domesticity. Remembered the shade of the giant, ancient Muir Woods when there were only the two of us, Priscilla and Dan.

As a rest from Bob Dylan records, and because we were serious people, now and then we put a classical tape on— maybe it was the Coasters or Chuck Berry. Later Bob Dylan would be a golden oldie, but some of us kept busy remembering those years when we witnessed lots of famous rock bands— It's a Beautiful Day, Jefferson Airplane, even the Grateful Dead before Pigpen died of drink and the usual high-liver liver breakdown—all in San Francisco at the Fillmore Auditorium, or in Golden Gate Park, or at Chet Helms's Avalon Ballroom. The late sixties and early seventies were made for ending the war in Vietnam to the rhythms of love, drugs, rock and roll; by that time we were taking Jeff along in a basket as fellow witness. We were happy. Danger, danger.

Priscilla bought a flashlight to keep under the bed in case an earthquake caused a power outage. We've got a child, she said. You can't tell what might happen, she said. Who can predict the future, she explained.

Just once in a while she took on extravagant tastes; not too often. She couldn't decide which granny dress she wanted, so she bought three although she would only wear one. I yelled a little, she cried, I apologized. Next day she gave the two dresses she didn't like to the Salvation Army, but I knew enough now not to complain that she could have tried returning them to the shop. Like every marriage, ours moved down the road to normal, rich in daily drivel. I looked at her in her Amish housewife drag and said I felt sad because we didn't have a horse and wagon. Although it was over, I felt sad because we had had a quarrel. There were times when she felt sad and I didn't know why. "A little postpartum privacy, please," she said.

With our house key I scratched our two sets of initials inside a little heart in the wet cement of a new sidewalk out front. It was a childish thing to do. I wanted our names to be marked together for all time, entwined in cement, and I wanted to come by now and then and peer at them and peek at her and say, "Remember?" and then ask again, imperatively, *"Remember?"*

But of course the utilities people are always digging, so one day the old cement was gone and new cement was wet in its place with the whiff of a secret cave. You can't do a childish thing like that again and again. It's gone, the single heart with our initials, but it's not gone.

In the meantime we were having conversations like (me), "I think I'll grow a beard," and (she) "That would be not shaving"; and then (me), "What a keen logical mind, but unless it's a rough kind of hippie prophet deal, I'll still have to trim." So then stuff about electric razors and energy and whether it's masculine to do so and she's behind me all the way as I find my path in life . . . The daily fare of married folks joshing and negotiating at the same time, fending off the married-folks boredom.

Personally, I didn't need to fend it off. The flat times were almost relaxing because I knew I was just waiting for the happiness to rise up again so I could legitimately grab her. Marriage means another person's fart sneaks out from under the covers sometimes in the morning. Marriage means your own fart gets commingled with hers and the blame is shared. I didn't mind. Our morning farts could fill the sheets like sails, and off they might lift into skies blue above bright-sparkled seas. Carrying us with them like windsurfers, lovesurfers, in the free sulfurs of the empyrean.

Can't speak for Priscilla, of course. That's the inevitable dilemma of two hearts, two farts entwined.

Sometimes Priscilla had nightmares, which astonished a husband who had watched her ride through the years triumphant in her strength and gaiety. One night I was awakened by moans. She said she had dreamed of a long-legged running bird with a beak like a pelican's. How big? I asked. Not a giant, as tall as you are, but that beak . . . Another night I shook her and she went on with those shuddering sobs and didn't seem to awaken, didn't want to, even when I murmured in my own sleepiness, said her name. I held her swelling and subsiding in breaths that came like sobs. I kissed her back and shoulder blades, swaddling her from behind. What a lonely tenderness to comfort a sleeping wife, comfort her like a hurt child, comfort my own griefs by sharing hers. I may have been ignorant of her sorrows. I didn't fully know my own, either. I was happy to lie that way against her back. I brushed my lips across her shoulders, saying, Shh, sleep, sleep. She woke, muttering, "Oh, bad dream," and I said, "I know, I tried to make you feel safer," and then she suddenly sat up, demanding: "You proud of that? Is that your job? You'd rather just turn over and snore?"

"Only snore sometimes if I sleep on my back."

But her head was in the pillow, her arms flung around it, sleeping or pretending to sleep.

Look down from heaven, look here, God of Christians and Jews, observe and judge how hard we try in the department of loving each other forever. Loving forever is a difficult procedure. We only do it the best we can.

Chapter 9

For a while I avoided the outdoor terrace of Enrico's because Karim was always there at lunchtime, wiggling his eyebrows at me so that the antlike dots from recent plucking between the clumps bounced above his nose. By rights, ants shouldn't be scurrying and bouncing between a man's clumps and tufts of eyebrows unless he's in the business of forehead sugar storage.

"Mr. Kasdan! Mr. Kasdan!" he would call across the tables between us.

I waved my hand. "Busy," I said.

"You're only reading the paper, Mr. Kasdan."

"Got to have it all read by two o'clock, Mr. Abdullah."

"Karim, call me Karim." He got half out of his chair. "We're old friends by this time, Dan."

A friendship built on refusing to hear his offer. He seemed to treat it like a challenge. It was a courtship; he intended to win me over.

"Karim, why me? You can find people who *want* to do what you want."

He appreciated the question; he just didn't like having to answer it. "Those people you speak of, my friend, they are rotten already. You are not. Dan Kasdan, a man to trust, that is my motto. All I need is for you to feel what I feel for you."

"Should you trust me?"

Karim sighed. I could see the little nose hairs blowing.

"There is one thing I don't like about you," he said. "You do ask questions. You don't believe I have sincere feelings, many desires, I am a person like you, stubborn." And because words failed him, he touched his chest, the traditional casing for all that trouble of sincerity, feeling, unspoken desires.

When I told Priscilla about these meetings, she said, "He made an impression. The champagne, that was cute. Brought it himself, not a waiter. What a comedian."

"He's a dealer."

"I thought you said he ran a porn theater."

I explained about having several enterprises, a conglomerate, girls, porn, maybe fencing, certainly drugs. She listened alertly; she took an interest. I explained about things she already understood; but she didn't mind. She said, "Not that I want you to do anything really illegal, but isn't there a legal side to it these days when people start to get rich? Since he's not stupid?"

"He's not stupid. Owns a few cops, Alfonso said is a probable. Provides for that nun, I think she's his daughter. Definitely thinks ahead."

Her eyes glittered. "I wouldn't mind a Genie for the garage . . . You could play that Handel piece you like, 'La Folia,' and your Dylan records on better speakers . . ."

"Corelli, not Handel. Are you putting me on? I don't get his appeal."

"It's not because I like pretty things, lover."

"I didn't say that."

She looked dreamy, cut the dreaminess with a grin, the way she often did. "But a little extra cash—"

"Tax free."

"—to pick up some, I don't know, maybe we'd just have caviar in front of the fireplace."

"See? Can't even think of a thing you really want. Money's not your thing."

She stopped teasing and stared straight into me. "We've

got a kid. School's coming up. Nest might be my thing, Dan."

For a moment I heard her saying "next" and felt terror and then, as an after-echo, I heard her real voice, *nest, nest*. Pray God "next" was not her thing.

She was amused watching the tracks of listening, not hearing, the twitches of distress as they crossed my face. She didn't need to know what I was thinking. She took a stab at understanding, even consoling me, in her teasing, stubborn way. "Not that he isn't pretty, got his own style—all that linen, jewelry, the notion store he carries around his neck . . . Brings some fun with him, doesn't he, lover? If a person is susceptible?" She stopped, she meditated on it, she reached to pat my hand. "Not that I'm susceptible that way, dear. To Karim Abdullah."

But she did take him seriously. Even as a nonfanatic shopper, Priscilla, like most people, liked a man who could give her something she wanted or thought she wanted. Like everyone else, she was a person in want—and so was I. In this case I wanted no part of Karim and she was open to thinking about what part of Karim might be helpful to her.

"This is America, you're a new daddy, may I make a suggestion? Think ahead. That's the schedule. And I have to say he's kind of cute, blowing and dodging and that champagne idea he got from the movies, and his eyebrows going at us a mile a minute—"

"We don't need money that bad."

"Of course. Since we're rich. Since our son is rich. Since this new daddy is still willing to live day to day."

"I've liked the days so far."

"What would it hurt to hear his story?"

There were things I didn't want to know. I didn't think Karim was wired, I didn't know what his most bad connections were, but I believed it was better not to know and to stick to my low-tech investigations and retrievals; lost kids, deadbeat daddies, missing data. I liked what worked for me.

Priscilla was asking: ". . . and why not? It's a sign of respect, it's the game patriots play in America." She was talking about money. "We could use some more, husband."

The waiter at Enrico's, Chad, made a special lunch for Karim when he went on one of his diets. He chopped fresh cherries over bananas. He dug out the pits and chopped the little cherry bits over bananas with cream. The cream, Karim explained, holding my jacket, was because when a man makes sacrifices like this at lunch, he deserves a little pleasure as consolation.

"Tell me what's so bad about a regular check, my friend. For a little collection now and then, just picking up the funds."

"Thank you." I said it to mean I didn't need collections, transfers, transport over state or federal borders—no.

"You have a problem with me? If I was Kevin, not Karim? Or Sammy?"

"No."

"So why not?"

With two fingers I plucked a cherry bit out of his bowl. It was sour. I licked my fingers. "No," I said.

He liked that. He appreciated dumb stubbornness. He gave me a broad, heavy smile, eyes glowing within their framing edges of eyeliner. He had his heart set. He was a man who enjoyed challenges. "Dan, Dan, Dan," he said. "Friends-to-be, am I right? Maybe soon?"

Despite happiness, I kept track of some of my old traditions. I still lacked full appreciation of the embarrassed kind of habitual male charmer, those shy San Francisco inherited-money lads with long thin legs and a permanent sailing and tennis tan; they were healthier, fewer-martini, nonsmoking versions of East Side Manhattan walkers to rich ladies, who were in turn trans-Atlantic remakes of stammering English aristocrats with uttah inability to pwonounce the letter *r*. Priscilla's friend Xavier, a fellow docent at the Museum of Modern Art, had a self-made career, but the self that made it was his great-great-grandfather. His father had restored a gold-rush-era warehouse once used for shipments of coffee, the massive grinding of beans, and this Xavier had upscaled into a gaslight-lit Aulde San Francisco shopping village (don't ever use the word "mall" in Xavier's presence).

Priscilla came home giggling from a meeting at the museum. "Someone asked how to clean the Pomodoro—you know, dear, that thing that looks as if Henry Moore were showing Rodin how to do a 'Maternity' for astigmatic sculpture viewers—?"

"Huh?"

"The Pomodoro in the lobby, you know. It gets greasy from all the public breathing and stuff. So Xavier suggested cleaning it with Windex. Windex! I couldn't believe I was still sitting in that meeting while my darling husband was sending the sitter home and might be longing for me, or at least hungry."

"Both."

"You were! I knew it! But quality time with Jeffie passes so fast, doesn't it, and he was so *funny.*"

Xavier and I were not destined to be friends, but I appreciated that he brought some extra comedy into my alert wife's life. It's easy for a new young mother to slip into boredom or blues when she is suddenly burdened with a new husband, a new child, and new and many obligations.

Then one day she said, "Xavier, you remember?"

"How could I forget."

"He's always there when he needs you."

"He contributed a case of tax-deductible Windex to the museum?"

"No, seriously. He wants to talk business with you."

I couldn't imagine Xavier had a long-lost child he needed finding, or that he lent money to the kind of folks who scurried off into the Federal Protected Witness program. More likely for Xavier to be searching for the best full-bodied hair conditioner in the civilized world, a kind of treasure hunt out of my line.

"My business is thriving. I'm inspired by a happy marriage to do more and more investigations. Do I need Xavier?"

"Talk to him, dear."

We met on the terrace at Enrico's, although he suggested coming to my office upstairs. Somehow, and this irked me about myself, I didn't want him to see the shabby garage-sale look of Dan Kasdan, Private Investigations, World Headquarters. So we sat at the faux-marble table, Chad the waiter serving, while Xavier stretched out his long legs and reminisced that we had seen each other so many times around town but this was the first time we were having a real chat one to one.

I enjoy sentimental reminiscence as much as the next guy. But I found a way to hint that he should get to the point: "I've got to see somebody at Vital Statistics, the Death Certificate Bureau, and parking around City Hall is a bitch. Do you mind getting to the point?"

He smiled winningly; terrific teeth, champion gums. He appreciated the gentle subtlety of my approach.

Although he preferred to link business and social life, thereby making all the days and nights of his life a festival in keeping with the spirit of encouraging the carefree use of major credit cards in The Factory, his restored Aulde Town museum with shoppes (*not* to say "mall"), he did know how to get to the point. He was, after all, not just a native son of the golden West but also a renowned environmentalist, a gourmet cook for small groups of treasured friends (Would Priscilla and I . . . ?), a guardian of San Francisco gold-rush memorabilia, and a savvy investor who had re-restored his father's warehouse just in time for San Francisco's emergence as a tourist destination like Venice, St. Paul-de-Vence, and Virginia City.

The Factory had become a traditional Barbary Coast destination for sophisticated tourists. The walls had survived the earthquake of '06. Now there were flickering gaslights, the Donner Party Saloon serving the Hangtown Brunch on weekends, an art gallery with authentic miniature player pianos, pressed sawdust statues of Enrico Caruso, nuggets from the Sierra, and, as in mall art galleries everywhere, lithographs signed by Salvador Dali. Xavier was opposed to the latter, but the gallery paid its rent and what could he do?

His responsibility was the basic property, keeping it maintained, the bricks rough and authentic, the view elevator that lifted high above Fisherman's Wharf clean and smooth-running. He delegated the leasing jobs to a management company. As the fifth-generation here, his role was mostly that of curator and guardian. Sometimes an authentic brick crumbled and had to be replaced with a new authentic brick. Sometimes the view elevator got stuck and a tourist family was stranded, snapping rolls of film of Ghirardelli Square, the Cannery, and the Golden Gate Bridge, when they really had an urgent need for Softees, walkaway crab cocktails, and T-shirts. Xavier also took responsibility, because he had developed taste over his years of developing taste, for making the decision to preserve the tracks on which the train used to run, carrying coffee into the factory. He had to fight City Hall on that one. The old narrow-gauge rails, embedded in cobblestones he treasured as individuals, were guarded against politicians who always wanted to lay down heartless asphalt; it's their nature. Herb Caen gave him full credit for that one.

People credited Xavier, correctly, with a sense of San Francisco history. He accepted his Oso Californio Ribbon from the Yerba Buena Forever Foundation proudly but graciously. Tradition was not a burden; on the contrary, as he expressed it at the Hangtown Fry Brunch in his honor, it was a privilege. For Xavier, the gold-rush days were still alive, vibrant and as full of resonance as his time on the tennis team at Stanford. In a toast to the Yerba Buena Forever Foundation, he raised his cup of campfire-boiled miner's coffee, eggshells thrown into the pot to precipitate out the grounds, although in this case it was Italian espresso. ("That's a mere detail," he said, and the assembly chuckled appreciatively. Xavier turned out to be one of their most entertaining après-brunch speakers.) In San Francisco terms, Xavier's was an old family, although he allowed that five generations isn't really a lot if you think of the crowned heads of Europe; even of Monaco.

Xavier's photograph collage of The Factory as it was, workmen in heavy leather aprons, pre-1906 non-union expressions on their beefy faces, and as it is today, visitors with Factory shopping bags, made a popular postcard in the Barbarie Coast Shoppe. The original, entitled "Les Ouvriers Then & Now," hung in his office. So he knew from experience what it was to be creative. The arts had a friend in Xavier; the museums, the chamber music, the theater, the more civilized performances (not that garbage washed into San Francisco by the sixties, of course).

"We need to organize a better security system. Shoplifters these days, you know—there's a whole race of them. Absent deterrence, they even try to rip off the gas jet gizmos—they're from Belgium, cast in a foundry there. I just don't know what they want with a piece of rare industrial sculpture, try to sell it, I'm sure."

"Sounds logical. Unless they're collectors."

"Not to speak of the prints—I've lost an original 'Vue de l'Entrée de la Baie de San Francisco,' provenance Thierry Frères, hand-tinted—the thief could even tell which was the original lithograph, not a copy. Gave me a bad day, let me tell you, Dan. To make a sad story short, my insurance carrier says I've got to set up something that . . . Well, you know, you put a green uniform on a ghetto kid, you badge him, you bond him—he's still a ghetto kid."

Shook his head ruefully. What a century we live in.

"You want me to be your security guard?" *Absent deterrence? What is this guy?*

"Dan, please. No, I mean hire a crew, just run the drill—train or manage, whatever it takes. I want to protect the restaurant from check-beaters—they even crawl out the potty room window at the Hangtown Fry, run down the up escalator—offer complete security to all my tenants. Listen, we had a flock of gypsy pickpockets during the Christmas rush, we also get Colombians and Bolivians who go to school for that sort of thing, plus the Mexicans don't even need to attend Snatch Academy—"

He was rushing, he was eager, he had innate zest when he got into it. He also had tact. He smelled reluctance. His antennae were more sensitive than your average-issue San Francisco trust fund baby's.

"Chad," I said, "offer the man a refill."

"Actually," said Xavier, "how about a double latté?" He didn't specify caf or decaf, nonfat, lowfat, or whole milk, cinnamon or a sprinkle of chocolate; he was tending to business. "So?" he asked. "You just draw up an informal plan, I can assure you I trust your judgment of what I'll need—just cost up the estimate and we can revise it as we go along—"

"Xavier," I said, "I appreciate this vote of confidence. But I have to tell you something about myself. There's a reason I'm a private eye. I write my own checks. I only use part-time assistants when I stumble into something over my head. I like to clean up messes where I control it personally."

"I don't think of you as a snoop, Dan."

"I'm sure you don't, Xavier."

"Priscilla thought you could be tempted, *challenged* . . . an *opportunity*—"

"I don't do security. I'm small-scale, small-time if you prefer, for a reason. It's personality, maybe it's even character if you want to put a grand name on it, it's the way I am. Priscilla probably told you I'm a loner—"

"All she said is that you're brilliant at what you do and you could do more."

"She said that?"

Xavier was nodding across the terrace at Enrico's to Karim Abdullah. San Francisco is a metropolitan village. I waited until they had finished their pantomime greetings.

"See, Dan," Xavier went on, Xavier fortifying his argument with every serendipitous moment, "not only your absolutely ravishing wife but also Karim recommends you as the best, the top, the crème de la crème—"

"Of things I don't do," I said. "I do investigations, personal matters. Lose a child and I'm your guy. Need a bill collected from a deadbeat gone out of state, I got frequent flier plans on all the major airlines. For getting in a deadbeat's face I got a knack. But I don't want to get into big business, what I call. Not even medium big business with tax forms, payroll plans, health insurance, hire a bunch of guys with phony badges . . . Am I making myself clear?"

"I understand you completely. Secrets are really private and nice."

"Bearing down on them. Solving a riddle for parents or convincing some greedy ex-father to pay up, even if he's hanging out in the French Quarter in New Orleans where he thinks nobody—"

Xavier sighed regretfully. "Karim told me about you." Deep sadness, almost like a yawn. "Said you were the most truly talented solo practitioner in San Francisco, in the entire Bay Area, a really stubborn entrepreneurial individual—"

"I'll bet that's what he said."

"But said I should try anyway."

There were various ways to express my annoyance with Xavier, even with Priscilla for something that wasn't really her fault, trying to do the right thing for all of us, introducing him to me. My way was to insist on paying the check, but the classy asshole had already had a word with Chad and the bill was on his tab. Another entrepreneurial individual, that Xavier.

Karim shrugged dramatically, grinned happily as I left,

heading back and around, up the Kearny steps toward the entrance to my office. It was a double shrug and grin, chocolate sprinkles on top, intended to do for both Xavier and me. Xavier crossed the terrace to join Karim for an après-lunch bit of fellow entrepreneur bonhomie.

I came out of the world's splashing and thrusting. Xavier lived in the eddies, inherited space. I had won a statistical miracle to be a lawfully wedded husband; we had a blessing son; why drift into Xavier's shallow pool when I could dive in my own stream? Decent reputation. Business okay. I could afford to say no to a friend of Priscilla, her fellow docent, because we didn't need to move up from a Honda Civic to a BMW, not even to an Accord; and I didn't care for the lean, ever-young lad with the surprising acquaintanceship with Karim Abdullah.

Priscilla didn't mind at all. "What need have we to climb into the upper rungs of the middle class?" she inquired.

"He's a creep, your friend—only my opinion, of course."

"But you respect the opinion of yourself."

"Thanks a lot. I wouldn't have guessed he knows Karim. This town, nothing surprises me."

She explained that Xavier hung around a lot. He liked to be in touch. She laughed and pulled my shirt straight.

"But the poor boy, I like him even if you don't, it's the charm of—"

"Of what?" I asked, impervious to Xavier's charm.

Priscilla gave it a long full think, brow furrowed, very earnest, and I loved her also for her ability to cut through to the heart of things, even if she was sometimes reluctant to do so. For me she would do it. "He's known far and wide as harmless. The charm of being charming, I guess. What's intriguing maybe is the unknown depths and neediness, unlike your depths, which are at least known to me, dearest. He's so used to getting his way and not being satisfied."

"I see why he's a friend of Karim's."

"Explain, please."

"Well, anyway, I have a conflict of interest about Xavier. I know his friend Karim too well. I've said no to him too much."

"Do PIs have conflict of interest?"

"Now they do."

"Explain all the above, please, dear. I want to understand you through and through. You have to explain the whole little list of everything you just said, start there, how about that?"

While Jeff napped down the hall, Priscilla and I had a family conference on the floor in front of the fireplace. There was no fire, it was still daytime, but it was a spot with memories for us both. We tended to fall together here. We had a sweet half-sleepy afternoon talk. I told her I really didn't like Xavier. I told her I even preferred Karim, a sleaze gone public and unashamed. She laughed. She enjoyed my company. Oh, my business was doing well enough and, besides that, I adored my wife.

A little later, after a lot of thought and a couple of reluctant sighs, she continued a conversation she seemed to be having with me but without my full participation. "And then about Karim . . . I think there's something else I should tell you."

Married men learn to beware the sound of these words. I snapped out of afternoon low-blood-sugar doziness. I was on guard, stomach fluttering, more alert than I wanted to be. I asked what the "something else" was.

"Oh, not *that,*" she said, highly amused. "What do you think of me?"

I wasn't sure what to think of her.

"But in a way, even if it isn't another man—really, Dan, don't start that one—but in a way, yes, but not what you're thinking. Let me explain."

"Please do."

I was sitting up on the floor in front of the cold fireplace. She sat up also. She reached for my hand. "Come on, come on. You look like you're ready for a jungle battle to the death."

"Sorry."

"Okay, your humble and eloquent apology is accepted. Just listen to me now. I've heard that in certain lines of work, creative things like investment banking, the movies, the private investigator business, there exists something they call the 'big score.' "

I'd heard of such.

"And in a tribute to you, if only you'll take it that way, I think you not only deserve one but also are capable; if you'll take the time to listen to your loving wife—you are fully capable. That's why I married you, I knew it right off, you're nice, you're fun, you sincerely liked me, and your big score was sure to come your way when you simply decided to reach for it, like a true American. Of course that's not the only reason I married you."

"Thanks."

"Soulfulness is nice, too."

"I'm still listening."

"I'm still conversing. And as your true American wife, surely I deserve to get what you promised me—what you seemed to promise—and to help you along the way because it's for you and me and now it's for Jeff." Her eyes were gleaming in the late-afternoon light. She liked taking charge, and since I didn't know what she was doing, she was entirely in charge. "For us," she said.

She waited for agreement or disagreement. All I offered was waiting. She moved right along, saying, "Karim."

"Shit," I said.

"No, just listen to me. He's terrifically impressed with your talents. He likes your independence."

"He likes my clean record."

"Dan, he's *fond* of you. He has that wonderful ethnic tendency to fondness."

"Whatever the hell that means. So the two of you have been having meetings about your mutual fondness."

She made a little exasperated sound. She was leaning against the cold fireplace screen. She shook off the irrelevancy, the jealousy, the general off-balance behavior of a husband, in order to get to the point. "We've met a few times. In public, I assure you. If I flirted with him just a tiny, it was only to work my womanly wiles on your behalf. Young mother. He was touched by my plight, Dan."

Terrific. A chance for Karim to spread his fondness around the neighborhood.

I asked if she made herself pathetic for him. No, she did not. Her plight was to be optimistic, cheerful, undaunted, a young wife and mother whose husband was this close—*this* close—and she made a graceful little gesture with thumb and index finger. It made me think of someone talking about the size of a prick. "This close," she said, "if only he'll reach out to accept the big score that would make everyone feel so much better, plus pay the future bills that will come due."

"You're not satisfied with your standard of living? If not Xavier, then Karim can help?"

"Oh dear, how stubborn a man can get. Especially my beloved husband. Put it this way, Dan—halfway I'm prudent, I think of schools for Jeff and the future and maybe some nice things. We don't have to get specific, but a car that goes vroom, vroom? With a rag top?"

"That's pretty specific. Do you have the color red in mind?"

"—and halfway I'm a red-blooded American girl who knows her husband can provide the best, the very best. We've had our fun, Dan. Now it's time for you to reach."

"For what? Vroom, vroom?"

"You can be so much more."

"A money launderer? A drug courier? Maybe the arranger of hits?"

She shrugged. My tone was so negative, so unnecessary. But Priscilla was a woman who respected her own power, and therefore she could recognize my tone but not be daunted by it. "I wouldn't, surely, Dan, ask the father of my son to do anything—would I?—that isn't exciting and challenging and probably the kind of dancing on the edge that's at least as safe as the parachute jumping you used to do in the army. Dan, you remember—we were on Mount Tam having a picnic—you told me how military parachutes were really small and you came down really fast and it was like jumping from a second-story window? And you really enjoyed it?"

"I was nineteen years old."

"Would you just listen to him, Dan? Pay attention? For me, too?"

Her eyes were both dreamy and bright and her face was flushed. It was as if we had just made love. Anyway, Jeff was about to wake up. We could hear him stirring.

Naturally a man capable of a big score did not see the need to rush panic-stricken into mere behavior. Setting things straight with Xavier had been entertainment; but Karim might be pushing my luck. Consideration was called for. I wasn't going to seek him out, confront him with a jumble of charges and reproaches, such as corrupting my wife, which of course was not the case at all. Priscilla was incorruptible by others. Priscilla had her own integrity, the best, the highest, and any corruption she required could be taken care of by her own efforts. I would not pursue Karim. I too could rise to a high standard of independent conduct.

So I grabbed him next noontime on the terrace of Enrico's, where I knew I would find him, around the corner from my office up the Kearny steps, across the street from the second-story parlor, A-ONE MASSAGE, OPEN 24 HOURS, which catered to lonely Filipino gentlemen but did not disdain others if they came up to normal all-night massage parlor standards. Karim wasn't involved in this business except for providing the opening lease expenses, accounting services, and the girls.

"Now you're a good friend of my wife?" I asked. This was my version of calm consideration.

"Sit down, sit down," he said, offering great hospitality, my choice of chairs, his palms open and concealing nothing. "She said she would speak with you—"

"She did."

"Now we must learn to defer to a woman of her quality, Dan. All men must. Your wife, a quality woman. And I congratulate you."

"As a good friend."

He took this comment under advisement. He was busy weighing the facts. "As a close acquaintance," he offered judiciously. "We both keep your best interests close to our hearts." Touched his own heart with thick, hair-sprouted, but trimly manicured fingers. Practiced sign language indicating sincerity in case words did not suffice. "Pris-ceela, myself, we are thinking about your future, my friend."

"You're not going to make deals with my wife, Karim."

"Would I ever do such a thing? Without seeking full agreement from you? Since only your trust and confidence provide us with all the satisfaction we seek?" He was startled by the hint of duplicity I seemed to suggest; he was shocked, shocked. "My friend, Pris-ceela appreciates to make an arrangement, but only, only on your full behalf, and only if you freely desire what all your dear friends want for you—the best! Surely you must understand that my interest in your quality future equals hers. If you don't fully appreciate my friendship, let me help by assuring you. My respect for Pris-ceela is profound. My admiration for you, Dan, and the respect which follows admiration, is only doubled and redoubled by this quality person in your life who wants nothing more than . . ."

Than what she chooses to want.

"Than what is right," he said, completing the thought after a moment of pursed-lip humming to himself. "So we must trust each other more, my friend. Can you accept this challenge? Can you, Sir?"

Karim's profundity of feeling was worth nothing if not communicated in all its great humidity. Hands fluttering to chest, mouth winsome with smiles, black-edged eyes poring over mine with little jumps and starts and then a steady high beam, all the generously proffered bundle of deeply human emotion informed me that this was a man I could truly count on for love, respect, and full employment. He sought to divert me from my Kasdanish slothfulness of spirit. He sought to inspire me with hope and greed. He was preoccupied with thoughts of my best interests. He liked challenges.

As for me, I was still getting used to the best interests of Priscilla as worked out by Priscilla without terrific reference to her spouse. But did her surprising (ambushing) me mean she wasn't right in her intentions, since I had always thought her intentions were both sometimes surprising and certainly right? She saw no reason for me to think any differently, so why should I?

It seemed that my wife was not merely a marvel of intelligent gleam and tenderness; that she was more than the statistical miracle I had found as if by God's help in the middle of my time. She was also an American woman, wanting some fun, wanting some goods, wanting some changes to be made. Others must have seen this coming and encouraged her renewed free choices in life. I was in the great tradition of blind lovers. Suddenly I was a little less blind.

"Please, if we can talk," said Karim. "Let me report once again . . ."

I heard the words "respect," "admiration," "quality." I heard the word "deeply."

"Together you make, what? A truly spicy combination. Perhaps cuisine is not the way to think about learning to accept a higher reward for talent—"

"I had a wife I loved," I said. "I fell in love with her."

Karim touched my arm in that way some men have, gentle, sharing, paying attention, and alert to how they look doing so. He shook his head heavily, mournfully, from side to side, and it came to rest with a heavy mournful smile. He pitied slavishness in a man, but he also meant to honor love. "So full of feeling," he murmured. "Kudos, Dan, kudos. You are a man capable of a rare devotion. I offer kudos and respect." Encouraged by my not squirming away under his fingers, he gripped my arm; he too enjoyed intimacy, hoped to learn kudos. "Now you must leave room for the woman to express a woman's devotion, woman's needs. You must listen carefully and consider, my dear friend."

Usually so concentrated on his enjoyment, greedy for his meal, Karim today picked at his food. Yet when I looked again, his plate was clean, with a decorous few brush marks where his fork had missed something. He must have been getting what he wanted. I was sure he enjoyed our little chat.

"Listen carefully to me," he said, "and above all listen to this unusual woman."

And so I said to Priscilla, "I don't want to do business with Xavier, and I don't need Karim either."

"It was only a thought, dear."

"I don't want to."

"I can dream that you'll change your mind though, can't I? Even if you love me truly, as I know you do, you can't take away a girl's right to dream."

"You're an American."

"You said it, I didn't . . . Of course, I've said it on occasion in the past. I do believe I even uttered those words to Karim and he was charmed. He just went on, totally charmed, about how much he admires your skills."

New reasons kept coming up for Karim's persistence. It wasn't just Karim. Xavier wanted me in his employ. Priscilla wanted me in a better line of work, one that brought in more interesting amounts of cash. They all had an interest in filling my life. Flying ideas were buzzing around my head. The concept "tax free" came to me without clearing off the buzzing. "Are you in some sort of trouble?" I asked.

"You'd be the first to know."

"In trouble with Karim?"

"Give me a little credit, lover," she said.

Instead I gave her a little time. Sometime with a client you just wait and he speaks, he incriminates himself, he caves. Priscilla wasn't a client and she didn't cave.

Finally I spoke, and told myself it wasn't that I was caving.

"I don't think I want you to be out scouting jobs for me. If you need things to do, there must be other things."

"Didn't you say we're partners?"

"Probably I thought it, but I didn't say it like that."

"So there! I read your mind, dear. Oh come on, everything has to move along, doesn't it? Just look at Jeff, how he changes every day. Let Jeff be an inspiration to you, isn't that a good idea?"

I didn't want a quarrel. The last thing I wanted was a quarrel with my wife and partner. I let her say "There, there" and run her fingers down my arm in a petting motion, although there was something about the touch I didn't enjoy. The difference between being loved and being indulged.

The subject wasn't fully closed. That's marriage. That's something I would need to live with. At least Karim and Priscilla were happy, feeling they had planted a seed that might grow in the right weather.

Chapter 10

Nowadays a person seldom feels the instant sea change when a woman stops loving, closes the door. There may be a whiff of draft that the person calls "mood." ("Hi honey, how was your day?" No answer, mumbly nonanswer; no further questions, please the court.)

She took my arm as if she loved me, her eyes washed their blue all over our lives, she made the picnic and said, "Let's have cheese and wine and other good things, because we're lovers, dear man." Yes, let's, and forever.

The door closes silently in a house that is suddenly still. At first, no clashing of walls, shaking of foundations, just the quiet munching of dry rot, which means invisible termites. Not even a big fight over take-out-the-garbage or drinking-a-little-more-lately or shit chores with Jeff. She might draw on an afternoon joint, some old-fashioned Acapulco gold, the sort of pleasure a person finds when perturbed and alone but shouldn't find when alone and upset. She might draw on a little easing smoke and, like other people, give herself leave to repeat herself, inquiring again about Karim, just out of curiosity: Isn't it nice to be respected, lover? By a very successful business person operating out of a white linen suit he probably has dry-cleaned after one day's wearing? Hey, what about your bride having to open the garage door loaded down with an armful of groceries and Jeff? A Genie would be nice, Dan, works like magic on FM frequencies . . .

One day I came home and the wiring in the house was different.

"Oh. Hello. Hi."

Was that a greeting I just heard? Was it?

So I hugged Jeff and went to the bathroom and washed my face carefully in cold water and made the claim to my pink face, wet beard, that this was "mood." Jeff and I would roll on the floor and she could just be as much a part of Daddy-comes-home-from-work as she chose to be.

The next day something similar. And the next.

"What's the matter, Priscilla?"

"Nothing."

I pick up Jeff. He laughs. I throw him in the air. He laughs wildly.

"Someday he'll hit the ceiling," she says.

"Never yet happened. I was a pitcher. Softball in high school."

"I know a kid lost his teeth that way, his father showing off."

"Not me, Priscilla. I think my dad did this to me. It's a free ride in the air. Not showing off, I promise."

"Would you know? Define the terms."

"Hey! At Lowell I was all-city—"

"This isn't softball. Just be careful."

I could feel the frown gather on my forehead. This is hardball. I undo the creases with my fingers. Then I say to the other happiness in my life. "Jeffy Jeffy Jeffy, don't you like to fly?"

He says, "Daddy Daddy Daddy," that's what I hear, the spirit of pronunciation still at an early period of dadadada*da*. Pretty good, Jeffy.

Then I turn to my great love, my miracle blessing. "Want to go out to dinner?"

"No sitter. We can't just pick up like that anymore."

Why is she explaining that we now have a child? Don't I know?

"We can get one. The kid next door. Or we can take Jeff."

"That's no help."

"I'll take care of him. He'll sleep."

"No."

The word that launched a billion shipwrecks, the all-encompassing no, the lips no-ing white at the edges, the eyes no-ing hard in their blue clarity, the face and body finding other places to be in a small house when the husband walks toward her; the no-in-chief; the no of no-ness.

Or it might have filled the air of another day.

Or been just gradual, like leukemia, a leaking of illness into the lymph system, capillaries wriggling for cover like worms.

Dimly dumbly dying, I took notice of something I had named "mood." It was more than mood. Emergency call to KCBS: our marriage was injured up to the point of asking to be considered dead. There was a thrill in the unmoving air of a house, something brutal, not quite fully happening yet, being prepared; like a lynching in the neighborhood, or an unannounced lightning war, an attack precise in scale but total. Priscilla was a brilliant antagonist with a pure heart, maybe the only pure heart I'll ever meet.

With such power she loved and didn't love!

We had dinner, talking to Jeff and not each other, and then put Jeff to bed. As I bathed him, watched him splash, dodged storms, Priscilla came into the bathroom; she had something to say; she chose not to say it. She opened her mouth and shut it. This was not Priscilla's way, this silent scream. I supervised the brushing of the Jeff teeth. I urged the putting away of the Jeff toys. I told the story. Again Priscilla came toward us, her lips parted, then shut, and then she bent to kiss him. Goodnight, Jeffie. Goodnight, Daddy. Goodnight, Jeffie. Goodnight, Mommy.

I thought she should have the last goodnight. Sweet dreams, Jeffie.

She shut his door carefully and listened. It was one of those evenings when he was drifting off nicely. Good.

She came out to tell me she had been wanting to mention something, and I was relieved that she would finally be mentioning whatever it was that needed to be mentioned. Again her mouth opened and shut with its barricaded scream.

"Please say it," I asked.

She shook her head. "I'm not sure how."

"Just whatever comes to you."

"What comes to me," she said with a tentativeness unlike Priscilla. Violently, with a gesture of violent head-shaking no-saying, she planted her legs in a hard straddle in front of me and shouted: "What the hell makes you think it's *my* job to clean up your friend's dog shit?"

I stared.

"Mingus!" she said. "Your goddamn friend's mess!"

Now I knew what she was talking about. "You've got a memory like an elephant."

Her voice turned cold and quiet. "No I don't. I only remember what I need to remember. We'll see if you like it better that way."

I didn't yet understand; it was too simple and pure. She was looking at me in a way that made me think she was staring at someone hidden by my body. I turned to see. No one there. She didn't laugh. But now that the ice was broken, she felt easier in herself, she was on a roll, she spoke with her usual calm and almost amused control, finding exactly the words she needed in order to make her point. Some kind of logic had been distilled and purified by her long silence.

"I didn't think I'd grow up to cook dinner for a black cop and a Jewish private snoop, no disrespect intended, dear—"

"Of course not. The surprises life brings."

"—and wiping up after their pet doggy."

I couldn't answer. I had no answer. I wondered if I was supposed to have an answer. "Is that how you saw it?"

She looked genuinely pained. "Dear, I don't remember how I saw it then. Probably not like that. But that's how I see it now."

She was moving backward; there must have been a reason for my graceful wife's bumping against a framed double photograph of the two of us on a table, knocking it so that it fell like a shot bird, wings flapping; she looked frightened and puzzled. I stopped advancing on her—I realized I had started violently forward. I ran into the bathroom. I turned on the cold water and splashed my face with it. No disrespect intended. No disrespect intended. I didn't want her to hear me so I let the faucet run.

She was in bed when I came out. I picked up the double-framed photograph and unfolded its wings. The glass wasn't cracked. That was a good sign; it would have been too much. I reinserted the Polaroid of Jeff where it had been stuck between the glass and the frame. I stood the hinged frames back in place next to the lamp on the table and wondered if she would leave it there. I spent the night in the normal place of a husband in a whole lot of trouble. On the couch, no disrespect intended.

And the next night she was breaking a hairbrush over my upraised arm when I refused to believe she had decided to separate our lives. "I just want to live apart, I need you to move out, I don't want to be married just now."

"Just now?"

And the hairbrush was cracking on my arm because I refused to understand.

"Just now," she said.

The routines of sudden departure, in my case, did not send me to an all-night movie or a hotel. I spent the night in Alfonso's high-rise in the Western Addition. Then I found a room. Then I started looking for a place to live. Sometime soon I would learn to sleep alone. So far I was just learning to sweat and turn alone, stare into the unfamiliar black ceiling above me, hurtle toward nonsleep in a place where unfamiliar house creaks and appliance noises seeped through unfamiliar walls. I shuffled toward dawn. It didn't help when Alfonso advised me that all this was normal, a stage. I had difficulty understanding the drill.

The drill would be an uncharted path except that so many have walked along it, worn down the territory, that only the tops of heads are visible.

A week later Priscilla surprised me with a telephone call, nothing on her mind really, just a suggestion: "Want a cup of tea?"

"It's late."

"I know." She waited. "Everyone's asleep."

Well, maybe herbal tea, a mouth-refreshing Mint Medley, would be a good idea. So I spent an hour in her bed, which used to be our bed, and then got up because I didn't know how Jeff would understand it if first I was gone and then I was there, first I was moved out and then I was waking him for breakfast. He could pronounce Daddy perfectly now. "Daddy? Daddy?"

As I got up to dress in the dark, she was saying sleepily, "You going?" I wondered if she would add "Stay." She didn't.

Here was the table, here was the chair, here was the things in our bedroom. This was the bed where Jeff's brother or sister might have been created; this was the bed Jeff used to climb into for a hug when he had a bad dream. I moved clumsily, still sticky, as silent as a burglar in my former house.

I was lacing my shoes. Priscilla sat up and she was whispering to me in the dark. "I can't imagine," she said.

"I can't hear you."

"I can't imagine not ending our lives together."

My hands shook on the laces. I wanted to hurt her. I pulled a knot. I'd have to cut the lace later. I said, "That's only the movies."

"What?"

"Where people separate, get divorced, and then after

many years, when they are elegant and old, no else is in their lives, time has stopped, they are beautiful, the same as before because they're stars, not people, only there's a little gray in their hair . . . That's only the goddamn movies!"

She sat there naked, a pillow held to her chest for warmth, and said, "You mean it stops?"

She was shaking her head helplessly. She was crying. I left in the middle of the night and looked back to see her face at the unlit window as I started the motor. A neighbor kid, cruising, looking for a parking place, was glad to see me go.

Chapter 11

Therefore it was a miracle Priscilla worked in her heart, something even better than separation, annulment, or divorce—the forward progress of forgetting. History could be wiped away, bringing a new chance for a woman who was young enough to be still greedy for her future, not her past. "Do you remember spotting Jesus Christ Satan on Polk?" "Sort of. The crazy." "Do you remember when we . . ." "I don't have a good memory, Dan." And the eyes ruefully smiled.

How alert she was to her own beauty. How wondering and shy in herself because she didn't know why she did what she did, knew she had to do something, whatever it happened to be—an impulse welling up in her like groundwater flooding out all at once, eroding the foundations, a force of nature, the rushing underground stream refusing to be dammed. Something wanted her to end her marriage, which also happened to be my marriage and our marriage, and she assented to this something almost joyously. Even if it hurt her, made her feel alone, lonely, tearful, offering no explanations except the one she suggested through clenched, denying teeth: "I thought it was only my period. It's never only my period."

She didn't have to believe anything she said. It was others who seemed to need words. She adapted to their habits. Out of innate courtesy and good breeding she could be persuaded to provide words. She didn't have to believe them, not this wife and mother. Not Priscilla with the eyes that gave blue certainty back to a needy and uncertain world.

Reluctantly she sat with her husband at the kitchen table while Jeff finished his nap. He would wake eventually, but her husband refused to climb out of his own sleep. I knew it did no good, but incomprehension kept me asking the questions again and again, clutching the coffee mug I had used for breakfast since we started living together. Dutifully she tried to give me words, since I seemed to require them; refilled my cup; left her own filled and untouched.

"You know yourself and you're lonely," she said. "I don't waste time knowing myself and I'm no more lonely than you, so what's the difference? Who has the advantage around here?"

She grinned. She liked winning the discussion if I insisted on having one. She listened, hoping that Jeff was stirring or the phone or doorbell ringing, anything to end unnecessary post-conjugal explanations.

"We could keep each other company."

"About what?"

"You said about loneliness."

"Oh. I did. Okay, we could infect each other. Hey, that's how different diseases all get to do their stuff, isn't it?"

Maybe the disease was just being human. But her patience for remarks, for intimate remarks, the disease of remarkism—for what lovers tell each other—was strictly limited these days.

No soul union these days. "Maybe it's just hormonal right now," she said, "comes after mother's milk." She took a deep, relieved breath when the good news arrived for her from elsewhere in the house. "Can't be bothered, things to do. Okay, I hear Jeff calling and you don't even hear, he's up from his nap," and with a blessing in the form of uplifted hands, a shrug, a grin, a click of her lips, she was gliding away to pick up our son. He too needed to be eased out of sleep into the world.

Sometimes it happened that she thought other people

might have a point. They said things, they repeated things; things that were not her concern seemed to matter a lot to other people. She might try thinking of what others expected, such as explanations, justifications, afterthoughts, remembering. She knew folks did these sort of things. When they drank coffee in the afternoon, they had to do something besides drink the coffee. She wasn't really sure why, but she was willing to take heed and give thought before she dismissed the idea. She didn't mind being a puzzle to others and to herself. Perhaps it was courteous, though, to think things through or along, since it seemed to matter to them.

So there were these afternoon visits, at least until she would have to put a stop to them, and there was her husband again sitting opposite her at the kitchen table, hand grabbing his coffee mug, asking and asking at her. She shrugged. There's something that's real, clear, traditional, and well understood: shoulders hiking, then relaxed; pale eyebrows lifting, then back in place; ironic smile playing on lips. An intelligent woman had no prejudice against the futile exercise of her intelligence if people didn't drive her too far. So she finished the gesture with shoulders, eyebrows, smile, and then said: "Freedom belongs to not being in love."

"Are you sure you're not in love?" (asked jealousy, asked rejection, asked hope against hope).

"I get it, Dan. I'd figure it out even if you didn't get that shrewd, angry look in your face. You think it's something about *self*, yuchh, *esteem*. Well, no. Okay, maybe, but I don't think about myself any more than I think about anyone else. I don't like to think about myself. I don't like to think about freedom, either. I just want to *be* it—free, okay? Okay? Are you satisfied?"

That wasn't the word for my condition.

"You've got responsibilities as a father and you're willing to let them float by. That's not my idea of freedom."

"Are you saying that I neglect Jeff?"

"Why don't you listen? I think you like him a lot. But you think your way is good enough for other people. Well, I want more for him in the way of schools and everything else. I take being a mother seriously. Maybe I personally, myself, want more, too."

"My income isn't good enough. Is that it—income?"

She was exasperated by my pigheadedness. "For you it's good enough. For Jeff, for me—"

"It's not anymore?"

She shrugged. "Some people change. Some people don't."

I was changing fast now. "I haven't moved along enough for you?" I asked, which is not at all what I wanted to say (desperation may have been hinted in passing).

"Some people learn," she said softly. She was thinking out loud. "It's not just about Jeff. Dear, I really want to be honest with you, but there's a limit. I hope you can understand that."

"Understand what?"

"That's what I mean. You have your way and I have mine. There's a time just to be happy. I had that time with you. It's nice, probably very nice as I sort of remember, but it's a short time. Then there comes a time when it's just routine and I'm afraid that's the rest of life unless you take chances, and even then—"

"You want to be restless."

"Want, a nice choice of word. Okay. I don't know if I'm doing it right, but I've got to do it now. Something besides wife-slash-mother."

"You could go back to school. Maybe we could work out something like that—"

As inkiness spread over the Priscilla-colored eyes, the face changed virulently. "We? *We* could work it out? Hey mister, how about I figure out my own plans and projects—"

I couldn't look at her now. "You're figuring them already."

"—like maybe flat-out making some space in my life and money, there are ways I know about—"

"What ways?"

"I'm exploring, dear. I don't have to tell you."

"What ways?"

She didn't answer for a moment—it seemed she was thinking—and then she did. "Yet," she said, "being in love is nice sometimes." And then hastily, stopping me before I had a chance: "Hey! Not that I'd recall."

Sometimes she recalled.

Sometimes, at the stage of general human hunger and monkey need to scratch, stroke, tickle, or cuddle, and behind her brilliant hard-and-soft blue eyes—at the moment of fading light, maybe, or late in a glass of wine—she expressed a symptom of memory without needing to dwell in it. "Come here. Let me pull that down. No, *me*. I want to do it. Let *me*. Let me run things for now, lover."

Former lover. Former husband. My pants.

It was evening. I had given Jeff his bath, put him to bed. I didn't know what book she was reading while she waited. Maybe she found an idea in her book or was just bored with it.

"No, no, just relax. I'm in charge."

She was. I had no choice. I didn't mind.

This graceful modern woman, this woman of today with a good appetite. Let her study running things, it's her turn now. Hook the belt back and let her unhook it, beginning to end. Zipper. Shorts. "Those Jockeys stick when you're up like that, how can you walk, Dan?" A hilarious wonderment. "Why should my hand there change everything, that's what I want to know."

I might answer at another time.

"That's what I've always wanted to know, lover."

She would still be a great slayer of mine enemies if I needed a few enemies handily slain. And she might choose to hold my hand if I were slipping away into oblivion—a brain tumor, say, or some other tasteful disaster—provided she didn't have anything better to do that day.

No, even if better entertainments were offered, she would nurse me. Convulsions would not terrify, nor diapers repulse, even if the day were perfect for a bike ride out to the windmills at Ocean Beach. When certain things needed to be done, Priscilla did them in good spirit. Offered a task and accepting it, she performed better than anyone. Those blue eyes would fade and swarm at the biologic turmoil on my gurney, no sphincter control, no bladder limits, just as her eyes swarmed over me when we made love, she came, another biologic turmoil, and then we made love again to the sound of tennis balls plopping against a hotel court practice wall at dawn. And she would clean up after me if that were the program (contrary to fact thus far). Whatever was called for in this life.

And what a warm breath she had. I decided not to try for incontinence and paralysis as a test of her decent regard for duty. I've decided to live forever because God wants her kisses to be remembered and I don't trust anyone else to do it. I have my orders. Remembering Priscilla is my job, Jeff.

My mind wandered because she wanted me to do nothing while she was of service. Sweetly smiling, she explored this way and that, brushing fingertips and lips here and there. She put her finger on my mouth.

"Shut up, lover. Let me. Don't think. Let go. Let me do everything."

I was desperate to change the history of the future. If it were someone else's, I would know how this story unfolds. Inevitability is hard to avoid, even for the stupid and self-pitying. But since it was the story I didn't want for myself, I poked at the air, failed at the simple task of sleeping, learned about abjectness.

I stood in the kitchen. She listened politely. The lip that curled was not her doing; it belonged to nature. If a person waves at a fly or twitches an eyelid when a speck lands on the conjunctiva, it's not a moral flaw. She didn't choose to sneer; her upper lip was an independent contractor.

"We talk and talk and talk and talk," I said, "and when we finish talking, we're a little older, and then the words go walking around us, we remember so much, I do anyway. So everything's the same."

She considered what she had heard. My speech. This walking around of mine. "You talk so much," she said, "yes, dear, you are a little older."

I waited.

She grinned. "But I'm not."

Not talking, not getting older?

Not so much as anyone could notice. I noticed that *I* was older: the spots on the hand, the shaking of my limbs when I wanted to say, Please, please. And I noticed her, she was right, she didn't change; she was on the long plateau.

Please, please.

She looked solicitously into my face. She didn't want to be unkind. She was still smiling. She turned to her book but didn't say, Let me read now, I'm in the middle of my chapter.

Then she did.

"I'd like to finish this one tonight," she said.

Leaving her book with a marker in it, she followed me to the door. She was polite, solicitous. She was a responsible ex-wife who understood that a person might feel lonely in his new dwelling without the familiar household things that make a man comfortable. "Here, why don't you take your mug"—and she put it in my hands, shining and clean, coffee stains scrubbed out—"take it to your new place so you'll feel at home. Anything else you need just now?"

Chapter 12

Jeff didn't say much when I moved out. He tried to help pack clothes in suitcases and boxes. He found a new game, handing his father things—socks, shoes, ties—saying, "This. This. This."

This is what parents do, this is what a father did, this is how it was. Son joins dad in the rhythm of leaving. His earnest, plump-lipped child pout was the same when we threw a ball or worked a puzzle. The way of the world was to learn new games.

By mutual agreement we left a few socks in the sock drawer, examples of Jockey shorts in the Jockey shorts drawer, samples of Dad planted here and there in the house. I put a pair of Priscilla's panties in a drawer along with my shorts. This sort of confusion happens to the clothing of married folks. Maybe things would breed together. I wanted to believe in magic.

Now I was living in the earthquake cottage I found on Potrero Hill behind a row of houses leaning at odd angles, their foundations protruding. Behind a real house, Poorman's Cottage seemed to have been born in seismic shiftings like a rock out of the hill; the street had been forgotten by the city, so that the gravel-based cement was crumbling and it was gradually becoming a dirt road again. My original prefab, a room added with siding, was historically valid, one of the shacks rushed up after the earthquake of 1906 to get survivors out of tents. I believed in history; liked it. The extra room, joined illegally, demonstrated that some people had hopes of nailing up improvements in their situation. I could be their heir. On its hillside above the former meat-packing plant and not too far from the Projects, my new home had recently been occupied by coyotes, wild dogs, rats, field mice, and a family of raccoons. In the corners, tiny waify mouse bones and piles of hair indicated a struggle for existence, but not being a zoologist I wasn't sure who had crunched up whom. These days I had my own problems.

The owner hadn't really thought he could rent this property. He struggled to control his joy when I said, "I like it, I like it, I'll take it."

"Price I quoted, rock bottom, it was a slip of the tongue, you'll have to clean up the shit around here. We don't supply cleanup."

"With pleasure," said Kasdan without pleasure.

"You'll have to . . ." The landlord's voice trailed off. A wistful property-owner regret crinkled up the skin around the eyes where smile lines might be located in a person who had taken up a different line of work. Instead, destiny had given him slum real estate. "You'll have to," he said with greater conviction, thinking at high-interest, high-taxes, high-risk speed. Since this was a death-eyed loser he had in hand, it was a duty—these are the rules—to take him. Cat got his tongue, temporarily. The place was so hopeless, leaky, shaky—a falling-down outhouse that only regular inspection payoffs kept legal—that he couldn't think of how to pull something else from a stone asshole tenant.

He struggled and brought forth data. "You a private investigator? Self-employed? That's all?"

"My own little business, been doing it for years."

"How about a first month, last month deposit?"

I performed the savvy used-car-purchase tire kick at a loose board on the walkway leading to the front door. "That stairway outside is gonna wash away we get some rain, I like to do a little fix-up. That's my hobby." Then I shot him a ducking, sincere, money-little-tight-now grin.

Even Gabe Montana, real estate investor, had a heart. He himself had come up from troubles, come back from tight interest and untrusting loan officers. He hated to steal from mental cripples who should be parking their brains in the handicapped zone. Divorce was no excuse; happens to everybody. But he couldn't find his way to further squeezing of this schnookeroonie. Besides, Christmas was coming and the asshole looked like he wouldn't make it. "You'll take care of the gas and electricity hookup, PG & E, water runs a little rusty at first but they say iron is good for you, I meant first and last month deposit plus a cleaning fee is normal . . . plus damages to the premises."

"We got a deal," I said before he could think of anything else. "I'll move in gradually, starting tomorrow. I like the tall grass in the neighborhood, those fields. Reminds me of country out here, Mr. Montana."

"Right. Right. Gives me terrible allergies," said Gabe Montana.

"You a relative of the quarterback?"

"People ask me that. No. Maybe. People ask me that all the time. Probably back there someplace, Joe and me."

"Love doing business with you, Mr. Montana."

He cast his eyes downward. "Call me . . . Well, guess you better call me Mr. Montana."

In case he had to get after me about little details like six minutes late with the rent.

I felt like a kid freshly graduated from vocational training, ready for the weekend garage sales, ready to furnish his first grown-up dwelling, except that in this case the Goodwill couch would be for the use of Jeff when he slept over. No, for me; Jeff could have the bed. Priscilla gave me some linens; nice of her. Alfonso sent me a barbecue dinner by the Flying Safari; also no advice; nice of him. That first evening the raccoons with their cajoling baby eyes came to stare at me, realized that my garbage was not going to be rich pickings—takeout courtesy of Alfonso was as good as it would get—and departed the immediate premises. They might come back to make sure, raccoons being as stubborn as new bachelors.

I swept up the shit and buried it, pending scavenger service. Hurt myself, I asked silent pardon of all the slum and field animals whom I had now displaced, paying modest yet exorbitant rent, burying animal detritus so the place could tend toward smelling okay. Urban renewal on the local level has its price. I was not at one with the universe, but I intended to survive here on Potrero Hill. I was home. Chateau Mope in the City and County of San Francisco. I hoped the waify, chewed-up field mouse bones were now just a fond memory.

Shelter a settled matter, I intended to get on with the rest of life, such as making a living and getting a haircut. I'd reserve getting my wife back for dreamland. Let's be practical. I made a little list: answer business calls, refresh client referrals, shop for food, pick a lawyer. I decided to proceed with care, doing only what didn't lay beyond my capabilities at this time.

Getting a haircut gives a person a sense that he's doing something, like other real-world life matters, it has to be taken care of, can't be put off indefinitely, carries some aspects of nuisance, frightens tourists, causes talk if not performed, *und so weiter,* as any great German philosopher might say. I drove to Jimmy the barber on Bush Street and said, "Cut it all off."

Jimmy said: "All? Ugh."

"I mean like a drill sergeant from when I was in the army."

"Surely you have misspoke yourself, Mr. Kasdan."

"A GI brush, Jimmy."

Jimmy walked around me, circling the problem, appraising the territory. He preferred hair long, not that it was easier to cut, just that this was how Jimmy saw the hair situation in my case. As a trained barber-psychologist, he knew that folks are making a statement about life when they ask for an abrupt change in their vision of hair. "Drill sergeant?" he asked with distaste.

"You can think 'swim team' if you prefer."

"They wouldn't let me in the army, dear, but I'd love it, I'm sure."

"Cut the hair, Jimmy."

Jimmy sighed. "Roger, confirmed, over and off," he said.

I settled into the chair, feeling strapped down and floating at the same time, like a space voyager sailing out, spinning, about to lose weight, as Jimmy made the vehicle swivel on its bearings. My arms were crossed tightly under the sheet. I was pulling myself together. I closed my eyes and Jimmy took the hint: no more discussion. Total attention was respectfully requested. Concentration. The Olympic chaos competition demanded efficiencies in the body: immune system check, diet check, random weeping check, hair check, whatever I could control. The uncontrollable would unfold in its own way. At least I could manage a firm grasp on my coiffeur until I got a grip on the rest of life.

I listened with something like pleasure to the lonely clicking of the scissors and the buzz of a clipper. Hair was dropping and ahead lay a new life in outer space. I'll be a drill sergeant, that's the drill. The red fault lights on the metabolic switchboard temporarily stopped their flashing and beeping. This time spent in Jimmy's chair was something like sleep, it was a state of meditative grace, in the deep philosophical sense it was the best possible haircut. Take it all away. It was almost enjoyable.

When everything is going and gone, try to enjoy what's left. I didn't consider every consequence. Severe family out yonder makes for severe consequences.

When I appeared with my hair cut short, Jeff burst into tears, crying, "Daddy," with vast reproach. Who was I? He ran. Who was I now? I found him hiding in a closet, still sobbing. I put my arms around my son. The hot fists dug into my back and I could feel the tears flooding down Jeff's face onto his neck, the unsparing, rational hot tears of a child. What a stupid daddy, what a stupid time to look like a stranger.

I was living in a dream, which is a time furnished with self-pity and copious not thinking. I took Jeff to McDonald's. Extreme times require extreme temporary measures—let him suck the milkshake ooze from a fast-food nozzle.

In the mirror of the bathroom (ask cashier for the key, customers only, this is America), I didn't see a high school swimmer or army drill sergeant looking back at me. I saw a nerd with creased cheeks and a dusting of gray. All this loser needed was a shirt with a plastic guard for pens in the pocket and little notches in the short sleeves. Well, hair grows, like nails, even if you're dead and the body is shrinking. It'll do that; lighten up. I decided to cut myself a little slack here. I came back to where Jeff was making gurgles in his Monster-Good ChocoShake (appellation registered) and said, "It'll grow back. In a few months it'll be like it was."

"What?" Jeff mumbled through a ChocoShake mustache.

Nothing will, nothing, it's just hair. Love means even the ChocoShake smell on a son's breath gives proof of life. But I said, "That straw is empty. The noise is driving me crazy. Give it up."

"Some more?"

"No!"

Jeff grinned. Don't have to say it so loud, Dad.

To make up for the griefs of the ages, and also to reward that grin, those gap teeth which would need orthodontic attention and regular payments by the responsible father, Kasdan sought amid the noise of fast-food punch-out registers some way to express his interesting notion, survival. He was forming this resolution. He would tell Jeff about the raccoon family with their eyes surrounded by dark fur, Mr. Montana with his eyes surrounded by petty greed. He would promise that they could hunt through the old tires, discarded radiators, undulating grasses, wild weeds, and crushed yerba buena pungency behind Poorman's Cottage. When Jeff saw that he had a house, a kind of house of his own, for the two of them, he would feel better. In the meantime, just this once, Kasdan gave his son money to go to the counter for another ChocoShake oozing out of the Monster-Good machine like an endless brown soft-frozen snake.

And I stared at Jeff as he waited for the snake to curl into the container. From a distance I could see him losing the pretty baby look. It was just oozing out of him like the snake, and being replaced by the tough defiant exterior of a hurt boy, thanks to time and normal events. Jeff bore his prize back to his dad, remembering to ask for two spoons.

Chapter 13

I don't know what skunk lettuce is, but there's some-thing behind the toolshed that smells as if it should be; maybe it's skunk cabbage (on Russian Hill, it would be skunk arugula with pesto droppings); and there are wild daisies and dande-lions; and everywhere that filmy, veiny lank plant that sends up a whiff of licorice when I snap a tentacle. Maybe it's fennel. I hope it's yerba buena, which provided the original name of this village before it became San Francisco, filled in the marshes, greened over the sand dunes, and settled matters for the Indi-ans.

Sometimes kids from the Projects came foraging like Na-tive American ghosts in the urban fields and leftover hillsides near Poorman's Cottage. Probably the kids couldn't sleep for all the dope dealing and irregular bursts of gunfire; the hunters were junior high dropouts, DITs (dealers-in-training), learning to step lively over the minefields of the former Yerba Buena. When I snapped the lights on at odd hours of the night, they realized this light sleeper, somebody's runaway dad, wasn't a normal, responsible motherfucker. He didn't have any valu-ables. He probably had a gun.

Street-smart, urban-meadow-smart too (goes with the territory), they sensed rage in the tenant of the old haunted hut. Kept their distance. Surely a Glock, maybe an Uzi, tear gas, knives, and a mess-around temper. Since they slept by day, the kids seldom glimpsed the actual slumping person.

So they mostly left his turf to the raccoons. Shit, bears could eat that old never-sleep whitey, far as they were concerned. They kept pretty busy not going to school.

At night, when I was putting on the light, scaring off the Project kids and the raccoons, all I wanted was to deal with my insomnia. Dreaming should have interested me, but the dreams I offered myself were without egress. I could bounce off the walls better awake. I tried to read, but my eyes were too grainy with conjunctival road wear. Can't read, can't sleep. Can think as long as it's the thought polished by repetition and overuse, rolling around loose, banging against the skull and chest cavity, doing no good. Tread gone from my thoughts, too.

A Jewish beatnik private eye, former philosophy instructor, could be interesting at a certain time in a woman's life, when she was young enough, if the Summer of Love was near enough, if it was San Francisco and the weather was almost always good. But now she was a grown-up. She might like to find a job that could use her quick brain and focused attention. It wasn't her chief thought to find a classier man than this somewhat interesting one, but if that happened, she might not mind. Or she could just have friends, men and women, and love watching her son's progress. There was so much freedom and opportunity out there for Priscilla. She would lose it if she didn't use it. So now she would use it.

The point was: She didn't like it that so many important decisions had been taken away from her and made in the dark or on the slope of Mount Tamalpais when she was too young to know what she was giving up. Desire wasn't supposed to lead a person to loss of options. Priscilla wanted her options back; was that so bad? She didn't want to be unfair. She wanted to be fair to everybody.

Now was the time to be fair to Priscilla. Some of her coffee-in-the-afternoon friends, playground friends, also going through their discontents with marriage, described it as a

Woman thing, an issue. Priscilla didn't care to separate herself from marriage as part of a movement, although she listened attentively to Meredith, who pushed her daughter on the swing and raged about lawyers (her husband) who got to have power lunches with no spit-up on their shirts. She could see Meredith's point of view. Priscilla pushed Jeff on the adjacent swing, smiled dreamily, said consolingly to Meredith, "Maybe, maybe," not answering herself or Meredith. Maybe what? She would see; that was the adventure.

Lying on my back in the dark, listening to the rummaging of the raccoons outside, I had the satisfaction of knowing that my ideas, when I mouthed them aloud, were not being heard by anyone. They weren't even ideas. They were rummaging among fantasies, nightmares, dreads, scraps of memory, self-justifications, justifications of Priscilla too. Alfonso said: "Stop living her life."

Since I was having trouble living my own, Alfonso . . .

"Go to sleep. If you can't, do something else."

So maybe I would do something else. I could talk to Alfonso—he said to telephone him if I had nothing better to do—but at his age Alfonso didn't deserve to be punished for my sins. On the other hand, if Priscilla were there to listen, I wouldn't be talking to myself during the sleepless Potrero Hill night, would I? So the whole deal was a wash.

No, it wasn't a wash; it was something else. My argument with Priscilla accumulated in great circles over my head, like thoughts in a cartoon. I tried to revise her not as the love of my life but merely a great piece of ass. It didn't work. Tried again. I stood up and went to the door and stuck my erection outside to cool it down. Then heard a raccoon, imagined it lunging with its savage teeth, and decided to remove temptation from its path.

Then I failed to appreciate that no one was there to share this one-man anxious comedy. And probably she wouldn't be in any condition to enjoy the laugh at—what was it now—

nearly three A.M. A long, soft blanket of fog, glowing where the moon coldly stared through.

I considered masturbation. I gave it a long stroking think. But I wanted Priscilla's soul linked with mine, her hand on my arm, and jacking off wasn't the answer even if her pink and muscled butt was part of the question. I tasted sour in my mouth. My eyes burned.

I rinsed my mouth. I avoided drinking more than a swallow because a person starts to wake up needing to pee at my age, especially if he drinks water when he can't sleep. Here was an idea I could stand by.

Peeked outside once more, just the eyes this time, registering atmospheric roiling fogplay, empurpled by the city's glow, the laden air of San Francisco rolling over itself. Thought again of masturbation, nature's tranquilizer. Stubborn Dan.

Then I tried that boyish trick of imagining the lady of my dreams on the toilet, straining, succeeding, finally reaching back to wipe herself. It doesn't control the adolescent boy's perilous and desperate love. It didn't help me, either (how glamorous for her to fall off the damn thing with diarrhea, how lovely she would be, and how I rushed to help her).

Nothing unreal helps when nothing real helps.

Maybe I slept. Pretty soon, or more likely never, I would get over the bad habit of loving a woman who used to love me.

"He calls me Xavier's Savior," Priscilla said.

"Pardon?" said Dan Kasdan, legally her husband for a few more weeks.

"Because I'm so good for him."

I took this in without visibly gulping air. I didn't want to look like a fish. Fishiness is not a preferred presentation procedure for a man making the best possible impression on his wife-for-a-few-more-weeks. I tried to say something cautious and stripped of excess feeling. "Xavier. Xavier's Savior. Does he always talk about himself in the third person?"

"Oh dear," Priscilla said, "you're irritated and that always makes you sarcastic. About my hair, my lover, whatever comes up. But anyway, all he was doing was making sort of a little joke. I mean, meaning it but still a joke." She stopped and called Xavier back onto her screen. "I think," she said.

I tried the joke on myself. Xavier's Savior. My wife was Xavier's Savior. Yup, it was a little joke all right. "So why are you sharing this little joke with me?"

Now it was her turn not to gulp air visibly. Her control was not total. This must be serious. "Because, oh, if we move in together or anything—"

"You mean if he moves in with you. Since you're the savior, you'll also provide the housing—"

"—and it's important that you understand. Since we have a son and everything."

Jeff, he thought. That was everything. Surely by "everything" she couldn't be referring to the towels, the furniture, and a stock of ghosts in the inventory.

"Jeff," I said. "Our boy."

"Well, I want to be honest with you," she said. "Xavier hasn't had any children—"

What!

"—I mean, and you're the dad and all, always will be, but he wants to take an active interest in my son—"

Active interest, I thought. Her son.

"—not really parenting, of course, and I suppose you can't really call it step-parenting since we're not married yet, if we're ever going to be, and I'm not sure that's a relevant question right now—"

A question Jeff's father hadn't asked.

"—but I just want to check to make sure you don't misunderstand or have any serious objections, not to have some annoying surprise sprung on any of us, all four, I mean me, Jeff, Xavier, and of course you, Dan, but—"

She was nervous. How unlike her. How rude of her to be

nervous and therefore to be standing there with her hands clasped together and a very bright smile on her face, harshly asking my help. She had planned her end of the conversation but couldn't be certain of my end.

"Pardon?" she asked. "Dan? You're not saying anything?" She worked her eyebrows humorously. "Sleepy-time, dear?"

"No," I said.

Suddenly she was all briskness. "Well. Well. Well, Xavier wants to have a talk with you about, about, I don't know, but I trust him. And you know my instinct is good—I trusted you, too. Still do, Dan."

What a sweet thing to say. I was proud to merit her confidence. I didn't take all the pleasure in this scrap of praise that she may have hoped to give me.

Without spending the time to look carefully into my heart, I was pretty sure I didn't take any pleasure at all in this praise, sincere though it was.

"Make his point of view, essential decency, clear in a . . . in a predicament, I think you could call it, that involves all of us. He wants to level . . . the ground rules . . . sort of man-to-man, I suppose—oh, you'll see, Dan! You're always so . . . you're one of the truly . . . ."

"He wants *what?* To explain something to me? Ask me for your hand or something?"

Now she was on a roll. She was getting over the rough place. We could go back to comfortable banter about the newly important matter in her life and maybe, in some way she could not calculate, it was important in my life too. But my life wasn't really her business, was it?

"Not on bended knee, dear," she said. "I don't see Xavier falling to his knees like that, though of course you can never tell . . . No, not even as a joke. He'd be embarrassed. No. No."

I wanted to thank her for seeing the fantasy through to a happier conclusion. I also wanted to hurt the woman I loved, which was an odd desire I had begun to live with. I didn't like it, didn't approve, didn't resist. The desire was for her, to love and to cherish this woman of strength and self-possession; the fear was that I might hate her if she didn't stop denying that we had made our history together. She used to love me; I wanted her to remember that she used to love me. She didn't. She claimed the right to her own story. "I don't have a very good memory, dear." And: "Try to remember that."

There was some kind of buzzing going on, filling the space between the walls and between us. I knew what it was, that humming of thought, Priscilla's complicated intelligence—sometimes I called it calculation—and usually it meant something important was getting ready to happen. It was a kicking-in of new gears. It was Priscilla making sure she was still in control by taking charge of matters.

"Fact is," she said.

Uh-oh. Danger danger.

"Fact is, truth be told, it's a strange world."

Agreed. Duly noted.

"In my heart of hearts, dear, which isn't necessarily the deepest part of a woman's nature—"

I was worried that she was going to take Jeff elsewhere. I was worried that she was going to confess some awful intention that would cause great pain. I was not speaking, only receiving.

"—I know this might seem funny to you."

No. Not funny, whatever it was. I made the effort and croaked out hoarsely: "Tell me."

"Fact is, I'd rather be with you than with him, but you know everyone has to follow a road she doesn't necessarily choose."

"You're following your unbliss?"

"Okay. Okay. Sarcasm helps nothing, dear. But there's a job here and I've got to do it."

It was not very California of her, I thought.

"It's not very California of you," I said.

She grinned. "I think I must be from Boston. In my past life maybe, huh?"

Priscilla had found a winsome impotent lover with a habit of saying "I hear you" and/or "Thank you for sharing"—epitaphs for an age. Even I could see that Xavier was pretty, with those deep sad eyes and that romantic mane of white hair, long and clean and tossed by his fingers every time he caught his reflection in a mirror; but "Thank you for sharing"? His only physical defect or flaw was a sudden braking in the forward locomotion of his feet when he caught sight of a mirror. It stopped him, his eyes went tender, he stared, he fingered his hair. He gave the mirror an ardent farewell glance. He sighed and proceeded, for otherwise he would stay there forever and the world would halt in its revolution around the sun. Weep, dear glass, for this needy free spirit.

"Are you paying attention?"

"I'm here."

She was frowning and worried. "Just talk," she said. I must have fallen silent, as a person might do when thinking.

"Isn't that what we've been doing?"

"No, no. With *Xavier*. Xavier wants to talk with you. Just be civil and talk."

"Is that conversation necessary?"

Her smile was radiant and cleared away all worry. "Do it for me," she said, "for our whole family, Dan."

Chapter 14

For Priscilla, Xavier was a change, something old and yet something new. And now it was time for "Dan and Xavier Enjoy a Rational Grown-up Discussion."

Xavier's boyish good looks could appeal to anyone, male or female, but in this case they appealed to Priscilla and not to Dan. However, this tennis entity of tangled, healthy, maturely white hair, generous smile with shining teeth, darting boyish shy unease, long legs—the whole Town and Country Academy Alumni Association gathered into one good sport—had planned ahead and was ready to make his case to Kasdan. He asked Kasdan's okay. He intended to play square. All he wanted was to be an honest person.

I wasn't ready to offer a blessing to the man who wanted my wife, even if he looked me forthrightly in the eyes and said he really cared, needed, hoped; even if he confessed that this conversation made him nervous; even if he cast down his long lashes, blushed and moved his footwear uneasily. Xavier was giving it a best effort. Like many a handsome lad before him, he felt sure his personal appeal could win the day. How could I fail to be convinced? He was so vulnerable.

"This is really embarrassing," said Xavier.

"We can agree on that."

"Um."

"We can agree on that, too."

With a warm grin, a toss of healthy mop, a winsome gleam

in the eye, Xavier said, "You and I were sort of friends, sort of knew each other, so you could sort of think of this in terms of betrayal, or not betrayal, or maybe—"

Betrayal. Sort of. Yes. A piercing minty odor, alcohol and oil and tart, came off Xavier as his metabolism labored away, his sportsman's cologne excited by the heat of conflict, shedding itself with green and yellow implications into the air. Probably he wasn't really drenched in perfume. I was just oversensitive to my wife's lover's manly aroma.

Since I seemed unwilling to speak, cat got my tongue, Xavier had to do all the work around here, put the ball in play. "So I thought I should explain. It's not like you think. I didn't *want* to cause you difficulties. It's hard for me, too, Dan. I mean, it's not as if I had a choice about, about, about . . ." His voice deepened. "About Priscilla."

Politeness at least obliged me to say something, and so I strangled out a few echoes: "About Priscilla you didn't have a choice."

A shower of smiles tumbled off Xavier in my direction; a vinaigrette wafting in the stirred-up, riled-up air. It was a multimedia avalanche of gratitude and anxiety. He was so appreciative because I favored him with a comment. "Since you and I were friends," he said, prompting me to go on.

I was unwilling to grant him that. With the aid of all the therapy he had enjoyed, Xavier understood my wince and frown at the word "friends." He had insight, he paid attention, he practiced the art and craft of sharing. Therefore, he amended the word "friends." "Buddies," he said, "acquaintances for a long time," and peered hopefully up into my face. Would that be satisfactory? But trying to peer upward toward a being who was lower than he was gave this tall man an odd posture. Humble piety did not become him.

"I mean, anyway, these days, women tend to make their own decisions, too . . . Dan?"

"Listening."

"I mean a strong-minded person like . . ."

He probably meant Priscilla. I was pretty sure of that. "Listening," I repeated.

"Their own minds up," he said.

"Half a sentence," I said.

"Dan, I hear you. I'm upset, too. But it's so much better . . ." The sentence trailed off. The minty cologne level rose. He found it difficult to share with me what was so much better.

"Listening," I said. This was becoming my mantra. It was what I shared with him.

"Their own. Own. Level," he said, moving now from half sentences to single words. "Um." To a timid biding of time in the form of a sad, brave humming. A kind of grace note of vulnerability. An expression of Xavier's total good feeling.

And so he rallied. He had manifested himself today in order to explain and lay himself open and ask my comprehension and sympathy. He spoke forthrightly, lover to husband; well, hopeful lover to estranged husband; whatever. Words were not important; deeds were what mattered, plus honesty and compassion and whatever. In short, he had come to ask permission to court my wife, openly, vulnerably, respectfully. He took a deep breath. He was ready to lay his cards on the table face up. He was ready to serve from the deep court, if that was the proper expression—and it wasn't. He opened his mouth and then he closed it and then it came open again of its own volition. "I can't get it up," he said suddenly. "Dan, she's gonna help me. She says she can do it and I believe her. She had me checked out at this clinic they run at Stanford . . . ran through urology, diabetes, plaque in the arteries, all those options . . . Guess you don't need the detailed reports, but . . . Nothing physical wrong with me! I check out okay!"

He paused while I failed to congratulate him.

"So with care, with attention, with patience . . ." He shot me a Tom Sawyer grin. Shy freckles exploded on his cheeks. He twisted his hands together. He wished his kind-of colleague

Dan Kasdan would say something more, even something disagreeable he might overcome by love and understanding. It was my turn to share.

His kind-of colleague said nothing.

"So it's all psychological, Dan! That's the only problem! And all this time I was *worrying,* I was distraught, I felt actual *despair,* Dan!"

Now he decided, in this difficult moment for a man explaining that he would like to make love to his friend's wife but is having difficulties beyond loyalty and other such interpersonal concerns—he guessed it might be appropriate to make a little joke. He might try to lighten up. "You know what Priscilla said last night?" He lowered his voice to a respectful baritone hush. "She said a girl should train for oral sex by learning how to roll a bowling ball up a flight of stairs, using only her tongue."

His lips were wet and parted. His mouth was open. He hoped Kasdan would join him in a moment of male sharing.

"I mean, that's strenuous, Dan. It takes a real woman like Priscilla, not a girl—a woman. Point is, here I'll just say it point-blank, I need her a lot and since you were kind of separated already, nothing to do with me . . . And I really like, he's a terrific kid, Jeff, your son—"

I knew who Jeff was. My son. Our son, Priscilla's, Dan's. I didn't require this instruction.

"—because he's the offspring of a real woman who means the most to me in the whole known world, who really cares about me—isn't that something?"

"Something."

Xavier beamed. He was relieved that I was speaking again. He sought to encourage self-expression. "I fully recognize your rights of fatherhood, because you're the dad," he stated. "I mean, there's room for lots of relationship for everybody. I don't suppose I'll have a kid, though who knows? But I love him too, Dan, in my own way. I hope you appreciate that."

" 'Preciate. Sure do."

Xavier sighed. This difficult encounter was drawing to a close. He had carried it through in a way that a man destined to chronic impotence never could have done. "Not angry, Dan?" he asked.

It seemed that I didn't hear him. Xavier's face darkened a little and I noticed his fists clenching, fingers whitening. He had expected that I would fight back and since I was being—what?—passive-aggressive, it was time for him to rally other emotions, play the full organ of my humanity, get a rise out of me. "What you do, your métier, it's a fulfilling occupation—"

"Métier," I said.

"—for a man with cleverness, probably a clever man, had some sort of education, and Priscilla used to think it was glamorous, you know, a self-employed dick—private eye—but now she's a grown-up woman. Exploring people's secrets and dark sides might not be such a temptation anymore."

"You think trust fund is a more grown-up temptation."

"Say background, Dan." The smell I smelled was the vinaigrette smell of nice sportsmanship and appeal to better nature shutting down. "Say a certain tradition. Anyway, I've diversified my investments. You'd be surprised. With the real estate market the way it is here, I had to and I did. Whatever my family happened to be good enough to leave in my care, I've done more than increase it at market rates, I can assure you of this." (Didn't require proof.) "I have been enterprising. Venture capital you don't even suspect. Try to give me credit for being worthy of Priscilla, certain qualities I have, even as I give you full credit for making an outstanding choice in wife when she was young and easily impressionable."

This was a surprise to me. There was a man there for Priscilla despite his manners, his smug longing. The guy had an edge. Xavier played WASP wimp as well as George Bush did, but inside there was a killer. Kind of had to respect that. Before I came around, Priscilla saw a glimmer of firmness beyond difficult erections, something I was too prejudiced to see.

"I wish I could get through to you, Dan. We share a love, even if not in a temporal sense, so in some way we must be similar as temperaments. Despite appearances, don't you think, Dan?"

It seemed that Kasdan wasn't thinking. I was looking at a space just in front of me. *Temporal sense?* That couldn't have occurred. I saw a mote floating across my eye, I saw Xavier in a little cloud beyond. Fully confident that he was passing the test of masculine forthrightness with colors snapping in the wind, that he would want to tell Priscilla in detail what he had gone through, how he had led Dan step by step into the path of rationality and sharing, how they had consequently resolved the matter in a dignified and open fashion, Xavier showed me another boyish ducking smile, asking nothing more than understanding, fellowship, and decency in one of those complicated human relationships that so enrich our time on earth.

"So, not angry, Dan?"

And then I hit him. I wondered why I hadn't thought of that earlier.

After due deliberation, the former wimp Xavier, misinterpreted by me and inspired by love, would have hit back. Shaking his head and bleeding a little, thick blood oozing from a nostril, he would have risen. I saw him more clearly now. He was making the proper psychic adjustments after a jarring shock to the cerebellum. Deeper masculine needs were working their way to the fore as nose muck surged and the unseen mechanism of clotting strived to check in. It would take a moment or two. He was thrashing his legs and working to complete his thought about whether violence just now was really something to which he wanted to acquiesce. I hesitated above him as he lay awkwardly, still somewhat dimmed out. A sourness in the vinaigrette cologne. Then I didn't wait around.

Chapter 15

Many times I had wakened to the sound of the telephone not ringing, my wife not calling, but next morning it *was* Priscilla reaching me in Poorman's Cottage on Potrero Hill. The ringing filled Chateau Mope, where I was warming my sore hand over the mug of coffee while I looked out at agricultural and wildlife discoveries that could almost make me forget the aching small bones in my paw, the discolored knuckles and scraped skin, the geography of a fist probably foolishly used in one-sided, old-fashioned, outmoded discussion with poor Xavier. And Xavier had only wanted to use vocabulary with me. I hadn't noticed the braces on his teeth; in addition to everything else, I was a victim of orthodontia. Rational male-bonding asshole had gouged my knuckles.

Yesterday's cereal bowl was still in the refrigerator. With modern refrigeration there seemed to be no need to wash the bowl more than once a week, although a bachelor-in-training had to get used to facing ragged crusts of Kellogg's products and stuck milk at dawn, not one of the best sights for the lonely morning. Today I only wanted coffee. My right hand ached and so did my head.

The sun came up early and hot on Potrero Hill. Gorse was growing amid the tires of the junkyard slope outside my window. When I came home that night I had paced outside, kicking up the smell of licorice from the broken fennel plants. Had I thrashed about in the dark, I would have ended by catching my foot in the dry gulch network of my garden vista, so I had gone to bed, stretching, scratching, and farting with blocked rage because Xavier would not, could not, of course dared not fight back—against his principles. His large and giving spirit understood that violence is never an answer to violence unless you happen to carry an atom bomb in your backpack and even then your opponent might be into hydrogen or neutron. So let's give peace a chance.

Poor pretty loser jerkoff; sweet gentle egomaniac lover to my wife with the startled expression in his lyrical wide supplicant blue eyes.

In the fresh daylight now, I could see a blackberry bush, the berries still red as blood but inexorably ripening toward purple and tasty. A pigeon cooed. The pigeon shit (also gull) dropped on the hill and inexorably made things grow better. No doubt about it; they were part of the deal, along with the gulls sweeping across the bay. Gorse, Scotch broom, was a stiff plant once used to make brooms but not anymore. Bright yellow flowers couldn't fool me; it was gorse. Now we have plastic and don't need Scotch broom with its yellow flowers deeply committed to life among the fennel plants, blackberry bushes, tires, and spittle bugs flashing in sunlight when I stepped among them.

I kind of liked my lair. I was getting used to it. I was getting to know it. Poverty suited my soul just now. I was not tending to business, I was enlisting in the child-support ramble. I was poor. But I was already beginning to settle in like any other animal in a place it had not chosen. I even hoped the raccoons would come back; all was forgiven.

Sweet wife, sweet former wife; you did, after all, leave me living. Still alive after all, sweet lady.

Ring-ring-ring. Tight-lipped Priscilla saying: "I heard what you did."

"And what did I do?"

"He's twice the man you are because he didn't stoop to—"

"He fell," I said.

"You're proud of yourself. He didn't stoop to brawling with you. You realize, of course, he's younger than you are. He's just as fit, maybe more so. If he'd wanted to, if he'd had some notice of what was coming, or just if he *wanted* to—"

"Yeah. I know he could have fought back. He was down, but not out."

"Do you know how smug you sound?"

"I think so. Yes. Probably."

"You're still proud of yourself, aren't you, Buster?"

And then she stopped. She was thinking. Was she going to say "macho"? No, she would spare them that. She had an idea that this conversation was useless and unnecessary, yet there was some point she wanted to make with her former, very soon to be forever former, husband, now known as Buster. The point was her anger. The point was to let Buster know in such a way that he would feel it. The thought of my smug comfort distressed her sense of justice. No doubt I was sitting there with a cup of espresso, the morning *Chronicle,* my feet on a table, and a contented half-smile on my stupid macho face. Not a pretty picture.

Priscilla didn't believe in useless fretting, stewing, the destructive practice of anger. She believed in making points and moving on.

I could hear her breath on the phone. I could imagine the little motion of her nostrils, like that imperceptible minnow agitation after we made love—when her face was still, her eyes blank and departed, and then she returned to me with a smile, her nostrils taking breath eagerly, greedily. Her soul alive to herself and me, returned from its voyage. Her eyes studying mine as if our souls could be printed upon each other forever.

"I guess you know he had a problem," she said, "because I let you know, nothing for a real man to be ashamed of in my opinion, nothing to feel smug about if you're not, it's just human, just shows feelings, a sensitivity, an awareness. But

Xavier is fine, it's nothing physical. He's healthy. He checked out okay."

"Great."

"And about that problem, Dan. Sure, he needs me. What I do is I imagine I'm rolling a tennis ball up a flight of stairs—"

How wise of her to reserve this conversation for the telephone. Now that there was a precedent of my losing control, she knew enough to say certain things at a time when all I could do was break the electronic connection.

Macha. But I wouldn't break the connection. I wouldn't say anything that would make her hang up on me. I would just wait and let her listen to herself because she learned better that way than from anyone else. I waited to hear what she would say next about how Xavier impotent was more moving to her than Dan with machinery functioning and no need to roll a tennis or bowling ball up a flight of stairs in that special way.

But had I said something anyway?

Because she had hung up and I was alone, grasping the telephone in my scabbed fist.

Months passed, moons and cycles; unrelieved compassion tends to tucker out; even the joys of helping a man with a deeply human and normal male problem were passing. My hand healed. A person forgets, when he grows up, how long such healing takes, given the constant flexings, washings, general busy use of both fists and open hands. Or maybe the wounds from scuffles and accidents heal more slowly at my age, as do all other injuries. Socking a playground rival is boy's work.

In the mornings I once again awoke to the sound of the telephone not ringing and stared out the window at broom grass, yellow flowers, fennel; I grasped the mug of coffee, reached for my crusted cereal bowl chilled from the refrigerator, read the *Chronicle,* kept busy.

The telephone didn't ring and that was all right with me.

More months, the season of yellow flowers dropping, butterflies disappearing, and I knew from seeing Jeff, from watching Priscilla, that the pleasures of curing Xavier were passing like the other pleasures in life. When the mouth dies, what is there? So then a person has to seek out new pleasures.

Then the telephone didn't ring and I wanted Priscilla to call. But I wasn't merely waiting. I was also watching the yellow gorse sway in the hot wind across Potrero Hill and missing the raccoons, the wild cats, the kids from the Projects, all of life that had abandoned me. Probably I was the cause of this myself.

It seemed that my devoted friend Karim never gave up. He didn't abandon me. I tried to avoid him by avoiding the terrace at Enrico's, but since my office was just up the Kearny steps alongside, there was no reason to stay away from the terrace at Enrico's at odd hours. At odd hours was when Karim, nodding, nodding vigorously in greeting, was awaiting me. His eyebrow clumps worked; the ants crawled; he had five o'clock shadow above his nose.

"Mr. Kasdan, Dan! At least enjoy my company one minute of your time, sit down to celebrate, please! I must!"

I sat. Priscilla thought I should listen. Perhaps I could tucker him out by listening. He was working a plate of pasta at eleven in the morning—no sliced banana with cream and cherries chopped by the waiter, Chad. Some kind of pasta with a white sauce and a napkin spread like a tablecloth across his lap. A different diet.

"So," he said, "so, my friend. Please listen. All I need is what you do so well. Find things out, a little information, find people for me, a little acquaintanceship, talk to them, keep it between us, you and me, sometimes maybe a little flight to Phoenix—you like Arizona, my friend?"

"It's not Las Vegas."

Karim frowned, bringing the plucked-hair ants close together. "Why is it—?" He saw me getting ready to stand. He changed directions. "Why is it I have this sensation, deep inside my soul, in another life we were very close? Why is it not so in *this* life? That is my trouble, I ask you honestly." He seemed to relax after the pasta, encouraged by my lingering presence; he dabbed at his lips with the napkin; the guy was really enjoying himself and wanted me to have fun too, increasing the world's enjoyment all around. I couldn't fault him for that. He reached into his leather case, a kind of purse with a strap, and pulled out a package of cigarillos. He offered me one. "I don't suppose you smoke, Dan? I do. I like to enjoy harmless pleasures, even if they are a little bit"—he pronounced it *liddlebit*—"harmful, but in California . . ." He waited. "You prefer not to smoke, consequently I also will not."

"Go ahead. I've got to go up to my office."

"Not yet, not yet, please. I want you to judge me fairly, Dan, that's all, that is the plan. I need your skills, I truly do, and you can also use what I can offer, buy nice things for that lovely woman, your wife. Lovely young women always appreciate nice things. The girls who work for me are no different."

"No different from legitimate women."

"Ah, my friend, such an unkindness is beneath you. Such remarks." He shook his head sadly.

A harassed street person wrapped in a khaki blanket paused on the sidewalk near us. Karim beckoned him over, handed him the package of cigarillos, and waved him off. The transaction required no words.

Chad came to stand by the table and I realized I was not focusing on the matters at hand. I thought he had appeared to hustle away the khaki blanket, but he was bringing Karim his morning dessert—the familiar bowl of sliced banana oddly scrambled with cherries, not chopped this time. With two fingers Karim picked up a banana slice and dropped it on the cement. He winked at me with his eloquent black-rimmed eyes. Then he picked up a cherry, dropped it, and watched it rolling around underfoot. "You see?" he asked. "Cherries run away, but bananas hang in there. You are more a banana, my friend?"

The man in the khaki blanket was awaiting my reply. So was Chad. So was Karim.

"Too early in the morning to play games," I said. "I've got to get on upstairs."

"Never too early to play, Dan," Karim called after me. "This is America. Please discuss my offer with your lovely lady. The divorce isn't achieved yet, is it? Individual employment requiring initiative, discretion, and reliability always makes a good impression. Try to change your bad luck if you can, my friend."

Women, Priscilla was learning, had a grasp of the eternal flow and meaning of life; they had to; childbearing, child rearing (how it usually comes down), the health of the planet. No problem; no offense to men intended.

When Xavier began to whine about how his past and future were burdens on his soul, causing even the present to sag like a tired branch—so much sadness in a fellow's growing up (his mother, his father, his place in the family), so much sensitivity spilling out of the corners of his eyes whenever he thought about it—he soon found an empty space where he thought Priscilla had stood. She was on her way to being gone. He may have loved the pale filmy red hairs around her navel as much as I did, almost like feathers they were; he probably loved them according to his own needs, which were unlike mine, the way men are sometimes different from each other; but in any case he was fast losing his opportunity to enjoy them in Priscilla's presence. Like me, he could try enjoying them in her absence. It's not the same, God knows, and He therefore offered us the gift of memory.

Men, Priscilla noticed, had a tendency to throw their heavy thighs over a person, get comfortable, start snoring. A woman then found herself staring at the ceiling, analyzing the situation, wondering how she came to be weighed down by all this oppressive male gravity when all she needed to do was shake it and say, first, "Stop snoring," and second, once again: "I want out, Buster."

"Uh . . . unh? I was sleeping"—the thick mumble of a man awakened and unable to carry his own side of the argument.

Well, talk didn't help. She'd learned about talk with me, if she hadn't known it already. That dark warfare space of the bedroom—one snoring and one thinking—was as good a place as any for the one thinking to make his or her plans.

A fundamental tenet for Priscilla was to create no additional landfill of boringness. It was a Green belief, a matter of ecological principle, even more than saving the dolphins or the rain forests. After all, mammals and trees can reproduce anew, but boringness just lies there snoring forever, weighing a person down. Too much routine had already been deposited on earth by previous generations, geological saggings of boring. Was a person just supposed to yawn and tiptoe around it, dreaming of flying? She would smile and pick up the litter, deposit it in the appropriate can, fastidiously dust her hands together, and continue on her way.

When Xavier continued to whine about his griefs, he became litter. He had a way of saying "aggravated" when he meant irritated. A lad with a family trust should have a better grasp of the language. She was sorry. He had ways that belonged to him, as folks' ways do, but it wasn't Priscilla's responsibility to deal with them past a certain point. At that point they ceased to be an interesting variation on maleness and charming. Briefly they were just cozy habits, and then they quickly became definitely irritating (not aggravating), definitely boring litter. Priscilla was skilled at finding ends for her chapters.

She adored the plot of her life. It had romance, it had opportunities for nursing care, it had anger and pain, it was full of jokes and entertainments. She needed love even if she might consequently not love. In the exercise of authority and power, she required rhythms of communion and loneliness. This woman's natural work was never done.

In the cycle of Priscilla's nature, Xavier provided all the right elements for a time, plus terrific thick hair and yearning cow-eyes, although cows' eyes are normally brown, not blue. She could save him from this cruel world. That was normal, part of her deal with the great chain of being. If a sweet handsome man can't keep it up, isn't it a fine story when a woman can show him how? She made him this gift. Later she might choose to enact the cruelties of the world upon him. Just because a skier is innocent, he doesn't escape the avalanche; just because a man is pretty, he can't avoid fate.

So she offered Xavier the same menu she'd offered me— to become bright, new, perfect, and someone other or she would leave him. Out of the laziness typical of your normal man, he was slow to make the proper selection. It was her job only to kiss away the warts and hunkers of her heavy-thighed princes for a little while; the rest was up to them; and if they were not up to the job, she could always go smiling elsewhere.

"He 'can't get rid of those old tapes,' " she confided to me with a wince. "At least you never said *that*. And I asked him to get tested for sleep apnea, it's called, but turned out it was just plain old snores."

When Xavier asked how she could ignore their tender moments together on weekend mornings and daylight-savings-time evenings, she told him with her kind, confident, unembarrassed smile—the smile that seemed to raise the question of why evolution hadn't made everyone like her; things would be so much better—"I don't have a very good memory, Zave dear."

Xavier was history. Priscilla saddled up to ride into the future. But she must have taken Xavier's arm, too, as if she loved him.

Of course I was hardly present during Priscilla's final negotiations with poor deplorable pretty Xavier. But I would come to pick up Jeff, sometimes just after Xavier had left, or sometimes in time for uneasy hellos between the two husbands-in-law; once she let me show him courteously to the door (no more sudden punches out of the blue). She didn't run to the window to wave goodbye to him anymore, and she had a tendency to open and frank audible murmurs. She liked to comment to me because I was still a necessary part of her life; bearing love and not-love secrets alone is wasteful of energy. May I be forgiven for not forgetting her? Not everyone has the gift of poor memory.

And I felt blessed despite everything. "Daddy," said Jeff, "I got to use the keyboard today!" The love of a child, a palpable ongoing fact, counts for something in the permanent equation between man and woman.

After Jeff was in bed, and then after the cup of herbal tea Priscilla offered me, and then after we had made love, a speedy silent high school act on the couch, I asked her: "I'm not nuts, am I?"

"No, no." Priscilla drew a long consideration from her stock of watchfulness; there was a roguish glint in her eye. "No, I don't see you choosing that way to go."

"People don't decide. You think I deliberate everything."

Little mouth pucker, little pout. "Up to you. What I think isn't important anymore. Except to me."

But it was, it was. In the space of silence I was praying, without speech, Let it be as it was, let us walk down Russian Hill to dinner again, let it be a weather in the world where you keep busy touching my hand, you take my arm as if you love me.

"I've given you something and you don't want it, but I can't take it back," I said.

"What is it?" she asked cheerfully. "Of course I'll give it back."

I stared, stupefied. "My heart," I said.

"Oh, *that.*" She looked worried. "If I could, dear, I'd give it all back, every bit of it. It's up to you. It's not my problem. I wish you the best and fullest possession of your heart, besides."

She smiled at the playfulness of her own words as they emerged, rich with goodwill and good humor. Even I had to agree it was kind of funny, imagining her handing me one ventricle after another, along with adjacent arteries, connecting valves, packed cholesterol, every little morsel on which she made no further claim.

And then she looked away. "I'm sorry. I'm truly, truly sorry, Dan, as much as . . . I can't expect you to understand me, you're so busy understanding yourself. But I am."

She was, she was. Sorry.

Tachycardia, extrasystole auricular fibrillation, the usual responses to her kindness and cheer. She looked sturdy and slightly flushed from our lovemaking. She couldn't understand why a zesty exercise of friendliness didn't restore my spirits. Yet she did understand it, too. "Well. Well," she said. "You get a prize for not giving up."

"Are you surprised?"

"I'm surprised that you care that much." She reached to put her hand on mine. The smile was unaltered, but the touch was warm and unsure, not like the harsh good cheer of her words, the glare of amusement in her face. She let her hand rest there a moment. Stay. Stay. Then she took it away. "But I always knew you were stubborn," she said.

"Not stubborn. It's because . . ." I knew it would just embarrass her if I spoke what I was thinking. Instead asked, "Don't you want to live with a prizewinner? Can I show you the trophy?"

"Love it when you talk dirty, Dan."

"Priscilla . . . Let's figure it out. You used to care, we had times I remember, there's Jeff."

Mo-not-o-nous. She could hear that kind of stuff from Xavier.

Briskly turning away, she let me know I was again going

too far. With the power vested in her by both Nature and her own nature she declared me in bad taste verging on moral bankruptcy. "I don't need reminders of the obvious. Okay, suppose we say you don't give up what you want and I don't give up what I want. Suppose we stipulate that. But what I want—maybe I'll want something different another time—is still the same."

I felt stupid. I must have looked as stupid as Xavier, even if less pretty. I didn't understand. The hot ache in my chest understood, but Dan Kasdan didn't. The throbbing at my forehead understood. I clung to ignorance as if it were an innertube bobbing in the rapids.

"I really want all the way free, dear. Really and truly. Try to understand."

Her look of sympathy was worse than her look of anger. Her look of concern was worse than her look of hatred. The look she offered was of one lost to me. Even that silent lovemaking on the couch had no consequence for her except that she would better enjoy her thorough hot shower and a good sound sleep alone in bed after I left.

Priscilla believed in the clock. Time moves forward in its flight, but the rest of time was none of her concern. The past interfered with getting on with it; she had a duty to press the Memory Erase off-on switch. Her style kept her efficient in ways I could not fathom, having no gift for on-off; to me, nothing ever seemed over and done with, finished. I looked at our cups of chamomile tea, cooled where we had abandoned them. She drank from hers and waited.

She used to say she was proud that "Kasdan" meant something honorable and distinguished in Hebrew. Perhaps she still remembered saying it but wondered why she had felt this irrelevant quiver of pleasure and couldn't quite recall what the name meant, certainly not "private eye" or "tendency to hang fist on New Age chin." Dan Kasdan, now of Poorman's Cottage on Potrero Hill, had no faith in titles of nobility, although I was brave enough to face down the raccoons, the blowing slaughterhouse smells, the big-eyed free-range Project kids, and even the midnight blues, shakes, regrets. I had faith in memory, though, and her dismissal of it pained me so deeply, so deeply.

It was about who a person is. Who I was, who she was, who we were—who I am now. Please, Lord, bring on the raccoons and burglars instead.

What I am is what we were together.

If it turned out to be entirely up to Jeff to carry on the privilege of memory, that was too much to ask of our child. He carried it in his body, gave evidence in his walk, his straight challenging stare, his grin, his statesmanlike blending of two people who were now strangers to each other except that they had once been lovers, holding each other close in the night, making love and making a child to confirm the sum of their decisions to be alive.

Probably Priscilla was not the best maker of love in the world; nor was I. Who is the best is just an opinion, anyway, and opinions differ. The problem for Kasdan was that, to him, she was the only maker of love.

The waiting period for a California divorce was now in place, the ceremonial agreements lawyered, signed, filed, and final. I was celebrating the end of the one-year legal limbo by taking Jeff to buy a new Casio keyboard so that he could make more beautiful music together. He would probably not have a brother or sister, but there were other things I could give him. I came to wait for him in that house which I knew and did not know— the towels were the same, but the kitchen was rearranged— waiting for him to come home from school. I was early. Being affirmed and registered this day as strangers by the City and County of San Francisco, according to the laws governing the State of California, seemed to bring a degree of shyness between my former wife and present me.

We marked the day by telling each other that nothing had

really changed. Although nothing was altered, I brought her CDs of the Mozart Requiem, which celebrates all death, and one of Bob Dylan in his Christian phase, to say that things don't necessarily get better than they were. She was startled by the gift-wrapped package; this wasn't supposed to be a holiday. The afternoon was chilled, as close to winter as San Francisco gets, grayness and a blanket of seaborne wet in the air after the brief, bleak sunlight at midday. Reluctantly Priscilla opened the Tower Records bag. Normal good spirits were hindered.

"Thanks, you didn't have to."

"Probably shouldn't," I said.

"I didn't think to buy you anything, so I'm embarrassed, but thanks anyway. How about I make you something instead? A sandwich?"

"No, that's all right."

"I could reheat some soup and say I made soup for you. And not feel guilty. Yes, do me a favor."

"For you," I said, "I'll eat."

We sat at the kitchen table, warming hands on bowls, and since I didn't ask any prying questions, Priscilla began to talk. She was celebrating the occasion after all. She said she was beginning to see her life as it should be as a divorced mother, either with or without Xavier.

"Great, great."

She stared. She was beginning to notice that the name Xavier, the idea of Xavier, made me less friendly. She found this quirk of my personality a little peculiar.

"You've been sane all your life," she said, "so now that you're nuts, you don't know how to deal with yourself."

"I'm just how I've been."

"Only since you met me," she said softly. "I'm not proud of making your life interesting."

"I guess so."

She sent a questioning startled glance at me. Maybe I

wasn't listening, just gnawing at the word Xavier. "I guess so" wasn't my style. Oh well, not her problem, either.

"I may be a mystery and pain in the butt to you," she said hospitably.

I shrugged agreement.

"But to me I'm just myself. Just Priscilla Kasdan. Keeping your name, by the way, and not just for Jeff's sake. I like it."

I was flattered and mystified. Yes, she was a pain in the butt.

"Not even thinking of taking, say, Xavier's name—no, not."

"Great."

"You always say that."

So I added nothing. I spooned my soup. Priscilla hoped to entertain me as my hostess this afternoon. Since the embarrassed shyness was diminished, on her part at least, she decided to enjoy the occasion, too. She said, "Uh, Xavier. Wouldn't you like to know?"

"Not sure. Probably not."

"Well, you're just gonna, dear former spouse. It's a holiday for us, isn't it? And really, this shouldn't do anything—what I'm going to say—but make you feel, oh, justified if that's how you'd like to feel."

And so she explained how Xavier had learned about the human body, meaning his own, from twelve-step manuals and how he had learned about feeling from record album covers, specializing in sixties oldies. When CDs came in, he had nothing to read. And he neglected to find the twelve steps to a strong erection until she pointed out that he was making it *her* problem.

"He wasn't speedy enough," she added, "to tell me I was a co-dependent.

"I don't read those stupid books, but know that's how you're supposed to answer."

She thought I would enjoy some flattering social gossip. I

didn't smile because I was wondering what she had shared with Xavier about me during their earlier, cozier moments of après-sex release, a unique time of pleasure because Xavier, future loser, was so grateful and Priscilla knew she was running the show.

"At least," she was saying.

A scurry of floor bird caught my eye. What was that? Her foot, her ankle, a leap of dance as she sat. But all she was saying was, "At least you read books about proper vitamins and nutrition, and also William Butler Yeats and What's-his Tolstoy, so you have some lasting worth. Probably."

"Thanks."

"I still like you. I learned from you."

Her foot was unmoving now. When the light in her eyes suddenly came on, she didn't want to make love, not this time. She was merely saying that she cared. I didn't mind. She didn't care quite enough, but still, but still.

"I'm still learning from you, Priscilla."

"And about me?"

"That too."

Now she wanted to make love; no, didn't. The unexpected power-surge glow in her eyes switched off. She was trembling. Something else was working at her and it was not something she could settle by quarreling, lovemaking, joke making, or turning her back with that little clicking sound of exasperation—tongue, teeth—which had become her frequent means of communication with me. It was a percussion music she made mostly for herself. It was a signal that needed no answering signal. If I didn't like it, I could discuss my complaints with Alfonso—guys have these guy buddies, don't they, for such purposes? They have beer, buddies, and easy lays. They whine and get along, scratching themselves as much as they want. She was sure Alfonso would be glad to go out beveraging—the hard work of an old guy pal—and hear all about it, rumbling, saying the right things.

I stood up. Surely it was Jeff's time now.

She motioned to the chair and asked me to stay. She motioned to me to settle myself while she uttered the thoughts that were making her tremble.

"Contrary to what you think, Dan, here's my point of view. You're a survivor and I'm in bad shape. I'm sure that surprises you."

"Sure does."

"Shut up a minute, please. You're depressed and I'm cheerful, so you think I'm the satisfied party."

"Right. All you have to do—"

She raised her hand warningly. She meant me to listen. I meant to pay attention.

"So don't advise me about what I have to do to help you. I'd like you to be happy, really I would. Fine, Dan, even cheerful if you'd like that, not losing weight like you're so busy doing, let it drop off you. But now listen carefully: *Me too.* I'm cheerful, okay, granted, *stipulated,* as you like to say. That's my style. But I need to be contented with my life. Maybe even . . ."

She was shaking her head and the trembling was not relieved. The trembling was worse. I wanted to tell her to speak up and she wanted me to be silent. I obeyed.

". . . maybe even happy!" she cried. "Why not? Xavier has nothing to do with it, do you understand?"

No, I didn't—yes, I didn't want to. Her eyelashes were wet and her eyes were turned away. I was not to reach for her. She would not reach for me. My lips moved and I knew the words they were forming but I had enough sense not to pronounce them aloud. Poor Jeff. I'm sure she thought I was saying poor Priscilla or poor Dan.

Many blessings don't happen. Understanding each other was one of them.

Part Three

Chapter 16

At this edgy time for an edgy operator in the PI trade, I received another call from a man I preferred to do without. "Karim here," he said on the phone.

"I recognize the voice."

"You're not that smart, Mr. Kasdan."

He was right, I wasn't: but I did. I saw him at business on the terrace at Enrico's, talking loud, downing his creamy pasta and dietetic sliced bananas, working his clumps of eyebrows with the ant herd in between. He liked to be noticed. Karim still owned his porn theater on O'Farrell where the dancers climbed cordially over the seats to get at the clients and earn their tips. This was the legitimate part of the business. On the street he was known as a trafficker who avoided arrests, a diligent person who used the porn house as a partial means to launder his earnings. His daughter, Heather, ran a stag act for bachelor parties. I had seen her perform as the stripping nun when a cop colleague of Alfonso's got married. I hoped Jeff wouldn't follow in my footsteps the way Heather (cute sharp ferret face, blow jobs for the groom) followed in her father's, although he was said to be good to the girls who worked for him, allowing them to keep their tips.

"I hear you talking at times," I said.

"People say I have an accent when I converse."

I waited, denying or affirming nothing.

"Could we enjoy a coffee, a little conversing?"

I considered. I needed money. I ran the possibilities through my head—transporting, laundering, proposing deals with his competitors. Enforcing. I had PI colleagues who did pretty well with offshore folks. What did I have to lose? I wasn't doing well anyway. "No," I said. "I don't think your work is for me."

"How can you tell when you don't listen? For such a long time you don't listen."

"I don't do your sort of job."

"How do you know?"

"I look for people. Sometimes I find them. I do background checks."

"Maybe I need something like that."

"I'm lazy," I said, "going through a lazy time in my life."

He was the sort of person who was encouraged by rejection; it had a charm for a man who lived by being sure of himself. "I hope to persuade you, Mr. Kasdan."

"My wife doesn't like me to do this sort of thing."

"*What* sort of thing, since you won't let me explain? Anyway, you're not married anymore, Mr. Kasdan. You will be owing child support for Jeff. You do already."

He seemed to have made his own investigation. He surely knew I was on the edge these days. I didn't want to hear his proposal.

"She doesn't hassle me if I'm late with the check," I said.

"Would it be much better if you never had to be late?"

I thought it over and said, "Got to go now. Got a client on the other line."

But before I could hang up I heard him saying, "You don't have another line."

Normally I plan to be smarter than that; used to be, anyway. I was still smart enough not to like the way he tossed the name of my son at me. I tried to think what I would do when he called again or managed to see me. Pretty sure he would.

Where I liked to do my planning ahead was in my office in North Beach, up the Kearny steps, above Finocchio's and En-

156

rico's Coffee House. Enrico Banducci himself was gone, but the café had been reopened for the old-time mix of tourists, real estate hustlers, North Beach artists, and porn and narcotics entrepreneurs, the normal easygoing folks who enjoy watching the passing parade from a traditional San Francisco vantage point. Sometimes romantic couples sat holding hands on the terrace, proud to be part of the great world yet lost in their private universe. I had sat there with Priscilla, asking her to tell me why I was so lucky and hearing her answer, "It just happened that way."

Broadway was relatively quiet tonight, late, midweek, and the girl barkers beckoning in the doorways of the topless joints were shivering. One, in pink tights, frilled pink top, frizzled pink hair and a navel ring, called to me, "Come on in, your hands are in your pockets already, big boy, you're eligible."

I took my hands out my pockets to wave at her. She deserved credit for quick thinking.

At night, on the steep Kearny steps alongside Enrico's, homeless folks made their home (so they're not really homeless, are they?) among Safeway shopping carts, cardboard mattresses, and dogs sleeping under the stars on lower Telegraph Hill. The dogs, tucked against the curled bodies of their masters, flanks radiating warmth, probably wouldn't have been found in other third-world countries. In Calcutta, they'd have been eaten. So these outdoor dreamers with their animal companion pillows were not like the desperate homeless street sleepers of Calcutta.

I edged up the steps past the dormitory to the side entrance of the wooden building. In the hall, an ivory glow was reflected off painted slats. No fluorescent tubes; our landlord didn't care to save twenty-seven cents a month by putting in carcinogenic track lighting. At this hour no one was in the other offices—no bookies, graphic designers, midget tycoons with pyramid franchise schemes. This was where Werner Erhard began est, shouting at his first recruits. I used to hear him telling the gang they were all assholes but with his help they could become better assholes, maybe, if they shaped up. At night I was alone on the premises and liked it that way.

I could have checked my answering machine from any push-button phone, even from Potrero Hill, but I wanted to consider things in a strictly business environment. Pure stubborn stupidity wasn't sufficient to account for my life; I was looking for other explanations, age, malignant nostalgia, liver disease—something it would be fun to blame. Dumb pigheadedness wasn't really enriching to my self-esteem.

I never saw evidence of cleaning people in the building above Enrico's, not very much evidence of cleaning, either, but tonight a chemical cleaning smell welcomed me and a bucket of green powder stood in a corner of my office, near the filing case. The stench didn't taste clean in my mouth, but maybe it was busy smothering invisible toxic infections. I sat at my desk, switched on the gooseneck lamp, and picked up my memo sheet. I wrote: Priscilla. I wrote: Dan. I wrote: Jeff. That was about as far as I could go. Werner, where are you when I need you?

The smells from the cleaning bucket were worse than dirt. I stared at the green powder in the pail that was like Jeff's sand pail when we used to drive out to Ocean Beach, except that beach sand isn't green and doesn't have that chemical smell. Jeff liked to pick up sand dollars, those airy tracings . . . When I heard the closet door open, I was ready with a question: "You left your cleaning bucket, didn't you?"

"No shit," said the man in the closet, stepping out, a schoolteacherish person with glinty metal-rimmed glasses and no broom in his hand. My closet-dweller was a dark cidery brown fellow with a weathered sinewy body. He had not been napping in the closet. What he had in his hand was a stubby weapon, cut down from a larger one. It would make a big noise if it went off.

"I didn't hear you cleaning in there," I said.

"No shit."

"You find anything interesting?"

I figured it might be a good idea to keep the skinny Filipino schoolteacher or night janitor or illicit-entry enterprise-zone person talking, if possible. A man with a gun is best kept talking, from the point of view of the man without a gun.

He didn't answer the question about what he was looking for in the closet. He must have transferred himself there when he heard my footsteps outside. I looked him in the eyes—couldn't see the eyes—looked at the glint off the bottle lenses of his glasses and kept on talking. "So if you're not a sanitary engineer in the building, what can I do for you?"

"I am."

"Sir?"

"Sanitary engineer stuff. I save phone calls, that type action."

"Save phone calls?"

"Make a point—"

"You're making it, waving that thing at me."

"—hey, and you talk too much while I'm making my point. Mr. Karim ask me to ask you—"

In that schoolteacherish gun-toting way, he said "ask," with an effort, not "ax." His nervousness and his gun were for purposes of signifying. He was a little man with severe eye problems. Probably growing up half black, half Filipino kept him on his toes and he needed to do a lot of signifying with the neighborhood kids, flashing his roll or his piece or whatever he carried to impress the folks.

"Mr. Karim, he like to talk to you, *converse.*" He peered around the room disapprovingly. "Why don't you get a better lamp, beam onto things?"

"I'm not usually here much at night."

"So meet Mr. Karim at the farmer's market—he like that fresh stuff, no preserve in it—down at Civic Center? How about eight o'clock tomorrow morning?"

"I don't like to get out that early. I get up, but I'm just having my coffee."

"Tomorrow morning's an exception. Maybe you be up most of the night anyway, am I right?"

The weapon was just for show. The skinny fellow stuck it in his pocket. It probably didn't even have cartridges. The skinny fellow was just Karim's way of saving on telephones, not putting things on tape, plus making an impression.

"If you never done your shopping there, you gonna love that farmer's market, man. All those fresh fruits and vegetables and dried nuts in bulk."

He started out the door.

"Hey!" I said. "Don't you want your cleaning bucket?"

He turned, his goggles catching the light from my gooseneck lamp. "You say hey to me, smart-ass, I got to give you credit. But man, I think you stupid, too. How about your responsibilities? Don't you get a divorce from your wife but you still got a boy you didn't divorce yet?"

I called Priscilla and said to watch Jeff, not let him wander unobserved, and were there any strangers hanging around the neighborhood?

"Dan, is there anything I should be afraid of? Are you in some kind of trouble?"

"No, no, you know me. Just fuss and fidget."

"Will you tell me?"

"Nothing to tell, just thinking night thoughts . . ."

As always, when I spoke with Priscilla by telephone, my hand was shaking when I hung up. But nothing in my voice betrayed anxiety, I was sure of that, because otherwise she would have mentioned it.

I thought it best, perhaps even interesting, to meet with Karim as requested. Although the message was delivered by a man with a cleaning bucket who had found his way into my office in the slope above Enrico's in North Beach, and this wasn't the way messages usually came to me, I saw good reason for doing a bit of shopping at the Civic Center's farmer's market the next morning. It would have been wrong not to enjoy the nuts in bulk and hear the man out.

The little brown guy was right about my sleeping that night. Karim had found a way to keep the blood moving in my head, the lymph system flooded and alert, if that's what causes a person to mobilize himself. It was almost a pleasure to be forced into doing something again.

I parked illegally in a bus zone near the outdoor market end of the Civic Center. As long as I wasn't towed, I wouldn't worry; always intended to rotate into the set of Florida license plates a colleague in West Palm Beach sent me every year as a Christmas present, but never quite put the screwdriver to work. Onion smells off the morning produce stalls. Admired the Honda clunk shut of a well-fitting door. The clunk now had a bit of rattle, like a cigarette cough; someone once tried to pry it open at another bus zone, figuring he might as well make off with the radio since the car was illegally parked anyway. Must have been a fastidious junkie who didn't like smashing windows, all those pulverized bits of safety glass.

Not just onion smells; *nice* onion smells. Down here in the Tenderloin, amid the homeless, the Cambodian and Vietnamese immigrants, the old alkies, the geriatric giveups, the Wednesday and Saturday farmer's market provided earthy, healthy, vitamin-filled fumes. Not even the hot air inflating the dome of San Francisco City Hall nearby could kill the smell of fresh onions. Folks picking up their bulk raisins, sun-ripened tomatoes, strands of plump white garlic, and artichokes from Castro Valley temporarily outnumbered the folks in the nearby outdoor offices of the transvestite and transsexual, twenty-four-hours-a-day, we-never-close retail exchange of drugs and favors.

I looked back to find a woman cop with her foot on the

rear bumper of my Honda, taking out her citation book, and then waving, "Yo, Dan!"

"Yo, Wanda!"

She tucked the citation book back into her belt. Maybe this was another lucky day. I even remembered her name. If she'd still been a meter person, where she'd started out, it would not necessarily have been my lucky day. San Francisco was sometimes a friendly small town where people knew each other, such as Wanda and Dan, and didn't give citations.

I didn't know the farmers at their stands. Some of them wore mittens, plaid shirts, work boots; and then, beneath a sign that said ORGANIC SQUASH, there was the young woman wearing a tie-dyed Grateful Dead T-shirt, denim cutoffs so short I could see part of the triangle of hair between her legs. She had a cute face with bright kitten eyes under dark bangs. "What's organic squash?" I asked her, and from behind her cart—now, settled on its wheels, it was more like a country stand—she said, "Bugs, weevils, worms, all good protein when you cook it—no cancer-giving insecticides, sir?"

"That's terrific."

"We sell a lot of them at Halloween time. We call those over there 'pumpkins.' "

"Good name for them," I said. "I'll take a weevil zucchini if you got one."

"Eat it here or to go?" the kitten-faced, button-eyed farmerette asked. "That individual standing behind you wants a word with you, Mr. Kasdan."

I turned slowly. It was Karim, no surprise there, wearing a long knitted coat, a kind of overgrown sweater with folds and drapes that made him look like a thickened, foppish manager of dancers. Several colors in dark shades, purple, orange, were woven together. He was nodding and nodding, smiling, dense trimmed clumps of eyebrows working, darkly stained lids blinking, the voice oiling out: "You sure do mess up."

"Explain that to me."

Karim worked his lips in the fresh vegetable chill. "Prefer not, my friend, worry you unnecessarily." He shrugged under the heavy knit. "If it turns out to be necessary."

The important thing in a complex negotiation is just to be there, not rushing to have a say, just waiting for the opening. I have learned this, but I don't always know it. This time I partway managed. Karim put his fingers around a tomato at the farmerette's stand. He didn't squeeze hard; he was only enjoying the fresh yielding flesh. He was smiling, nodding, urging me to understand him, *care* for him. I needed to make things explicit. This need of mine had been part of what caused the trouble with Priscilla, my asking if she loved me at a time when the answer was not going to be favorable. Sometimes it's better just to let things slide along. I wasn't like that. I was an old-time nag and worrier.

"You ever go about things the normal way?" I asked.

Karim sighed. He put his hand on the knitted wool over his chest and then back on a tomato. "Like everybody, I have human feelings, my friend. I think it was eight years ago, summer. I was younger. My best girl was pregnant—was I pissed—but then she had a miss, you know, a late period, and she couldn't stop crying and suddenly, right here"—his chest again—"I felt something for her. Sad? Didn't want to fuck her or anything, just sad. For her. Isn't that the normal way?" He cast his eyes downward, long lashes fluttering, dejected. "And then I went to the mirror, my friend, see what it look like."

"I accept what you're saying, Karim."

"No you don't."

"I believe you."

"But you don't understand. Nobody does. You're so smart you think you do, but you're so dumb you don't."

"Stipulated. What does this have to do with me?"

Karim was still exploring the tomato, pressing into it, taking risks with his nails. It could squirt all over me. It could even squirt on him. "My friend," he said, "but I really was sad. Would have changed my life. Have that son, nearly eight years old by now."

I wasn't going to ask how he knew it would have been a boy. Karim didn't need the procedures of questioning. I didn't need the involvement.

The farmerette with the bright button eyes and the fringe of bangs was watching us both with a happy Future Farmers of America smile on her pointy little face. During the moment which gave her a chance, she remarked politely, "Normally when people squeeze the tomatoes, we prefer they buy. These are carried ripe, farm to town, and we're proud of their mint condition. We even drive in low gear so's not to bounce them around too much."

I reached into my pocket.

"Oh no, not you, Mr. Kasdan. I was just explaining our tomatoes in general. You're not responsible for what Karim does around here."

Now the nice fresh vegetable smells weren't much better than the green chemical cleaning smell in my office. Sniffing around should be more fun for a man with a healthy nose in middle life. For that matter, as a coffee lover, I had been stuck with rotten coffee since Priscilla and I split up—either bitter restaurant coffee after cheap Greek salads and souvlaki or, worse, instant brown paste when I was waking myself at home, climbing out of a bad dream with relief when the alarm went off. Sniffing around with a healthy nose in middle life was leading me to Filipino office cleaners and Junior Miss farmer persons without a lot of sincerity in their hearts.

This was a *complaining* man. Sometimes I drank good coffee at the Puccini on Columbus, and Alfonso made good coffee, and I recall a few times, visiting Jeff, picking up the kid, when Priscilla told me to sit down while she offered me a cup of the brew I remembered.

Karim called me back to business. He preferred that I pay attention. "Hey Dan, two things people like to have said about them, and since people say those things about me, I'm a happy individual."

"What's that?"

"You mean what's those. Okay, now we're conversing. First, I have a great sense of humor. Everybody wants to hear that, but in my case, I'm confident it's true."

"Stipulated. And?"

"And he moves with a certain grace."

"Pardon?"

"People say, Dan"—Karim bent closer to explain, patient— "people tend to say I'm stocky, not fat, built slow and easy, not a kid anymore, but, Dan . . . I move with a certain grace."

I would agree to that, too, a certain grace, plus lovely eyes, if it was required. I had no strong convictions in the matter.

"And Dan? Furthermore?"

I kept my eyes on him.

"You kind of tickle me. That's as good as have a way with jokes—better. And you definitely move with an average degree of style. I'd almost say, in your case, grace, if you will kindly permit."

"As you say, everybody does."

Karim shook his head. "Didn't say that, my dear. Said people like to *think* that. About themselves they like to think it, and sometimes like to say it to others, whether it's true or not. It doesn't have to be true."

"Okay."

"So Dan, you have this clumsy kind of charm. Your kid got that sort of quality, too, only more so. Fresh."

I didn't find this conversation enlightening or delightful. The conversation was circling something unsaid, and—in an open-air market with scales and bargain tables and organic certifications over the beans, rice, fresh vegetables, and bananas that certainly weren't from plantations in California—it didn't seem appropriate to be having a conversation where the disagreeable part was undefined. So I just stared. I didn't even like the farmerette anymore. She had no business knowing my name.

Karim was patient. He liked waiting. He smiled at the farmerette. His attitude toward her was different from mine.

"What're you telling me, Karim? What are you asking?"

"Jeff," he said. "Your boy there's not exactly girly, but he's sweet, you know?"

I felt the heat rush to my face. "That's not how I think about my son."

"No, you wouldn't." Karim was satisfied and glowing in his knitted sweater coat. "Some people would, Dan. I'll tell you what."

"What?"

Karim shook his head. "I'm thinking. I'm formulating. Then we'll converse."

While I waited, I smelled the onions and thought of poison gas despite the fresh salty whiffs of other vegetables, the sugary undertow of rot. It was only a memory. I should have been thinking of good things, but I smelled tear gas. Nothing but a memory.

"You know that kid they took away in Italy one time?" Karim asked. "Father, grandfather, whole goddamn family was zillionaires?"

"Getty," I said.

"Yeah, Eye-talian name like that. Gotti. Well, reminds me you got a boy, too."

"No money," I said. "No point in that."

Karim shook his head. "Local people around here wouldn't be sending you pieces of his ear, like those Eye-talians did. For the fun of it, around here, they'd be sending you pieces of his asshole."

The market seemed there. Karim seemed there. I was in a spot where people were buying and selling nice fresh produce outside and I could see the dome of the Civic Center. And my arm was reaching out to grab Karim by the soft wool of his collar, choking him while Karim twisted and said, "Dan, Dan, have a sense of humor, I ask you . . ."

Off to the side I could see the cute farmerette with a forked hammer, the tool a person uses to open crates of lettuce. She was bringing it toward me with a smile in her bright, unspoiled, girlish eyes. I let go of Karim and turned to her. Karim raised his hand to halt the descent of the hammer, the fork darting and silvery.

His voice was croaking and his throat must have hurt, but all he did was repeat gently, reproachfully, "Dan, that's not careful. People can do harm, Dan. Try to pay attention."

I stood there, paying attention amid the fresh onion smells.

"Go ask your wife if you want to, the kid is fine. Why would I do a thing like that?" Karim's hand was gently massaging his neck. "Hurts, Dan. Shouldn't get so excited with a man you might be considering doing business with. I was just horsing around, kidding, already told you about my sense of humor, but what I mean is I sincerely hope you will consider how you can significantly improve your situation."

"I don't want any business from you, Karim."

"You're a man in need and so am I. At least we have to make that clear. Where we go in the future is up to us. You owe me the opportunity to present my offer, Mr. Kasdan."

"I don't like the offers you're presenting."

"Hey, hey, a little calm consideration. All I wanted was to get your attention."

"You got it. I didn't appreciate it."

"As I said, Dan, hey, hey. Calm. I deeply apologize, but this is one more thing I like about you—a passionate nature, it so much reminds me of my own."

"Thanks."

"Now let us put that behind us." He made a sweeping assward gesture with both hands. "Truly I have so much to give, someone who appreciates your qualities."

"No."

Karim enjoyed the vegetables and spice air of the market, the view of my temper, the prospect of accomplishing a task he had set for himself. He was fully engaged in his project and in some way that commitment was reassuring. In my present frame of mind (stumbling desolation and the ebbing of an adrenaline rush), I could even find space to admire him. Yet I repeated: "No. No deal."

He was standing too close. He observed me with compassion. His warm breath reached my nostrils.

"I am sure," he said, "as you think, think fully, my friend, you will find time to consider the opportunities. In my heart I feel most positive."

I needed to take a shot at getting things clear with him. If he wanted me for laundering money or carrying goods, I wasn't going to do it. I suppose, yes, I could consider going along with finding someone for him. Maybe. Someone he really longed to locate. Or maybe even a collection. Priscilla had a point or two, she had a way of showing me things; but I didn't like Karim's procedures for approaching a deal. He wanted to start on top with an off-balance employee. I didn't need to be any more off-balance than I already was. I may have needed work, I could even see why Priscilla liked him—a man who had fun with his life, no matter what obstacles came his way, unlike others she could name—but I wasn't sure I could afford to be hired by Karim.

I headed toward the Mission with my feet jerking at the brake, the clutch, the gas pedal, forcing red lights, always the sign of a man who is absolutely determined, has his mind un-equivocably made up, but isn't sure about what.

Karim lived in a tall wooden Victorian house on the wide boulevard of Guerrero, not too far from the Spanish colonial Mission Dolores with its graveyard filled with vigilantes and their victims, including the hero or victim named King William of William. I remembered telling Priscilla the story of my favorite con man, Dr. Lovejoy, buried here, who was asked by the vigilantes about to hang him if he wanted to speak any last words. "Not at this time," he said. An inspiration to a man getting along in years.

Karim's stately Victorian made a statement about cash flow—Caribbean sloppy grace, vines, a palm tree, wooden steps through a jungle garden climbing a steep slope, rocks breaking through the planting on the hillside. The siding was rotten and splintered in honorable Victorian tradition; the palm tree had shed its leaves, leaving untended drifts to crunch underfoot, like some San Francisco version of snow, a peppery smell rising as my boots crackled through it. The high white structure and the leaf-strewn stairs looked like a house in Port-au-Prince. Quite a nice little ecosystem he had here.

My footsteps on dried fronds seemed to serve as a wake-up call. Karim filled the doorway, all in white, dazzling, a real beauty, white pants, shirt, some kind of almost-linen jacket, white shoes, and a beaded belt flashing tropical colors over a hard jutting belly. "Welcome, welcome," he said. "So glad! Be welcome."

His eyebrows were still carefully sculpted into wide dense thickets with clean outlines, the ever-present antlike dots of plucked hairs between the clumps. The eyeliner on the lids, with an added gleam of mascara on the lashes, highlighted his fortunate natural pigmentation. The effect was lively and bright, and certified that I was correct in my view—don't get involved with this enterprise.

"I just want to say," I began.

"Come in, come in first, how can we talk without getting comfortable?"

"I know what I want to say. I'd rather not listen. I'm cutting down on my business these days—"

169

"I know. I fully understand, so when a good opportunity can be offered a good man—please do come in."

I stood there, smelling the mixture of cologne and anger being propelled out at me by an absence of calm. I put on my nicest smile. Probably, if the wind was right, he could smell my own absence of calm. "I'm not looking for a job," I said. "No point in going round and round about this. I've taken care to let my friends in the department"—I meant Alfonso—"know about your employee in my office—"

"You're not paying attention to your opportunities. You don't listen to what I have in mind."

"That's right. Better if I don't know, also."

The mass of muscular, pissed-off, white-suited smoothness was no longer beckoning me in. It was now blocking the door. "I don't hire people to come to my house to threaten me."

"So we agree. Now keep your cleaning guy out of my office. He left his bucket behind, by the way. Okay?"

I stood there looking at the man's hide up close, the thick gray bristles under his chin, the creases at the forehead and the long deep lines in his cheeks, the heavy lips, and his odd green eyes, which gazed at me with something like concern. Jeff obeyed me when I said goodbye to him—"Eye contact!"—and knew it was important to meet folks' eyes. I met Karim's.

"In my heart," he said, "Dan . . . I cannot feel right about asking you for something that you don't want to give. For that reason I have to inquire if your license has ever been questioned."

He meant my private investigator's license. The answer was no. No harassment of runaway girls, no billing for services not performed; an occasional failure to fulfill the assignment due to excess psychopathy, as in the case of Jesus Christ Satan . . .

"Yet you have purchased brownies from a client, my friend."

As I've said, I prefer not smoking. When I enjoy grass, I

enjoy it in a form that doesn't leave me with a scratchy throat. "You can't do anything with that, Karim. If anyone gave me brownies, they're not a credible informant. Anyway, the licensing commission doesn't care about misdemeanor offenses."

"Oh dear, would I want to see you in difficulty with your license? No and no. And in Sacramento, all that paperwork in the office, oh dear, with hardly a blemish in your file . . . I am only saying in another way that I have no wish to make difficulties for anyone."

Of course he didn't. He only mentioned the possibility to let me know what a good friend he was. He only wanted me to appreciate keeping his friendship. Sometimes a person likes to eat a brownie and space away part of his weekend or an avoidable national holiday. Priscilla and I ate brownies together now and then, used to, once sat in the front row at the Surf to watch *2001,* huddled in outer space in the front row; used to, now and then.

"Are you threatening me, Karim?"

"No. I reiterate. No."

Only mentioned was all, just so I could appreciate him even more fully than I already did. Personally, it's how I am, no different from other persons, I don't like hassles from the IRS or the PI licensing board.

I would try to take all of Karim's suggestions into consideration. I needed to get on my way.

One more time, almost mournfully, he asked, "So I don't suppose you are ready yet—"

"Not even for my own good. You're right that I need work just now. But not even."

Palm fronds crunched underfoot like snow as I hurried down the steps. Steepness made me feel taller, the steep descents of San Francisco made me step lively when I was heading downhill, but it was necessary to hurry now. The man hadn't even said, Get the fuck out of here.

At my Honda I looked back up toward the stately old house on its slope. The door was shut, the curtains were moving slightly at the windows, and it was as if I had never been there.

Chapter 17

Some people, when they say no most firmly, most definitely, most angrily, teeth bared and jaw set—that's exactly when they are ready to say yes. Priscilla was not one of those people. It seemed I was.

Needing money was a good reason. Trying to become interesting again to my wife was a bad reason; so were desperation, despair, the dream of escape. But the bad reasons didn't cancel out that faithful old American decision to do something practical about trouble. I was in need, hungry.

I went crawling back to the house on Guerrero, reared up on my back paws like a foraging raccoon, but both Karim and I knew the real facts in the case. I was as empty as one of the Project kids.

Karim was gratified to see me without too much time having passed and his friendship for me growing cold. He promised it would be a happy day for both of us.

"Okay, one job," I said.

"To see if you like it. Of course."

"To get back to making a few bucks. But no drugs, I don't do narcotic jobs."

"Be of good cheer," he said. "Would I, my friend?"

"No drugs."

He looked a little hurt. I had hardly begun and already I was worrying at him. "Let me tell you all I ask," he said. "Not complicated, no outside travel, this is within your capabilities. It's only a collection."

"For merchandise delivered, someone didn't pay for? What kind of merchandise?"

Karim shook his head. It wasn't supposed to be like me to complicate matters by asking foolish questions. "If it helped, I would tell you," he said. "It would be normal to do so."

One job, I repeated to myself. I was hungry, I was greedy. Better not to spoil my appetite by studying Karim's needs. I had once given someone else, Priscilla, control of my life, and didn't enjoy the consequences. They had been drastic. So why shouldn't I make the same mistake with Karim, give him power over me—with the difference that I would take it back. This time I was going to end up in charge myself. I would buy something nice, maybe direct the purchase toward new transportation, something sporty, the way men in my situation like to think (ragtop, stereo, leather seats); things for Jeff; maybe even something for Priscilla if presents didn't make me seem creepy, abject—just so she would see me undefeated, able to provide and surprise. I too could take to wearing white linen suits (joke) or the new Ralph Lauren après-tennis scent.

To fulfill these complicated needs might take two or three jobs, but not a retainer, not a regular thing with Karim. No drug transactions that I would know about. Nothing on my conscience or in evidentiary records that anybody could discover. No sir.

Nothing that could provide material for the commission in Sacramento that oversaw PI licensing; no evident felonies, no misdemeanors if feasible; nothing that Karim could store up to use in asking for further services.

I was deeply engaged in the usual delusions that appetite provides.

Karim watched me with interest as thoughts traveled their various routes through my body, bumping into each other, lighting up, moving on. In his soul he sincerely hoped I was a sincere person, not responding to any threat about the board in Sacramento. He sighed, having things to do on a sunny morning under the palm trees on Guerrero.

Within my present capabilities was one job, for distraction's sake and to pick up some useful, probably tax-exempt cash.

Maybe it was just like a legal collection, merchandise, a loan, a matter simply too delicate to get all bruised and depleted from being pushed through the crowded dockets of the court system. Sometimes legal orders just waste everybody's time. Demands-to-comply and foreclosures are a pain in the butt to the entire society, an ecological disaster in how they waste computer time, legal-size paper, electricity, messenger boy sweat, process servers having to stand there and wait outside someone's door with hard-boiled eggs in their pockets in case lunchtime came and went—oh, the digestion is wrecked—the whole crudeness of an overgrown legal system. Whereas face-to-face human contact with the warm glow of personal threat . . . I could help Karim cut through the crap for everybody.

"Okay," I said. "Just point me in the direction we're going. We're in business."

Karim was a happy man today. The name he handed me, on a slip of paper, was G. Press, and the address was the Clay-Jones Tower. He let me look at it and then took the paper back.

"You don't need this. You'll remember," he said. "Twelfth floor."

"Almost like the preppy clothes, J. Press."

"What?" he asked. "G," he said.

I would think George. I knew the Clay-Jones building on Nob Hill, elegant old San Francisco, with a doorman. "How do I get in?"

"You'll get in," he said. "Seven o'clock evening is a nice time to call. Details I know you're good at."

"Tell me about this person."

"Do you need such answers, Dan? That's one more thing

I like about you—you know how to accomplish the job without unnecessary fuss. But it does take time for you to make up your mind, doesn't it, my friend?"

Karim had a way of staring silently above his fluent gab, remaining on a different plane despite the chatter; and now he was doing it in fluent silence, nodding a little at a passing thought, staring into my eyes, seeping his attention into me, settling in places where I did not want him. He trespassed. I had the right to blow up. Or, since he had won me over, convinced me, I wouldn't do that. I could still see hurting him for my pleasure. If profit came with the pleasure, so much the better.

I met his dark-lined eyes without flinching until he smiled again and nodded to dismiss my gaze. I could go now. "Friends?" he asked.

"Why not," I said.

The idea of giving him what he wanted had been late in coming to me. In my own way, for my own purpose. We didn't discuss fee. Karim's prideful expanse of chest and belly, the generous body type, convinced me he would not stint. I thought, What the hell? I could use some unstinting tax-free cash and distraction. I was starting over in life. I was starting from the beginning and bound to prove myself if I could. G. Press. Gee, pressed to prove myself. No problem remembering details if you've read the Sunday magazines about how the stars do it. I was in business again.

I dressed for Nob Hill and Le Club, the lobby restaurant owned by a scavenger king known as Captain Garbage. What his fleet of clanking trucks collected in the early morning was not necessarily what they served evenings in the hushed and opulent restaurant—white linens, little lamps here and there, a romantic rendezvous for old folks and their parents. The doorman let me in because I said I was meeting Herb Caen. That was a fib. Maybe my nose got a little longer, but who was measuring?

"He doesn't have a reservation," the doorman said, creaking in his shoes.

"Herb Caen," I announced, "doesn't need a reservation."

He looked at my clothes, which make the man. The man these clothes had made was no longer Kasdan, PI. It was a San Francisco personage wearing a gray fedora like one of the famous newspaper columnist's.

"Yes sir," said the doorman.

"Here, for you," I said, looking away fastidiously, putting the five-dollar bill in his hand, bored with all this haughty negotiation, then glancing at my watch—*Where's Herb?*

"Yes sir!" barked the doorman, now improved in spirits about the whole deal.

He went to blow a whistle for a cab (the parent of an old folk feeling poorly). I went for the elevator. G. Press, twelfth floor. Karim didn't know everything, but he knew I'd remember a helpful detail, such as where the perpetrator lived.

On the door there was a little plaque, greenish where it had corroded, and the engraved letters *GP.* Tasteful copper corroding, done professionally; how antique, how decorator.

Where did it hurt with the tension and fear when I knocked on this door? No place. It hurt no place.

I had telephoned, heard the phone pick up, knew someone was home—no worry there. I had the usual inexpensive advantage of surprise, the person being visited suffering the disadvantage of maybe eating onions and worried about breath, or needing to make number two, or in the middle of a nap. People don't enjoy neighborly drop-ins these days. But I was on track, no tension at all for me, and counting on some for the person heading toward a quiet dump when there's a sudden rapping, buzzing, or belling at the door. In some other land, I could just nail a dead cat to the gate, preferably black, and go about my business, but in the U.S.A. we like to make personal contact with the client and urge him to do what's right.

Why wasn't I nervous?

Need I be troubled by this phenomenon?

Unless I backtrack and maybe pay the doorman to let me *out* of the building, explaining that Herb Caen just called on my cellular phone—I don't see no fuckin' cellular phone, sir—asked me to meet him instead at Wendy's . . . unless someone answers real soon, I'm stuck and should let loose the nervousness I'm not feeling.

I heard a lock and then a chain being worked. Someone was there, someone was responsive to my mute appeal, someone was confident enough of security to open the door. My first words were sort of planned, like a beer commercial: "It isn't going to get any better than this."

"What?"

As I stepped firmly inside: "Let me explain."

That was the plan. I wasn't worried. I didn't care if the door opened with a gun stuck in my face. This should have made me nervous, not being nervous.

The door opened and a thick-waisted middle-aged lady in a gold lamé jacket, dressed for God knows what lovely occasion, maybe me, was stuck in my face. "Is Mr. G. Press here?" I asked.

"There's no mister. I'm G. Press."

"I'm from Karim."

Her eyes flicked over me. They were heavy-lidded fishy eyes, and I had to give her credit for rising above cosmetic surgery. "What do you want, From? Mind if I call you that?"

"Dan Kasdan. May I come in?"

The eyelids twitched, tired tiny muscles working beneath the untreated fatty tissue. It was very like a smile. "You wish to visit my flat? Why, if you wish to, please do."

I moved aside and she shut the door behind me. I was in a land of showroom antiques, someplace dark, densely layered in rugs, gilt, weavings, hangings, with no child, other human tenant, or animals except for one sleeping ceramic cat on the couch and another (they must have been sold as a pair) curled up and stagnant at a painted mouse hole in the corner where the Persian carpet, telling the story of Xerxes with his boat over the Hellespont, came to its logical end by meeting a deep green wall. The fleet stopped here. The woman had a sense of history or humor, but the woman didn't smile much. G. Press seemed to confine expressions of charm and amusement to subtle movements deep in the puffy terrains of her upper eyelids. A little slow-phlegm ripple, more alive by several layers of organic nature than her ceramic cats.

With the heavy curtains and myth-laden rugs, the heavy furniture, the general stockiness of decor—even the air seemed thick with heat and motes—I felt as if I were in Boston, Philadelphia, doing a job on the East Side of New York, not in breezy northern California. We don't do the Hellespont in San Francisco, we do Scandinavian or Japanese simplicity or maybe Spanish mission rusticity. The lady was overdressed for expecting no visitors, but maybe she had plans or liked to give herself early-evening fashion shows. There was a long mirror on one wall and reflections of reflections in a glass door behind me. G. Press could see around any unexpected movements.

She stood with a drill-sergeant spread to her legs, parade rest, watching me take in her "flat." Thighs apart, catching the air. Then she felt it was time to take control. "What do you want?" she inquired. "And get the hell out here."

It was essential that I not let her do what she had in mind, take control, and that I stop wondering why Karim didn't have the courtesy to tell me G. Press was a woman. Even these days, it can make a difference.

"Like to leave as soon as possible, ma'am," I said.

"Right now would be best."

And so with maximum precision I answered, "But not possible, since I'm engaged to leave with what I came for. Otherwise it would just be a wasted trip."

"Mr. Kasdan. You might leave with a lot less than you came with."

I wasn't going to fight a battle of the repartee with this thick-waisted person proudly modeling her gold lamé jacket and embossed eyelids. But I wasn't ready to go yet, either. I was preparing to stare at her instead. This basic PI move often proves surprisingly effective when I put my heart and soul into it. I concentrated. I stared. I spent the moment wondering why a person alone at home would wear this metallic garment, making her ineligible to pass through any self-respecting metal detector but of no use in case of armed conflict. Was it some kind of beauty motif in her mind? Gold lamé with beaded pockets? Her concept of a perfect design for living in her living quarters was also modified by the remains of a snack on one of those hinged monk's tables, a silver spoon sticking out of a cherry yogurt container that had been scraped pretty clean. But of course she hadn't expected my visit. Otherwise she surely would have put out a low-fat cherry yogurt for me.

I continued staring. The trick is to give the mind something to do while the eyes burrow in there. She nodded appreciatively.

G. Press didn't ask me to sit down, although the room contained ample chairs, an upholstered couch, a settee, more chairs, footstools, and that nice rug if we chose to squat crossed-legged amid the Persian fleet on the floor and negotiate her handing over to me what she owed to Karim. I didn't look forward to squatting cross-legged and catching intimidating glimpses up her thighs.

"I notice you enjoy my afternoon coat," she said. "Lamay."

"I can see."

"Is it too obvious? I feel better about myself if I look nice. It's a question of self-esteem."

Maybe she was a madam. Maybe she owed Karim for protection services. Maybe it wasn't drugs. Maybe he only supplied drugs for her girls. Maybe it was none of my business and only a real estate transaction that had gone bad, or down payment on a gold lamé jacket factory—maybe none of my business, inappropriate, better I didn't know. So I said, "Please stop shitting, ma'am. I don't work by the hour, so I'd like to do what I came here to do and be on my way."

She smiled. Buffed teeth, very white, just the few brownish edges of a smoker. "You're not going to get it, Mr. Kasdan."

I could have said, Yes, I am. I could have said, Isn't there a heavy-duty dentifrice for those nicotine tooth stains; said it nicely, open-faced, friendly. But G. Press was too easy with talk and therefore probably less so with silence. Old training in collections had provided examples of folks like this. They weren't usually Renaissance minds with equal skills in talk and silence. I was pretty sure a space of silence was the ticket. The eerie ceramic cats didn't move or purr.

She cleared her throat.

Good sign. A little self-esteem slippage.

She offered me a chocolate from a box.

I shook my head, not uttering "Allergic," or just "No," or even "Yes." Silence was now the ticket if it didn't drive her to call upon the weapon I was sure she kept someplace within reach or the assistant she might have had waiting in one of the other rooms. She let me in, didn't she? She hadn't seemed surprised or distressed. She must have been confident. She was easy in her person like someone used to dressing her own way, decorating, having things proceed in her own preferred order.

"Cigarette?" White cork-tipped cartridges extended from a ceramic dish with a cat embossed and baked into it; lady liked kitties though not necessarily live ones. Like a fisherperson handling bait, she jerked the dish toward me again.

Shook my head. Stared. Didn't give a fuck.

Lady couldn't anticipate I'm a nonsmoker.

"I could," she remarked mildly, "have you hurt, maybe right now. Might could do it myself."

I stared.

She might could; she didn't.

I pursed my lips in the old Black Panther, Muslim, Muhammad Speaks middle-distance stare, guaranteed ominous.

Surely she would prefer that I engaged in continuous conversation. Evidently she hated to carry both ends of the chat. It goes with the style, decor, tea or dinner jacket—preferred warm sociability even if inside she might be a cold person.

"Look, Mr. Kasdan—" she began again.

"No, *you* look, Miz Press. You talk. You stall. I wait. Finally you get."

"Wow," she said. "Scary, menacing."

I could see her cosmetically challenged eyes trying to sort me out. I had no obvious backup. I didn't seem to be carrying weaponry (in fact, wasn't). Yet I seemed absolutely convinced I was in charge of these Nob Hill condo premises. Only Dan Kasdan knew he wasn't, and didn't care, but she couldn't understand that, could she?

I might venture a merciful bit of conversation as a reminder of the cause to which I had hired out. "So if you've got a dinner date," I said, "you won't be late if you settle with Karim right now. I'm ready on his behalf. And then I'm scampering outta here like the Domino's pizza guy."

Strictly speaking, my commentary was unnecessary, especially since I was sure that with G. Press not talking spoke louder than talking. Also I wondered if she had a tape recorder going. A bleak old-timey Kasdan stare used to work with runaways. It might not work with Miz Press, but it wouldn't record.

Silence. Revving of a sports car down Jones Street, twelve floors below. City silence with no grandfather's clock ticking in the corner, just the unheard purr of a ceramic kitty.

"What kind of work"—I had all day, all night was the idea—"you do before you got involved with our friend?"

She loved it, loved it when I spoke. "Got people hurt who crossed me. Thinking of going back into that line of work."

I performed an appreciative half-grin, a little habit born

of vanity since I lost a back tooth after an especially active night of tooth grinding (Priscilla gone, Dan sleeping alone). I needed to make a little control statement. I wasn't going to punch up G. Press, push her around, but I needed something equally attention-getting. So I sat down.

A little understated as aggression.

If she was a madam, she had her armor watching over her someplace; same if she was a dealer; same if she was into loans or gambling, although I doubted either of those was her chosen field of financial and creative endeavor. Whatever, I believed in her violence and the idea that Karim might not protect me. By this time I fully merited being hurt in her cat-eat-dog universe. What would stop her could only be herself, her anger untickled to the point of explosion. Maybe I could help her both fear me and like me to the extent that cutting my balls out just wouldn't be worthwhile. Already she was puzzled that I didn't seem to care much. Knowing the terrain, I was puzzled myself. To lose caring while retaining desire might be the ticket to success around here.

I was getting better at holding my tongue.

She cleared her throat, drummed on her jacket pocket, which gave off a scratchy, metallic rattle, kind of tinny, this fabric, maybe no weapon inside.

I continued my present course of action.

She moved. Her heels scraped through carpet, then rattled on hardwood floors; she trotted through the glass door, down a hall, into another room. Hair sculpted but in motion, earlobes red; a lady deserves better security in her own condominium high on Nob Hill. Her little hooves sounded like Janey's pony. Maybe she would bring me her Medal of Honor.

If she came out with a weapon, well, it happens. I used to be a fighter, even if my best battles were fought to keep from fighting. I was different these days. I hoped it wasn't hormonal.

I stared down the carpet, keeping in practice. Little carpet eyes, tiny pony-hoof depressions, gazed back at me. She must have been truly piqued to dig in so deeply. Gradually the fibers sprang forward again, the carpet eyes faded. The shadow of G. Press above them kept watch over me and I watched it; that was only fair.

I wasn't worried. This worried me. In my line of work you're not good unless you know you're in danger and avoid it to the maximum. I didn't.

Jeff. A floor hockey game coming up next Saturday. His dad wanted to sit on the bench with the young mothers and a few other dads.

Maybe I did care. I couldn't do this. I was doing it.

I heard a snapping sound, like a flag in the wind. Adrenaline sharpens both the ears and the eyes. She could come out with a pistol, a knife, a friend, or an army. It was all the same to me. Then why the animal thumping in my chest?

The little pony trot sounds were returning down the hall. The glass door opened. She looked into my face with merriment, as if she had won a great victory. "Do you take Visa?" asked G. Press.

One side of my mouth went up in its shy smile to indicate adequate IQ; I got the joke.

"Sure you don't want a smoke before you go?" Nodding toward the ceramic dish with the cat design baked into it.

I stared. I let the shy mouth-corner smile go.

"I could," she repeated thoughtfully, "have you hurt, if not now maybe later?"

This was a question, but I only shrugged.

It was really bothering her that the cat—one of the cats—seemed to have gotten my tongue. She gave me her attention in case I wished to respond. I didn't. She took a deep, reluctant breath. She held out a plastic portfolio. The words SANTA BARBARA were printed on the side; it was a souvenir. It was sealed with packing tape. That was the snapping sound I had heard, ripping this flypaper stuff off its roll.

"For Karim?"

"Unless you run away with it. Wouldn't advise that."

"Thank you, Miz Press."

"And now get the fuck out of here."

And so I did.

At the grand Victorian on Guerrero, the morning sun glowed through drawn curtains, a dusty filtered tropical pearliness in a room with heavy mahogany furniture and layers of rug on the floor. When G. Press redecorated, her consultant must have shipped the treasured old pieces over to Karim. By noon this banana-belt neighborhood of San Francisco would be as hot as Ensenada; now it was just warm and densely humid. Karim kept lots of plants. Fresh pale green shoots in a tray on the windowsill had the spiky look of herbs for salad flavoring. Karim was smiling, resmiling, broad faced, broadly happy. When he took my hand, I could feel the lotion slipping between us.

He wanted me to feel welcome. He took my hand to draw me close to him. He was assured already of our success. Since I was only a partial success, he wasn't as good a judge of character as he thought.

"Please, sit down, and also I have for you—"

I didn't sit. I handed him the sealed portfolio from G. Press and said, "That's it. I'm going on to other employment."

"Oh, my impatient friend, and you haven't even yet received from me, with many thanks—"

"I quit, Karim."

Still warm-souled but exasperated, he asked, "Does this sudden . . . childishness . . . mean you want to know things we agreed you didn't need to know?"

"I'm finished, Karim."

"You did exactly what we agreed upon, and thus in return, for my part—"

"Resign, no more, finished, it's not my line of work, Karim."

He was shaking his large head. He put a thick envelope in

my hand and I took it. Because otherwise it would fall insultingly to the floor. Because I wanted it. Because I needed it. "Please, a coffee?" he asked.

"This is it."

"You accept without even discussing the terms?"

"I earned it. Okay. Now it's done."

"You did very well. No fuss, prompt, I like that. I asked myself why you waited until morning, but you didn't want to awaken me. You had to think, consider. I knew I could count on you."

"Stop counting. I'm out."

This would not be easy. Probably I shouldn't have taken the envelope, but I needed it. It was dense, stuffed, the most appetizing way for cash to be presented. It didn't help the process I intended.

Karim sighed and touched my hand again. Already the lotion was mostly absorbed. His hand felt hot and dry. "I could be like a father to you," he said.

"I'm too old to have a father. My dad would be drooling if he were alive."

Karim licked his lips. "And of course you have a son, so you know how a father feels."

"That's a joke I don't want to hear from you."

The good judge of character looked at Dan Kasdan and saw a man who didn't want involvements yet was capable of murder. His sigh was deep, like a yawn. "I apologize. We made a deal."

"So I apologize too, Karim. But I'm not your boy."

He spread his arms, opened his palms, grew happy again. "And I never *never* on this earth said you were. To be my colleague, colleagues, so much better, is it not? It would be—" He glanced at the envelope heavy in my hands, not yet a part of my economy. "As you can surely understand."

Karim and I didn't see or understand the same things. My clients and I usually did not. That's why one side offered and the other side took. The work wasn't about mutual understanding.

"There are other tasks for an intelligent and diligent person that come up from time to time. You have the temperament, my dear colleague. Reliable, honest, why do you imagine I have my heart set on someone exactly like you?" He glanced at my paw. "Also you have the appetite to sup at my table."

"Sometimes I'm hungry. I'm a little short these days."

"You see? I enjoy your honesty. You are a little short, so let me help you grow. Of course, we have already nicely begun."

He wouldn't give up. We were going around and around. I was out of there, dropping the laden envelope on the table by the door. A thick supple presence was relinquished, almost like a woman's body, but my sense of business was not entirely departed. I felt regret. In the blast of light through the open door, Karim stood beaming and joyous, rapid grief rapidly gone, disappointed in me but entertained by human folly, the best kind, as I also used to be, before the folly around here became mine.

He let me pass. He seemed certain this was only another step on life's way.

I wanted to rush, to proceed with noise and wind, showing heels and billowing shirt. But there amid the smells of riddled wood and drying palm fronds, I stopped and turned back. Karim was still fully equipped with both gloom and happiness to spare, nodding, encouraging.

I walked past him to retrieve the envelope off the table. It was mine by right. I had worked for it. We could think of it as the severance package. We didn't have to think. I needed it.

His lips moved, but I couldn't hear what he was saying. *Go ahead, go on.* He didn't stop me as I took the money. He didn't stop me as I finally departed. We had already agreed I was a little short these days and had to do certain things. Whatever that might be.

Alfonso Jones and Dan Kasdan sat at nearly clean Formica in Panchito Three (We Serve Luncho), a cop's burrito-and-coffee joint south of downtown near the Hall of Justice, 450 Bryant, eating rice and beans off paper plates on plastic trays. The plain-clothes guys were packing into mounds of fried fuel, guacamole serving as the vegetable, and grabbing their monster containers of coffee-to-go. Disgruntled citizens on jury duty were complaining to each other about the waiting, waiting, except for those who had brought plenty of reading matter. A few in the jury pool were staring at portable word-processor screens, trying to keep up with business while performing their civic duty and regretting they hadn't gotten a testament from the family physician that they were challenged by deafness or the early stages of Alzheimer's disease (they had forgotten to do so). A bailed-out defendant sulked at a corner table. His girlfriend was weeping and stroking his motorcyclist tattoos while the guy stared heroically into the middle distance. Probably an amphetamine bust. The only happy defendants were the Food Not Bombs crew, publicly celebrating their coming conviction for illegally setting up a feed for the homeless in Golden Gate Park. The men wore revolutionary, ecology-saving beards, except for their leader, who had a revolutionary, ecology-saving shaved head, using no hair or skin products to pollute the atmosphere; usually the women did the cooking in twenty-gallon cans and looked more businesslike.

Alfonso took in the familiar scene at Panchito Three, then began to shovel up what he had piled onto his tray in the line at the counter. He needed a little nourishment while I sipped my pink strawberry punch. Then he said, through shreds of pork, "You not tellin' what you up to."

"Not everything."

"Up to you." He refilled his face.

"Right." Of course he knew; it was his business if not his pleasure to keep track of me. Poor fellow accepted the heavy charge of an old friend.

Even in my present state of selfishness I had an obligation to him. I explained that I didn't feel very enterprising these days, and he asked if beggars have taken to being choosers, and I argued that maybe some other job would turn up. Nodding agreeably, Alfonso let me persuade him that transporting drugs or moving illegal money to a safe place were among the sorts of work that didn't suit me just now. Bad loans or payoffs, professional girls or shylocking, Karim's ham-and-eggs conglomerate was not a good place to put my energies. I thought G. Press most likely ran a house for Karim and wanted to buy out of the franchise, take her gold lamé jacket, and trot away on her little pony hooves into an enterprise that would be all hers. G. Press, ready to go for it. Maybe she was making a feminist statement; maybe arranged for new protection. A superb idea for me was not to do any more work for a man who made dumb jokes about my son. Alfonso's deep bass surged up at me: "You put it like that, don't sound so good."

Karim had made a smarter joke about the PI licensing commission.

"Something else?" Alfonso asked.

"No."

"Isn't there something else?"

"No, not now. Nothing I can't deal with."

It was up to me. "Okay, due time," Alfonso said.

I may have been hungry. I may have been scared. I may have forgotten how to say yes to opportunity. But I could still figure out how to say no to this opportunity. I could do without the new transportation and Priscilla wouldn't be happy with her surprise present anyway. Gifts from estranged spouses make some wives feel tender and regretful—not Priscilla. Sometimes I thought I knew her better than I knew myself, even if I also didn't know her at all.

I didn't want to depend on my new strength, being careless of whether I lived or died. It was the only power most of the Project kids ever learned. It may have been the power Alfonso's son had. Okay, thank you, Priscilla and Karim, thank you all. But the G. Press envelope was just tentative money, cash I came across, happened on in a game, not a real job. It was a speculation, just to see. It was a temptation, an easy win I wasn't going to repeat.

All this roiling inside, plus Karim's moldy Victorian on Guerrero, feeding at Panchito Three on Bryant, and the speculative bulk of Alfonso observing, parked opposite, helped me imagine I was still here on earth, still alive. That was something. Being still alive was progress in the sense that it was not retrogression.

I didn't mind lying to myself.

"So did you take the envelope and how much was it?" Alfonso asked.

I said nothing. Didn't like lying to Alfonso.

"We agree, don't we," Alfonso asked, "that Karim he full of shit? Not like some other folks?"

His laughter came rumbling toward me again, deep and worried. The defendant in the corner behind us at Panchito Three was goddamn tired of having his arm tattoo stroked by his blubber-faced girlfriend and gave her his stone-cold, steely-eyed stare, enacting the role of Man in Control.

Chapter 18

Alfonso was on the phone in a voice that stopped my breathing.

"I gotta . . ." he was saying. He was flying east and would I drive him to the airport? "There's this long-term parking if I'm parking there long-term, man, but I don't want to drive. I don't think I can drive, man."

"I'll be right there."

"I don't know if there's any use in going, but I'm going."

"I'll be there. Wait, I'm on my way."

His son had lived in Trenton, New Jersey. His son was being buried in Trenton.

I was thinking of the nightmares fathers have, waking sick in the dark, far from their children. For Alfonso it came true with drugs and a drive-by shooting. He didn't tell me if Alfie was one of the shooters, one of the dealers, or just a kid passing by on his way. "He was still in school," he said. "He was gonna make it."

I asked him if he was trying to fly east with his service pistol and if he didn't want to leave it with me. He asked if I thought he was nuts, but he didn't answer the question. Then he felt me reach across to poke at his hip as I drove and he chuckled as if we were playing our bachelor games again. He couldn't get it on the plane. He couldn't shoot his former wife. He couldn't kill himself.

"Hey man, I might be crazy, but I'm not nuts."

"Thanks for that reassurance."

Then he was being silent about his son and I was being silent about mine. I drove through the morning traffic down 101 to the airport, the San Francisco commuters heading out to Silicon Valley and the peninsula commuters heading into the city, Alfonso heaving wide-mouthed yawns. He wasn't bored or sleepy. His eyes were red-rimmed and heavy-lidded as he slumped against the door. Men sometimes yawn when they mean to do that thing they somehow forget how to do around the age of eleven, the skill of weeping, although rumor has it that they are learning again and floods are being released all over America.

Alfonso's breath was bad, sour meat inside. I wondered if, to make sure, I should pat him down, body-search him for his pistol.

At the terminal I pulled up at the United entrance. If he carried a weapon, he might could talk his way on, a cop on duty. Okay, that was his business. Most likely he wouldn't be carrying it on his person if he was thinking rationally. He might not be thinking rationally. I wasn't my brother's keeper.

He swung his bag out of the back seat. The grace of some fat men. Alfonso's caramel voice running thick. He wasn't meant for sadness, but I couldn't tell him that now; sadness wasn't God's intention for Alfonso Jones. He was meant to be funny and easy in himself, hard on me, but people don't always play their assigned roles. Even as a cop, he was no longer at Park Station. Life doesn't make permanent assignments.

"Call me from Trenton," I said.

"Yeah."

"Okay, where will you be staying? I'll call you."

"Never mind. I'll be back in three days."

He hoisted his bag and straightened his back, stretching. The bottom button of his shirt was undone. "Just before this came up," he said, "something else came up. Wanted to talk with you. I know Karim wants you to do some jobs for him."

"I got to get some money. I got to get some variety in my life."

"Don't."

"I might."

"Don't, you listen to me now."

But Alfonso wasn't Dan Kasdan's keeper, either. On the way back to the city I switched on the radio, KSAN, and before I could turn it off I heard part of a golden oldie that said something like, Hello hello, I'll be your lover tonight. Wisps of morning damp on the highway, wisps of asbestos and oil particulate and a touch of San Francisco morning freshness being undone by heavy morning traffic. Alfonso, my buddy.

Alfonso, my fellow father. Perhaps I shouldn't put myself in the way of accident, just as Alfonso said. A philosophy to live by, if we were choosing to live. Having other people in mind sure does limit a person's options.

Alfonso had his son, I had Priscilla and Jeff, maybe Karim thought he had me. No telling what makes a person fall for someone, willing to give his life for someone, a ruinous meteor elevatoring out of control down from the sky here at the edge of the Pacific or any ocean. With fiery edges crashing and sputtering out.

He used to have his son.

Chapter 19

It seemed that my friends were falling into trouble; maybe I was a carrier. The day Alfonso was due back from Trenton, Fred, Fred Weinberg, Doctor Fred, called out of the blue, saying, "Need to see you in my office."

"Sorry we haven't been in touch. I've been kind of busy—"

"Never mind, now you better come in right away."

"What is it?"

"A little health problem's come up."

It didn't sound like any health problem I knew about. I said cautiously, thinking that blood tests ripen a little faster than this, "Hey, it's been months since my physical. How come you just thought of it?"

"I'm in my office. You can get down here right now."

And before I could point out that it was Wednesday afternoon, religiously his midweek afternoon off for catching up on the medical journals (golf), he had hung up on me. Didn't like this, but headed out to Fred's office on Sacramento.

There was no receptionist, this being Wednesday, but Fred buzzed me in. The waiting room where ailing patients and dead magazines kept each other company was dark. He came to the window and without a word beckoned me into his office. He switched on his desk lamp and said, "Karim."

Karim was sagged comfortably in a chair, half out of the

yellow circle of light, nodding and nodding, enjoying my surprise. There was a smell of cleaning powder in the room, that green chemical smell.

"Your friend, Dr. Weinberg, and there are so many doctors in our city, happens also to be my doctor."

"What a coincidence," I said. "Since when?"

"I thought I could ask him to help me," Karim said.

Fred looked sick. He wasn't wearing his on-duty white smock. "Do it! Do it, Dan! Do what Karim says."

Karim was shaking his head. "No, no, such a negative way from my good friend Dr. Weinberg. Do you think he sees too many people who are ill, sometimes seriously so, and that makes him feel negative sometimes? What he means is—"

Fred was standing by the tools of his trade, books, instruments, devices, a wall of diplomas and framed certificates, as if they should give him strength and authority, but they seemed to be choosing not to. His mouth was working but no explanation came out.

"What he means," Karim said, "I need someone to help in my business and you, sir, have no good reason not to be the one."

"I told you. I explained already. I don't do the sort of things you like to have done."

Karim spread out his massive arms in his linen jacket. "Exactly! Exactly! We have already seen! And that is why you are the most marvelous person."

I looked at Fred. I couldn't understand why a doctor didn't find his own drugs. What was he using? It shouldn't have been necessary to go to Karim.

But then it was also difficult to understand why I was considering Karim's request again. I couldn't need money that badly. I needed it, but not that badly. I needed distraction from my life, but this wasn't as good as some distractions. Karim was threatening me. He was promising reward and threatening punishment. Like a vulnerable soft disc between the notches of the spine, worn down by use and abuse, caution was wearing thin. I had relished the visit to G. Press in her gold lamé jacket at the Clay-Jones Tower and he knew it. Karim had figured me out. He didn't plan to be the loser in this courtship.

"I am so happy," he said.

"I didn't say anything."

"But I see you are thinking logically at last. I am so happy for that, dear friend."

He was right that I was thinking, even if I wasn't thinking with top-grain logic. I was considering. I was entering a full condition of off-legal estimation of gain, a state of mind not unknown to my profession. Launderers, hiders of fact, revealers of nonfact, there were operators like these who filled out the ranks of my colleagues. Why should I be different? I had already taken a share from the visit with Ms. G. Press. Like Fred, I needed a remedy for this time in my life; I *needed*. And today, whether I could use it or not, I was getting a down payment in amazement. Fred took my two paws in his, holding my hands together, and said, and begged . . . Fred was the man who had consoled me, made notations in my chart, eased a rubber-gloved finger up where no man's finger should go and told me my prostate wasn't too bad. I felt as dizzy and seasick as I had been in those post-forty rectal encounters. He was whispering, choked, "Dan. Do it for me."

I barked at him. "What! What!"

"Oh dear," Karim said. "Please instead do something for yourself. I'm not in the business of threatening your friends or your son—"

"What the fuck you say?"

Karim backed off. "No, no, for your own benefit and gain, my dear, this time all I want is for you to transfer a package, just once to see if despite so many difficulties we can work so well together . . . Be my friend just once more, and then we will see."

Fred fell to his knees in his own office, amid the textbooks, charts, files, diplomas from Swarthmore and Case Western Reserve University School of Medicine, certificate of successful completion of residence in internal medicine, souvenirs and trophies of friendships and hobbies. His face was wet and swollen as he pulled at my hands: *"Please."*

I wouldn't fall to my knees even to bring Priscilla back—not noisily, anyway—no, definitely would not. Pride must be the last thing to go in certain cases. My addiction was different from Fred's. I might walk on my knees, but not fall to them. Not in public. Not with that craven plopping sound. Or if I did, I would explain it to passersby as an athletic event, tryouts for the Olympic knee-walking competition.

Fred and Karim were waiting. I needed to answer Karim and he offered soothing music to help me on my path: "I am the first son of a first son, dear friend, and I strongly prefer to get what I think is right. You have the qualities. I have studied your nature and I am sure of that. I am stubborn. Just like you, I have feelings, I am strong in that field. So, your favorable response?"

"Okay."

"Isn't that what we all need?"

"Okay, just once," I said. "One delivery, okay, and it's understood I'm to be well paid."

Fred pulled himself lumberingly to his feet, whispering, "Thank you." I didn't meet his eyes.

"Very happy, very pleased," said Karim.

I looked straight into Karim's face with my own lying one. "Understand I'm only in this for the money. I may do this only once. Please specify exactly how much."

"I understand exactly, that's best, my friend. Now are we once more good colleagues and friends?"

"How much, Karim?"

His breathing was audible, that of a heavy smoker burdened by both lung blockage and financial consideration. He was engaged in thought. In and out the breath, up and down the chest with its layers of linen. Finally inspiration arrived with a slow beaming grin. "I have a wonderful idea. Let's say this, Dan. I'll be appreciative."

"What fun," I said.

"Dan, don't spoil our association with bad sarcasticness. I'll be very, very . . . I don't want to say 'generous' because that isn't the way I want it to be between us, I want more of a democratic feeling, two partners, equal in spirit and other ways . . ." He seemed to run out of breath but not out of smile. The grin was fat and tireless.

"Let me think."

"Of course. As a friend I value your fine mind."

"How can I turn down a friend?" I said.

Fred sat in his chair, staring at the framed photograph on his desk of his former wife and children, the wife in her haircut from better times, the children still babies when the photo had been taken and encased in its gold and velvet frame. "How can you?" Fred muttered.

Chapter 20

Alfonso was staring at me across the table at Ensenada on 16th Street off Valencia. That's more chic than saying 16th off Mission. He was thinking and thinking and not talking to me about Trenton or Alfie. In the two weeks since he'd been back, his son had been our main subject of nonconversation. If he wanted to talk, and when he wanted to talk, he would inform me.

What he wanted to say was something different. "Okay, so the man don't want to leave you be. He nagging and nagging at you, got a bug up his butt. I think he handing out what we in the law enforcement field call an opportunity. Will you listen? Ain't hard to 'splain at all. Why should he be the only one with a plan?"

I listened and after a while felt my head moving up and down. It meant I chose to follow the line Karim had in mind. You could say it was fate and my state of mind. I'd prefer your saying it was my choice.

"We get a free shot," Alfonso said.

"I don't know if I like this."

"He need you not just 'cause he treasure your funky soul, man. No encumberments, nolo encumbered, amigo. You clean so long, you like a fucking virgin to him."

"Thanks a lot."

"Not to me. So we don't know if it's skag the man into or maybe he delivering some of that frisky dog kibble to the yuppie pups on Chestnut Street, our good buddy Xavier help him out with that, or the gay clubs down on Folsom. They sure 'preciate that friskiness, don't they?"

I needed to take this in—"our good buddy Xavier"—without giving up too much in the way of surprise and off-balance behavior. "Don't like this." But I could allow Alfonso a little peek. "Don't need Xavier playing stupid games with my wife."

"Uh-huh. Uh-huh." My buddy in his pigeon salesman mode stopped his rap to consider what I had just brought up, good bargaining, nice recovery. "I promise, word of faith, your wife—ex—don't know nothing about it. Listen up, pal. Even if she know—"

He had all my attention.

"—even if Xavier let her in just for the fun of it, she don't know, y'unnastan what I'm sayin'? She not gonna be implicated any way or form."

"That's a commitment."

"Even if she is, she isn't. Your friend the junkie doc, neither." Since I wasn't responding, he looked at me tight and unfriendly and sincere. "Word, man."

Shit, shit, shit was what I was thinking. In this spot a person gets down to basics: *Shit*. "Still doesn't feel good, Alfons."

"Uh-huh." He was relieved. He tossed me a bone. "Partake of entrapment, that kind of bother you?"

I tried to figure if Karim and Xavier were entrapping me. I was supposed to be snaring them. This wasn't my usual way of life, not the way my career was supposed to shape up, but then my life wasn't a usual way of life either, especially in recent times.

"I've got that bad-taste feeling."

He brooded upon this. Matters of taste are hard to argue with. A man gets a bad taste, his pal really can't tell him it tastes good. It seemed that Xavier might want to do me harm, but on the other hand I had already done him a little harm. It seemed that Karim just wanted to enlist me as a soldier—well, low-ranking officer—in his enterprises. It seemed I needed a new and stupid path at this turn in my late middle age.

"Sometime," Alfonso mentioned consolingly in that caramel rumble that served him well even when he was doing harm, "you deal with certain people, sometime you got to get down to certain people's level."

"My own level isn't too good these days, Alfons."

"That's an opinion you want to change eventually. You goin' do it?"

Karim didn't mention figures, how much I might walk away with. The police didn't mention reward, what was in it for me. It was as if I was just a good citizen for one, a good soldier for the other, a loose hire for everybody in sight. I was pretty sure the satisfaction I might feel about taking Xavier down wasn't going to cost him any lasting trouble; he and his lawyers would find deniability in ample amounts. I tried not to dwell on Priscilla's opinion, especially if she knew how Xavier was filling the idle hours in San Francisco. "Right. Right," I said.

Having sold his encyclopedias, Alfonso now took a rest and measured his client for what conditions he could offer. "Uh-huh," he said, just passing the time. Then: "You don't have to be wired. Clumsy like you are, probably you electrocute yourself on the battery. You just go along with him, I'll be there, the narc detail be there—"

I wondered how he knew the cops weren't under Karim's control.

"Man, you are suspicious. Trust me on this."

That was always a recipe for disaster, wasn't it? *Trust me on this.*

"If it's a delivery, we'll have people watching. If he got people watching, we'll have people watching the peoples. Just go along."

"Why am I doing this, Alfonso?"

"You a loyal American. You want the reward money. You looking for *something.*"

"I don't like him threatening me."

Alfonso heaved one of his juicy sighs. "Now you got it. I knew I give you a chance, you figure it out."

"Okay, okay," I said.

Alfonso just grinned. "Be interesting."

"I said okay. Don't oversell."

But for Alfonso and me, "interesting" was a factor not to be passed over at this wedge moment between our troubles. I wondered if my brother, who usually thought so intelligently about everything but his eating habits, was thinking up to par these days. The same question could be asked about me.

I also wondered if I was rectifying any personal rationality deficits as I drove past the Mission Dolores, where I remembered showing Priscilla grave markings one Saturday when the sun slanted over the walls where the tombstones stood in a garden that celebrated both the vigilantes who killed the men of violence and the men of violence who were hung by the men of peace, strung up with their bare feet tickled and teased by torches as they jerked and tried to climb up the ropes. It did the men of violence no good. The men of peace cheered, rubbed their hairy chins, and watched the men of violence bubble and cook.

I was on my way to tell Karim yes, I'd do one more job to see what it felt like and to meet a few bills; just one for now, just to see, with no permanent commitment.

On the wide boulevard a sidewalk sale was closing down. An offbooks merchant with drooping mustachios was loading his used Lawrence Welk LPs and his new SKI CANCUN T-shirts back into the Chevy station wagon. He had a face that expressed bearing up under the injustices done century by century and day by day to all part-Aztec peoples, plus traditional tribal confidence that someday, someplace, someone would surely need to complete a used polka repertory or funny T-shirt collection (skiers swooping down a beach around a sitting-up sleeper in a wide-brimmed tasseled sombrero). In the great spirit scheme of themes, sun-warped and scratched Lawrence Welk didn't sound any worse to him than any other Lawrence Welk.

I was uneasy about this visit to Karim. I drove slowly, trying to work matters through. Karim seemed to have convinced me, although I wasn't convinced. I turned out not to be as right about people as I thought I was: Priscilla, Xavier, Fred Weinberg, now Karim. I still believed in Alfonso. But did I really need to protect Priscilla with immunity if she had gotten into some stupid, profitable, *interesting* connection with Xavier? I didn't even know for sure, but I knew one thing about the lady. Having her best interests in my heart would be considered dire meddling. I was already a confirmed meddler of the dire kind. I put Dan Kasdan along with the others—Karim, Fred, Xavier, Priscilla, maybe even Alfonso when it all came out—in the category of folks who weren't what they seemed to be.

A bongo crew was working its goatskins in Dolores Park. The audience of men holding their beer cans, doing beer can isometrics, was drifting in front of the crew, sinking into wet grass, moving as if they had to pee but didn't want to break the rhythm by heading elsewhere. Some looked too blissful for mere bongos; they were deep into the day's ration of reindeer dust. Even from the street, trying to get clear in my own head, I could smell beer, stepped-on grass, marijuana.

Then, no matter how slowly I drove, Karim's house stood there on Guerrero, high and towered, with its wooden turrets, projections, and overhangs—jagged carpenter gothic decorations—a falcon perched on a branch near the gutter, red paint flaking from its beak; carved gargoyles with drool added later, probably a relic of communal flower-child squatting years ago. The driveway slanted steep in the sunlight. The house looked different today, its eyes blinded, shades pulled. I parked on the street (didn't want to be blocked), hurried out and up the steps. My right big toe hurt sometimes, a little arthritic; this was one of the times. I bounded up the slope, twinging at the toe but wanting to seem as young and agile as if I were really agile and young. I was sure someone was watching. It wasn't necessary to locate the shadow behind the curtains. Here in the Mission District, with its semitropical microclimate, the light of sun through palm trees made the neighborhood look like a Caribbean port, Port-au-Prince in a good decade.

Alfonso had changed his mind about the wire, but I refused to wear it. Alfonso and his buddies thought this was a mistake, but just shrugged and looked bored when I said I knew what I was doing. Most serious police errors come when a cop thinks he knows what he's doing. Well, I wasn't a member of any strike force.

Up the steep incline, set with stone, a rusty iron railing at the left side of the steps, I followed the rules and checked out the terrain. Karim wasn't left-handed as I could recall, but someone who built the house must have been. No guard rail on the right. There were no longer farms in the Mission District, but sudden heat smells of compost wafted under the high eucalyptus and skinny palm trees. Branches stirred and let things fall. There were flying motes of light, dusty eye glints, a cloud of insects in a dense shrub shifting and tumbling in the air. I had never seen so many fireflies lift off in a hovering heap. The filmy bugs reflected the sun; not real fireflies, which didn't exist in San Francisco. Chickens weren't supposed to exist in San Francisco either, but I was sure someone around here kept them, maybe for ceremonies in the back room of the Botanica at 20th and Valencia.

It seemed that Karim managed to import his own climate from someplace else. A coo of doves from a dovecote sounded like the pulsing of a heart, but more shrill. The falcon with the glaring pink eyes stared down at me as I knocked. Falcons don't float among palm trees. Wooden pink-eyed falcons don't float anyplace. This falcon with its painted eyes was rotting on its perch and one day would come crashing through the branches.

All I wanted in the whole wide world was to get back what I had lost.

I knew Karim had seen me. I rapped on the door to give him the satisfaction of receiving a polite social call. *Okay, I've decided.* No panic, but apprehension is a normal safety mechanism. *Okay, just like everybody, I can find a use for money.*

Karim opened.

Okay, in my abnormal way, I'm a normal person when it comes to wanting things, will you take that in?

Karim stepped smiling and nodding onto the porch. He closed the door behind him. It clicked hard shut. There was someone in the house he didn't want me to see.

I always want to say something nice to people when I can, so I thought about saying to Karim, What a lovely clump of hair you have in your right ear. Instead I said, "Okay, I'm ready. I'm ready now."

He didn't seem in a hurry anymore. He was dressed in a dark pinstriped suit, with a vest and white shirt and a yellow tie, a Karim version of business-meeting attire. "You enjoy?" he asked, nodding at the falcon in the palm tree. "I'm planning external restoration, gardening plus, for my property. My bird will retain its character, I promise you—"

"Let's talk inside."

"Good point, an excellent point, my friend." He extended his arms in the gesture of all-this-is-mine. He was stalling. Then he opened the door to let me enter and I sniffed something familiar, a tang like mint and sweat and anxiety. This was an item of interest I should have worked out before now, because it would have been a helpful inclusion.

I was sure Karim's partner was upstairs.

"I'll do it," I said. "I can use the helping hand money sometimes provides. One more job, okay?"

"Oh dear, when you see how uncomplicated, my friend, I am proof positive you will choose to continue—"

"Once," I said.

Karim beamed down at me. How can a helping hand, once taken, be refused? "Within your powers, dear friend, to come to an intelligent judgment. Please take that chair, it's my favorite."

Cologne left behind evaporated out into the heat of the room. No need for the man waiting upstairs to hide while we settled the preliminaries. Karim's associate in this business was that old acquaintance of mine, wearing something like Sportsman, For the Guy Who Knows From Regattas—the assiduous investor, manly scent-enthusiast, and sharer of feelings. It seemed he diversified both his love life and his investments, financing a little trade in go-fast powder. It seemed he liked bringing me into his deals, himself moving out of sight, not wanting to confuse me, while once again his vinaigrette wafted into the stirred-up, riled-up air.

I should have known Xavier wasn't just an Enrico's terrace acquaintance for Karim. As Priscilla assured me, in his lazy way Xavier liked to keep in touch—would she settle for less than a man with an edge? The gaslit tradition of Aulde San Francisco included the fragrance of both coffee processing and the opium trade.

Xavier, depths I hadn't wanted to allow him, just because I felt petty envy of his great teeth, long legs, lovely smile. And I gave myself an excuse for jealousy only because my wife was striving mightily to help him do what less-well-bred men often do on weekends, national holidays, idle afternoons, or just when there's a fine woman in the vicinity and the impulse strikes them both.

"You can tell him to come downstairs, he doesn't have to hide," I said.

"That won't be necessary. He's comfortable up there."

"This is strictly business."

"We understand that. But not strictly—please, Dan! You're a practical person, so I'm happy to reach this quality in you at last. Sometimes, isn't it true, friendship can be both difficult and practical?"

"Xavier! Hey!" I yelled. "Come on down."

He didn't answer. Filling the silence were Karim's warm and loving words. "He doesn't want to. I think you hurt his feelings, Dan."

Chapter 21

Blue-and-white trail-cruising landwhales lay beached near downtown Greyhound America just south of Market Street. Steam rose from a spout. The lot gave off motor oil and septic tank smells, plus eddies of troubled fast-food oxidation, ancient fish in cracked Styrofoam, errant small animals caught under wheels, crowds engaged in the worries of transport and inner flux. These days folks can travel Greyhound and enjoy all the comforts of home, but I wasn't sure about some of those homes. Just ahead lay the depot itself, the proper place for my stupid job, delivering a stupid package to a not-very-intelligent locker for which Karim had given me the key. I didn't know what was in the package because Karim said it wasn't necessary for me to know just yet. I could guess. I could figure it out. I could also figure that someone had a duplicate key. I hoped it wasn't Fred, my doctor and trusted pal, who had been putting his finger up my butt to test for rust on the prostate every year since I turned forty. If someone stuck a finger up there, I wanted it to be for a good purpose. Making me feel seasick didn't suffice. This job gave me something like the feeling of prostate pokery.

The Greyhound building off Market Street was an experimental space lab for pimps, hookers, runaways, outpatients with no in-clinics, a clubhouse for State Aid to the Totally Fucked. The urban concept "bus terminal" was only part of the idea. Heavy-metal junkies, speed, crack, and ice freaks, smokers, drinkers, inhalers, injectors, and fed-up philosophers who had settled for their daily methadone ration glumly kept moving, waiting for a relieving fit of violence to break the monotony. There were child bag brides, not so much anorexic as evaporated by crack, willing to take commuters off into a shady corner for an expeditious blow job that wouldn't delay their travel connections; moonfaced zombies on idiot chemicals; and the usual go-fast operators with beepers on their belts, talking into cellular phones or chattering at the ceiling, in case God was listening. At video machines, no-hip Southeast Asian kids, born not so long ago to mothers who only took off an hour from the rice paddies, now played at Western-style genocide with their new electronic toy guns, waiting out the months until they could get up to speed for the real world. It didn't take long. A few veteran Thorazine cripples herky-jerked by, trying to make the moving parts of their bodies follow along in other than random order.

The crusaders bound for Jerusalem may have looked like these folks (I was too young for personal experience of their trek across Europe and the Middle East). Maybe the lineup at Lourdes or at one of various blessed waterfalls in Africa attracted a crew like the one I was joining, carrying a package and the key to a locker. I was carrying the package and key because it served the purpose of my good friend and doctor, Fred, and also of Karim; and Alfonso and the police; and, it seemed, Xavier; and then there was Dan Kasdan, who had an oral contract that his former wife would not be named in any way. Not all these purposes were in any better arrangement than the purposes of the normal population of the depot.

A smell of Deep-Fried Pig Belly McNugget Slimsies advised the Vietnamese and Cambodians that this was America, get with the program, learn to eat like regular folks. A doughnut stand sold doughnuts and mysterious pale, skinless, meatlike products. Refugees making a new life couldn't be expected to know what kind of tree the McNuggets had been plucked from;

hadn't crossed the briny Pacific to choke their guts with alien stuff; didn't trust what they smelled. If Xavier was here, even his Regatta scent would be overpowered. "Kin help yew," said the hooker on the corner, an offer she repeated while her manager/trainer, Giants cap on backward, observed her technique from across the street. "Kin help yew? Hey, kin *help* yew." I gave her an A for effort—garters showing, sticklike legs, a full adolescent bosom, perished eyes; she staggered when she tried to move toward me on regulation stilt heels. I held my silvery duct-taped package tight, the key in my fist. No, lady, can't help me.

A woman I hadn't noticed (must have been distracted) touched my arm and said, "You're kind of cute in your own special way. Sir? I got lots more similar remarks if you liked that one."

The loudspeakers announced departures to sets of twin cities, paired concepts. Stockton and Denver . . . Sacramento and Eureka . . . Transcon Express. These were destinations to please the most picky patron. Muffled by tunnels, buses began the mission into the outside world with deep earthquake creakings. A salvationist screamed into a battery-powered megaphone: "You! Abandoned by the Lord! Do you have a moment to change your life?"

On track, I thought. Just now I was looking to find Karim, Xavier, and a crew of plainclothes cops, none of them in evidence. My nose was in overload; couldn't smell anyone I knew, not even Alfonso. I pushed into the waiting area. An unseen missionary with a squawk-box, licensed by Freedom of Religious Noise exemption laws, competed with official Greyhound destination announcements and his colleagues packing only a low-tech megaphone: "Join me on line with the quality Savior, brothern and sistern, Who asks whither you think you are fleeing in such a hurry with your bargain tickets . . . That's *Jee*sus, and without Him, do you think you can ever, ever, *ever* git there?"

Where I was going, I didn't need a ticket. I was like Jeff with my skate key tight in my hand. SAY HELLO TO MADAMA SOPHIA asked a sign above a former nuts-and-raisins stand. Madama Sophia, in return for this hello, would read my future in my hand. She sat nursing her baby, who, if I grasped the future correctly, would grow up to be a boy or girl. I kept the key in my hand, my package under my arm. I wished Alfonso would make himself visible. A black guy, a do-gooding peddler volunteering for the Tenderloin Self-Help Society, wore a merry row of condoms around his Bob Hope–Bing Crosby porkpie hat. "Condoms! Free rubbers! Get your free condoms now!" He was hawking them like a priest distributing hot-cross buns and paused before a pimp who said, "Yo, man, no use for them things. I got sharp sperm, they cut right through that rubber, swim right through that lube, man." Neither of them was Alfonso. "Barrels right through, man."

I didn't want to drop my load in the locker and head away. I wanted to see results. I wanted to know if Karim was there watching, if the plainclothes guys were there—maybe the plainclothes women, if Alfonso was properly looking after his buddy. I didn't feel easy with my ignorance. I stalled, still holding the package with a sense of clumsiness, as if my thumb were caught in a bottle. Something was caught and making me wince.

A person in a hurry or very careless had left a muddy Nike near Madama Sophia's mitt camp. He had gone running so fast after his fortune or his bus, been chased so imperatively by his fate, that he lightened up by one foot. Maybe it was all he had time for. Sophia had predicted he could fly if he chose to, or he was trying to flee from crack brawlers or chattering geriatrics claiming attention, leaving this shoe as guarantee that he'd be right back. I headed in where the lockers were stacked, headed through the thickness of hot pork, frying grease, used air. A drunk lurched against me, too preoccupied to demand an apology but blew his green thick gasp of liver disease into my face.

I wasn't happy here. I could do nothing about the amplified instructions crackling from the loudspeaker (another bus for Sacramento, departure imminent) and the pathless trekking of terminal wanderers. There was no way to close down my ears or my nose. Here I was, standing in front of the lockers. I found my number.

This was my lucky day. I had remembered to load my pocket with quarters. I plucked the coins from my stash, inserted the key, looked around for company. None visible; some invisible.

I dropped the quarters into the slot for number 49, as instructed. They made a parking meter music going down. The key fit. Now I didn't look around guiltily; I stared ahead guiltily and stuck the package into the locker and shut it and turned the key and that was the deal. No lightning struck me; today was still lucky. Now to get out of here.

After I'd gone twenty short steps, back toward Sophia's palm-reading outpost again, curiosity got the best of me and I turned to see an old friend, not Karim, inserting his copy of the key into lock number 49. Dressed for a safari with Ralph Lauren, with his usual lounging grace, he made no compromise with the Greyhound environment in these premises. My husband-in-law was playing funny games with me. Not Karim. Not Karim. Xavier, the early-stage divorcée's consolation. Congratulations, old chap, now we have the same beloved and duplicate keys.

"Hold it! Freeze! Hold it, hold it, hold it!"

They came from behind Sophia's mitt camp. The palm reader must have predicted they would be there since she already knew all things, past and future. They brought their palms with them, their badges, their weapons.

"Hold it guy, don't move fella, hold it!"

About a dozen of the depot-dwelling Greyhound people wearily took familiar positions, hands flat against the nearest wall, ready to be felt for guns, knives, or plastic bags of illegal substances. They looked bored to be bothered again, and then perturbed, peeking around, all their conceptions of race, color, hair style, and dress sent flying as the cops rushed the sportive, lounging, grinning, untattooed Xavier.

Xavier was entertained. A lock of hair fell becomingly across his forehead, emphasizing boyish and bemused and having a curious time of it, old chap. His scent made no effort to get through the terminal fry, dirt, and cleaning-fluid smells. He was standing with the package under his arm, ready to return to sender.

None of this seemed like normal procedure. I was wondering why Xavier didn't wait for me to get out of Greyhoundland before he used his key, why the cops were circling him as if he were dangerous prey, what Alfonso was doing here, keeping us all company. He might as well have been a tourist from Stockton with his family's Instamatic. The Greyhound folks didn't seem to want to talk about the events in our vicinity since all discussion was quieted except for the continuing drone of arrival and departure announcements. In general, cops were taking over. Xavier was happy to see everybody.

A meaty sergeant with a refrigerator bulk said, "Hand it over."

Xavier enjoyed his life. He looked me up and down, saying, "Those shoes, they promote a lot of athlete's foot, don't they, Dan? The heat, the humidity. Tend to?"

Wearing a suit, a matching jacket and pants of some sort of worsted fabric, just hanging out while he awaited an arrival, Alfonso watched from a proper distance. He was dressed for medium civilian success. The deep furrows in his forehead, skin almost folding over itself with concern, told me he was figuring something new about this whole deal. Something wasn't going how it was supposed to. He came closer. "If I may ask, may I ask what you doing here, sir?"

"You may," said Xavier.

The sergeant was pulling at the tape on the package, just

loosening it. He was planning to open it in front of witnesses.

"Visiting the bus station," said Xavier, "which is a public place, I believe, although not a public utility. The ground transportation depot, a recourse for those who prefer not to fly."

"Where's Karim?" I asked.

"Karim? Oh, *Karim.*"

It was clear now. Karim was trying me out and Xavier was here to watch my performance and for extra fun. The refrigerator sergeant nodded to his partner. Then the duct tape screamed as he ripped the top of the box, which was filled with glassine envelopes containing a white powder. It would have been cocaine if it wasn't baby powder, corn starch, powdered sugar . . .

"We're gonna take you in," the sergeant said to Xavier.

"I bet you think so. I bet you think so. I bet you want to," Xavier remarked.

"Okay, mister."

"For Dr. Scholl's? Relief for hot itchy toes?" Xavier was hugely pleased with the turning of developments, showing teeth white as teacups and, for all I know, real. Under other circumstances I could determine the answer to this question by knocking them out of his mouth.

Alfonso grumbled unnecessarily in my ear, "Foot powder, bet it is," and I didn't even need to agree, and he added, "That's part of the game sometimes." He put his hand on my arm. He didn't want to see me jumping the happy lounging fellow who stood alert and comfortable in our little group. Up close there was a new smell: a slosh of underground sewers and bus exhaust seeping through the odds against their seeping through, plus nearby Greyhound cooking and cleaning combined with the even more nearby tang of a tennis cologne.

Xavier looked to me as if he were photosensitive, a papery person-substance waiting to have interesting events printed upon him. I'm sure he was not a blank sheet to himself; as far as he was concerned, he had a soul that required aid and comfort from Priscilla, recognition from Dan Kasdan, public acknowledgment of personal distinction. In his heart of hearts he believed he had the right to all of the above.

Alfonso held tightly to my arm. As a warning. To keep me on earth and not jumping. I snapped loose and he grabbed again, hard and angry. "Try to think," he muttered. My friend Alfonso was a meat-filled restraining order I had better obey.

A band of orange-clad Hare Krishnas, all wound up and banging away, chanting away, blissed away, steered itself through the terminal like a single organism of marauding leaf-cutters. Their shaved heads and shining orange robes—a smudge of reddish grease on their foreheads—made them look alien beyond the tinny, overwhelmingly sincere, mouth-breathing chant. One of them had acquired a brown stain across his cheek. He seemed different from the others, an imperfect earth being, growing along with his birthmark, evolving through time, the bearer of a scaly crust due to fungus, sun exposure, or parental flaws on delicate Celtic skin.

Behind the Hare Krishnas stood a large man in a white linen suit, shoulder pads, generous tailoring, with dark eyes seeming to be augmented with eyeliner, saying, "So now, my friend, is this what you want?"

"That's it."

"Nothing, and you have it now?"

"That's my program, Karim."

He bowed his head a little. It was a moment for him to seek out his own privacy. Then he raised his face toward mine and the smile was full of joy. He offered to share his pleasure with me. "I'm not even offended, Dan," he said.

"Couldn't resist though, could you?"

"I was sincere," Karim said. "You are still learning the benefits."

When he lowered his head again, I could see a shiny pink bald spot like a scar amid ample surrounding fur. Sharp teeth glinted in his smile as if a morsel were stuck there he still wanted to share with me. His mouth was strange, smiling, not smiling. Whatever further thoughts he had, they would not be offered at this time. I may have lost my chance with him. He really liked me, he had contempt for me; it was up to me to sort things out if I could. Karim was disappointed that our friendship was coming to this.

Alfonso cleared his throat; hated to interrupt. "You too," he said to Karim. "I think Captain Nolan wants you to trot along to the station house. This is Captain Nolan."

The man in uniform, as thick in the waist as Alfonso, stood spraddle-legged in front of Karim.

"I cannot believe you need me. I have another appointment."

Captain Nolan did a slow stare. He had not achieved his rank by repartee. "I've got a pair of handcuffs here," he said. "Do I have to use them?"

Karim lifted his shoulders toward me—see what trouble he put himself to on my behalf?—and strolled off with the captain, leaving Alfonso and me standing alone together with not much to say. I could see Xavier lounging in a blue-and-white, having an experience in the no-parking zone. I was checking down the menu of possibilities and options and finding nothing more here in the Greyhound terminal I really wanted. Xavier waved at me; still enjoying his experience. Alfonso grinned. This wasn't what we had planned. "Now everybody happy?" he asked.

Part Four

Chapter 22

Much of my recent work experience had consisted in not working for Karim. This didn't pay the bills; working for him might. But if not working for him was so much trouble, employment might be worse. I wasn't ready to take a retainer from Karim Abdullah or Xavier, his semi-silent partner.

I needed to keep events registered with Alfonso; elementary prudence. Then I needed to let Karim know events were registered. He was still playing his Karim games with me during these not very busy times, proving that he lived on a plane above that of, say, mortals. It was occupied by avoiding, side-stepping, ducking, weaving during a slack period in the PI freelance trade. By now his hint about paperwork trouble with PI licensing in Sacramento was adequately discounted. Good sense would tell him not to bother. After our Greyhound morning together, he knew I had protection and he didn't like trouble, either. Karim's life wasn't about trouble. Home free.

I sat in Alfonso's office while he rested his feet on the desk during a call to Trenton. He was saying into the phone, "Much oblige, much oblige. Much oblige." Then he turned to me without explaining about the call and said, "Yeah. Listening. Go on."

I wasn't sure about going on.

"Karim," he said. "I heard you. Goddamn, let's just get to it."

He would soon be finished with the grit and stink of this San Francisco Police Department office. After returning from

Trenton—"about my kid" was how he put it—he looked into his pension benefits. He was taking retirement a year or two ahead of time. At his rank, he could have waited, but he was starting work for the Pinkertons instead. Since all life had changed, Alfonso decided to change his life, too.

"This isn't a good time for you," I said.

"Shut up."

"My problem can wait," I said.

We sat there among the smells of disturbance, dust, papers, angry men. "No, it can't," he said. "I'll tell you what. I got your problem in the computer, but that's all I can do right now. Yeah, and Terrence knows, down at Central. How about we grab a bite tonight?"

Since he got back from Trenton, Alfonso was getting fatter, downing his barbecue or his Korean pork with kimchee and a cranky glare, stuffing himself for a reason beyond a need to lay on inventory in the ass and shoulders. I said, "Hey, let's do something else besides eat," and he looked at me, still cranky, chewing a toothpick, and asked, "What else is there?" I didn't think he'd want to hike on Mount Tam; not the type. Maybe a movie, but he didn't want that, either, even with the popcorn bucket and don't spare the butter. A sociable visit to Janey and her pony at the Medal of Honor—no. Major drinking might work out for him, but I didn't see it as a big help. Getting on with our routine of stuffing the gut seemed to be what he had in mind.

"So what do you say?"

"Alfonso—"

He stood up and I stood up. I wanted to tell him something about his son. I think he wanted to tell me something, too.

His phone was ringing. "I'll pick you up," he said, "get outta here," and turned to the phone.

I stood waiting outside Poorman's Cottage because he said he would roll on by, slow down and open the car door, didn't want

to see the mess I was no doubt living in; and since he was buying, he would pick the place where we might eat, might drink,
might pursue the little hints and jostles I was putting out.
"Course, we been hinting and jostling a whole long time," the
oozing caramel voice of Alfonso intoned over the phone.

"Do I have to hear a lecture?"

"You take your chance on that," he said.

I stood on the crumbling pavement and breathed the air.
The Potrero Hill butcher smell was gone with end-of-day wind;
early-evening thermal inversion was bringing in the usual wash
of sea damp and fog wisps. Kids from the Projects were playing some kind of beer-can hockey in the last daylight in the
street down the hill from me, but they kept stopping and pointing my way, probably a nervous habit picked up from running
illicit medicines for their dads, live-in uncles, and big brothers
temporarily out of jail. When they saw Alfonso, they scattered
in every direction, leaving the evidence behind—a crushed
beer can.

I climbed in. There was a smell on the front seat of wrap-
ping from some of yesterday's bag lunch. I could also smell
advice coming on. At least Alfonso had not replaced Mingus;
animal companions didn't do it for me, either. As he drove,
keeping that wary cop eye on the street, he paused and looked
longingly at the Thai Barbecue near the corner of Missouri and
Eighteenth. The oysters, the rice, the cute thing done with
strong coffee, cream, and sugar, iced, in a tall skinny glass. "Always remember where this must be," he said, " 'cause Missouri
loves company."

Ha-ha.

"Here, get out." It was some kind of Filipino joint on city
patronage landfill near the barge and houseboat encampment
beyond the Fourth Street Bridge. There was a garden. There
was blowing sand. For the pleasure of Alfonso there was a settling down for a South Pacific fried grease feast. I tried to tell
him about cultures over there that take to burying pigs in the

ground, building bonfires over the grave, and then eating what they dig up with many a lick, spit, and grunt and maybe twigs through their noses. But he wasn't going to let me get off with anthropology gossip; he had an agenda for the night.

"Bein' in the civil offense line," he began, having given his order, "you're not used to so many offenders in my own idea of offense—my department, I mostly deal with legal offenders, criminal justice system type. What you are mostly, your line generally, is civil offender."

I might as well spread my cheeks and let him search me. He seemed to have prepared this tangled little speech. I didn't see how it was any help.

"You know what I'm saying," he said. "Not on top of the situation is where you are not."

"What do you want to do about it?"

"You're asking me? Suppose I ask you what to do about my own kid, my prostate, weight problem, how you feel? We got most of an order of lumpia too much—want it to go? . . . It be your job to tell me, supposedly a grown man, how to cut the crap and get on with the rest of my life? You want some golden-ager senior kindergarten counseling, brother? From me? Get real. You hear what I'm saying?"

I stared. I tried to feel sorry for this good cop hanging out with a known civil offender. It would be a relief from feeling sorry for my own lonesome legal self, wouldn't it?

"Better," said Alfonso, and he poked me. "I saw a glimmer across your face."

"I don't eat that stuff out of the microwave. I don't know how you can."

He sighed. "Subject ain't my dining habits," he said, and stared longingly at the lumpia oozing and seeping oil all over itself. "Hey, maybe you glad about not having the responsibility no more? Live a little poorer, okay, pay the child support, feel sad for yourself—but don't have to please the lady? That spell relief? A little, hey?"

He continued staring shrewdly, pig-eyed, wrong but meaning to be wrong, my wrong pig-eyed pal. Knew I didn't want to duck out on this one, not Priscilla, not Jeff. Giving me a shot of adrenaline, I guess, for conversation's sake.

He wasn't allowing me to talk about his son; wouldn't permit it. He wasn't allowing me to ask about Alfonso; didn't let it happen. I knew enough not to push him. I wondered if my friend in his cunning was using his grief to make me feel shame. I was specializing too much in my own sorrows, and for one reason only—they were mine.

"Get set, ready, *go*," he said. "Eat." He sure could scarf the family-style South Pacific dishes with his delicate absorbent little Japanese chopsticks—carried sets of them like toothpicks in his jacket pockets for emergency chowing down—sharpening them first and getting rid of the slivers by rubbing them together. Hungry. And then he'd go ahead to some fancy Italian coffee place, a "caffé," and have a creamy, sugary, mortal tiramisu, some new edible spansule for filling the arteries with goo. But the chopsticks still in his pockets, just in case, like the toothbrushes and the condoms.

"Coffee?" he asked. "You ain't uttering much in the reply mode, are you? Coffee's good, suppose to be, for the blues. You might could use some blues medicine."

"You need your dessert."

"Cutting down on the drinking, so I do tend to like the sweet stuff. Say what, there's compensation everywhere you look. Hey—can I help?"

"You do," I said, my throat constricted. "You do."

Alfonso's inappropriate laugh rumbled from deep in his belly. "That's a good sign, pal."

Appropriate laughter, the usual from Alfonso. It was okay. Something's got to be okay. *Hey—can I help?* He had caught me by surprise with that one.

He wanted to get back to normal buddy bullshit before we were both embarrassed. Words tended to ooze easily out of Alfonso's rumbling belly. The program was to get by and enjoy a little holiday every day. Over the years he had learned a thing or two, how to handle chopsticks, for example, even the washable Chinese plastic ones that let the chicken and noodles slide onto the shirt or lap. In the course of chopstick training he had developed certain experienced-older-guy tricks. Ate Tommy Toy's Chinese with his own little disposable porous genuinewood Japanese tools, the sweet-and-sour dishes, the slimy noodle dishes, the oily MSG dishes, the shrimps, the scallops, the many, many Chinese mushrooms. The mu shu pork he rolled into papery folded crepes like a San Francisco pro, truly a gourmet with other resources in his repertory besides mere ribs, rice, and fries.

"Back off," he was saying. "Here's my advice. Move, keep your hands in front of you, watch where you're going, not where you been."

"Am I under some kind of arrest?"

Suddenly he waved gleefully, using both hands. Whew. Waving away his burp, waving it off. His tongue was purplish, like his palms. Food and drink were not the real celebrants here. It was the gathered years. A little extra wiggle in the thighs and arms came with the times. He was trying to be a happy mortal man. Alfonso had no quarrel with the personal inevitabilities. Globules and corpuscles could set forth to rove beyond the digestive tract. Muscles might even go into hiding, although he knew they weren't yet ready to disappear into the great chain of nonbeing. Disappearance would come in due course, the uprooting of the trunk. In the meantime, better a happy tub of gut than a wired complainer.

"Hate to get personal, man."

"Go ahead."

"You perpetrate, man, that's okay, but you know what? Some people learn. You keep on doing it."

"I can't help myself."

"They all say that. We call it, used to, recidivism, pal. That's for kids with lots of time. Not you."

"What's for me?"

He was thinking of his son. I was sure of that. "That's for them," he said.

"What's for me?"

"Try to enjoy. At our stage that's what we got to use ourselves for."

He gave me a full dose of late-middle-aged, high-IQ, ethnic-racial barbecue hospitality, covering the check with his paw. He was buying. Priscilla was right. It's good to have at least one friend who understands when you're down and you need to be treated as if you're down. For dessert we didn't go for the key lime pie; we had another couple beers.

Since he had filled out his retirement form, no more fitness standards to meet, many ethnic barbecues were having their way with Alfonso's thighs, ass, belly, chins, but he could still move fast when he wanted to, especially his tongue. As a Pinkerton consultant, minority hire, he figured that they liked everything about him, including his heft—additional evidence of minority preference. He had gotten comfortable and could recommend it. He dipped his finger into the bleeding, mahogany sweet-and-sour sauce, licked it, and commented, "You're going under"—sometimes a merciless tongue—"*not.*" He contributed a wheezy growl for emphasis. "Trying to go under, which is worse. Telling yourself how miserable you are."

"I guess that's self-pity."

"You said it, I didn't."

"That's what it's called."

He sighed. "You're still mixed up with that wife. A Boy in Love."

"That's not prohibited, Alfonso."

"No. But Jesus, you *admit* it."

In this barbecue courtroom I felt like the defendant, the

one with the long hair and the tattoos. Alfonso decided to take a little enjoyment, sucking on a rib. Regretfully he put down the bone. "It's called boring is what it's called," he said.

Was this the discourse Priscilla envied among male buddies? She was right to do so. His nagging made me feel better or at least alive, part of the world's shared noise. Alfonso shrugged and made an ethical, moral, psychological, and therapeutic decision to let go another of the wet burps he generated through the greedy sucking of clotted grease inappropriate to our arteries. He didn't intend to hold anything back. He was sore at me and that relaxed an experienced cop.

"Upside the head you toxic, man, y'unnastan what I'm sayin'?"

"Come off it, Alfonso."

"Okay, miserable's your job. But you do it overtime, you hear me now? How about some dining or some Q tomorrow?"

"It's too early to be hungry already for tomorrow. I can't think about tomorrow's eats."

Alfonso looked astonished. "I'm always thinking about it these days. You like Mongolian beef? Sounds kind of naked, but then again it ain't. You don't think about it? Usually Q or Chinese from the carton, I might be in a hurry, or that other stuff, dining, *cuisine* they call it, this being San Francisco. If I got plenty of time. I got to get you off your subject, buddy—think about it."

"Thanks a lot, Alfonso."

"I got the time. So how's about some *cuisine* then?"

I smelled grass, new grass, and then I saw tufts stuck to his black high-top cop shoes. Even as a Pinkerton, he was still involved in investigations. I wanted to smile because I deserved congratulations, my nose working all right, smelling tufts of new grass, and my brain, adjacent to the nose, coming to conclusions about it.

"So?" he was asking. "Cat got your appetite? . . . Why not

try to feel good about yourself, it's the latest thing." He stared, bug-eyed and angry with foiled friendship.

I thought I saw my chance to get to him in the way he wasn't letting me. There weren't any words and words were all we had.

"Alfonso, what can I do—I know this doesn't help—about your troubles?"

"My troubles are over."

"Come on, pal—"

"I said it's over. He's dead. That's it."

I started to speak but all I managed was a breath before he stopped me.

"Wanna be my pal . . . *pal?* Okay, I'm dealing with it and you can deal with it. It's over. Just let it be."

He bent to the littered paper plate. I kept the peace. I wondered if this silence was anything like standing graveside in prayer. Neither Alfonso nor I knew much about such things.

He let us both off the hook a little, he cut us down, he allowed that I had spoken to him. "Funny how misery can put you at the center of the world," he said, "all by yourself there, but then turns out it's a crowded place."

Okay. That was a lot from Alfonso. I don't know if I or anyone could be lucky for him, but how lucky I was in life with this friend, fresh tufts of grass on his shoes, no dogshit in evidence on this occasion. He had a further question for the defendant: "You still like to perform, don't you?"

"Perform?"

He was embarrassed. When he blushed, there was a purplish color across his cheeks. "You know. Down there."

I scrunched up my face, not even pretending to smile. "It's not a performance."

Alfonso sighed, rumbled, groaned. "I know. When it's with her, it's not an act. I know the feeling I'm sure you think you got. That feeling when you're there with the woman, dark warm busy place, it's not a test, not acting, performing, but you remember everything about being together and explosions happen behind your nose in your head when you're remembering . . ."

He made it sound like a sneeze, but Alfonso really did know the difference. Normally he wouldn't let on, probably wouldn't let himself go through that thing, that process, field of traps, festival of disasters—*love*—again. To him I was living proof that his own procedures were the correct ones. But just because he was now immune to my disease, it didn't stop the steady flow of consolation. "When you're remembering how it was and how you think it always gonna be."

I don't have a very good memory, dear . . .

"What?" Alfonso asked. "You still here?"

"I've known you for a long time."

"Yeah, you were the same guy I enjoyed different things with."

"Now I'm different," I said.

"You think that's good? Different if you got to, but find a better way, okay? That's the short version."

I waited. He didn't say anything. "So?" I asked.

"Okay, here's the long version. There's always a risk. You might get old, tired, pass on over. I guess we better look at that possibility. But my way of thinking is, there's no hurry, okay, just no hurry, you understand what I'm saying? *No hurry.*"

Outside, bouncing off the cast-iron Fourth Street Bridge, came the high insect whine of a motor scooter, someone back from his vacation with a new toy. There was a stretch limousine with smoked windows, high school splurgers trying to act like rock stars, the eighteen-year-old version of the thirteen-year-old playing air guitar. There was the city straining at its seams in roadways against the moat of the San Francisco Bay and its estuaries. We'd all been here awhile now.

As Alfonso drove, he was saying, "Me personally, tell you what. Don't want to perform no more, that's a fact. I did my ex in Trenton that one day a couple weeks ago—now I don't want to no more. She did me, was how it went. Thought we didn't like each other."

"I know how that is."

"No you don't. Kid gone. Kid gone."

"What else, Alfonso?"

"You're home. So get out this vehicle."

Chapter 23

I wakened to a general stickiness and heaviness in the eyes. When I stood, I lost my balance and lunged against the wall. Motes floated in the air. My shoulder hurt and I thought, Is this a heart attack?

Then the dizziness subsided. Oh, it's nothing, just getting old. Transparent fish swam across my sight. I watched them in all their slow grace. Not a heart attack, not a stroke, only what it is—clumsiness. I'm an older person. Nothing more. So that's settled.

Having dealt with this trivial circulatory system matter, I wondered why there was a young woman's name I couldn't remember and also couldn't remember why a vague message about her had sparked in my head. It hadn't quite gotten through. Why anyway did I need to remember her name? (Green eyes, black hair, liked to play squash, wore cutoffs and an Ektelon T-shirt—not Cynthia, not Linda, something else.) Of course, not remembering the name of a squash partner twice a week, sex partner on her birthday once when she had broken up with a lover whose name I really didn't have to keep in the meat computer file (better squash player at the Bay Club), all these missing puzzle bits are not proof of Alzheimer's disease. They're only a sign of memory loss. They merely indicate the meat computer gets overloaded. However, when someone asks my name and I look in my wallet for my driver's license, that will be evidence to be taken seriously, unless I can excuse myself by claiming it only means I've had a few strokes, just a couple cerebral accidents, mere fender-benders.

Not dizzy anymore, but the legs felt heavy as I headed for the bathroom with sticky, heavy-lidded eyes. Not wonderful balance.

One hundred; ninety-three; eighty-six. I tested myself for Alzheimer's by counting backward by sevens. Seventy-nine. Seventy-two. Okay so far. My brain may not have permanent tenure, but I can still find sixty-five, fifty-eight. Is that okay so far?

I peered into the mirror. Sticky conjunctiva, burdened lids—happens to eyes. The crease to the left and right of them seemed only a little deeper—I must be smiling, for these are called smile lines—but the eyeballs were mottled red, with bits of yellow muck oozing from the lids and sharp dried conjunctival bits in the corners, clinging to the lashes. Thinner lashes. Oh well, hot soaked cloth should take care of this, and baby shampoo swabbed across the eyelids, or some neopenicillin prescription if the body's immune system didn't rally to the rescue. Supposedly there are mites, almost invisible mouthy worms, clinging to the eyelashes and sometimes they go hog wild, taking over and eating hairs, generating mite spit, littering what had once seemed fresh and relatively clean in the center of my face. The mirror of the soul was greasy with mite dumps.

Makes a person feel out of whack, trivial as it is. I've noticed that some psychopathic street people also have conjunctival eyes, but some don't, so there's no rule about it. I began to suspect myself of wearing that peaceful-old-man's slight smile, ingratiating and accepting, of continual mild depression. I was smiling too much at nothing. I was too welcoming. I wasn't expecting anything good for myself.

A panhandler ambled, unsure, toward me on Polk Street, his hand with the Styrofoam cup outstretched but not fully operational. His mottled, gray-bearded chin waggled toward mine.

His conjunctival eyes tried to blink some moisture on the seeing parts. He asked: "Are you one of them or one of us?"

I gave him a quarter.

"One of *them* gives us a dollar," he called after me, and let the coin roll into the street where someone could pick it up for use in a parking meter. Since he didn't have a vehicle, he needed folding money for mental transportation by Thunderbird sugared wine or amplified malt beverage.

Rejection by a wife seems almost normal, part of doing business in this ragged end of the century, but being put down by a homeless alcoholic was an insult. My pride wouldn't let me run after him, waving dollars, though he might have been gracious about it. I didn't want to risk further reproach.

My balance on earth is what dancing is all about, and my best memory of dancing is jumping out of an airplane, suspended by a military parachute, coming down fast with a pack on my back, high boots laced up, murder in my heart and the wind hiding the smells and sounds of hostile fire. If you landed in a tree, it would hurt. If you rolled the wrong way, you could break your back. Once, in a practice jump, I sprained an ankle and they followed the wartime practice of the period—morphine it, tape it, and now back to duty, soldier.

Occasionally, years later, I get a twinge in that ankle and remember it's okay, but history marks the body throughout and inexorably. And it's only a twinge of weakness, not a fall or break. I can still run, jump, walk, though I hate to look down from high places. More accurately, I don't mind at all, but my stomach lurches and I get a sick taste in my mouth. When Priscilla said she no longer loved me, it was like looking down from a high place onto the distant earth and falling, falling, dying.

Maybe this occasional totter when I walk is only a touch of brain tumor. After an extra dose of coffee, or one of those good night's sleeps that come out of the past like a visit from an old lover lady, or a day with scudding clouds and clean winds, or just some unmeasured, unmotivated, unnatural good feeling that surges through for no good reason, I like to stride and stretch my skeleton in fast hiking. The sleepy tottering is concealed. As long as I don't see a mirror I'm twenty-two years old again, a paratrooper vain about his boots and his just rages.

I was running for the Polk-19 bus, down between Geary and Post, and I remembered running off the bus a few years ago, the bus down Columbus, when I spied Priscilla with her long stride, Jeff alertly bobbing in the pack on her back. *Let me go, let me go, that's my wife.*

Okay, maybe I'll not fight the totter if I'm tired or sad. Maybe I'll give up to nostalgia, what was, what I think was, what might have been. I'll need my nap and blink awhile at the pocked ceiling before I can rise from regret once more. Oh Lord, let me continue to walk in the world; if I have to die, let me die running.

We were sitting in the kitchen where Priscilla and I had often had our most interesting conversations, good or bad, and this was one of them. I wasn't sure which category it would come to belong in, but I had an inkling. She was curious about the deal with Karim and how it all came down, this bus terminal transfer of athlete's foot remedy. Sweetly she inquired, "Willing to be a snitch?"

"That's not what it was."

"Maybe I don't understand these things, the menace of drugs in the fabric of Western civilization, outraged citizen private eye only doing what's right on behalf of the common weal. So you're not a snitch, not even Accessory to Snitch, you're just a cool professional, dear?"

"It may seem simple to you."

"On the contrary. But in the interest of full disclosure—" She took my hand, tugged a little, and led me into the sunny front room.

No immediate full explanation was required. For the moment I was engaged in registering Priscilla's uncharacteristically silent visitor. Karim sat there in one of his nice tropical-weight linen suits, silk tie, topcoat draped, smiling reassuringly, nodding happily, offering a heavy little lurch forward in the chair in order to get up to greet me if this seemed called for.

"You know we're friends," Priscilla said. "You know I like the idea of broadening my horizons."

"Friends," said Karim with emphasis. "Like you and me, Dan."

That's so important these days. But I didn't say this aloud. Karim kept smiling and smiling, wearing me down. He really wanted to be a winner when he started to play.

"That's so important these days"—but when I finally spoke, Priscilla and Karim glanced at each other, not sure what I was referring to after my period of silent thought.

Usually first impressions decide whether I'm going to like a person or not. In Karim's case, it had been not; but then there were second and third impressions, and now this, and I could see why he had won Priscilla over. The man took pleasure in his life as a man should. He saw something in me that I might want to find in myself. Since other procedures were lonely, turned out lonely, I was considering the example Priscilla was pressing on me. *Hey Karim, it's kind of lively in your vicinity.*

From where he sat, defenseless in an armchair, natty and at ease and contentedly defenseless, he fixed me with the eye-linered eyes and waggled his heavy head. "I have been explaining, my friend, and to persuade. That has been my intention. Perhaps now you concur. Pris-ceela understands and so must you. This is America, which gives rewards for good work."

The man doesn't give up. "Sometimes," I said.

"But oh, my friend, you have been difficult in your time of troubles."

"That's always my way."

"Change your way, my friend. Such is my mission."

I didn't thank him for his example, his devotion to mission. Perhaps I should have thanked Priscilla.

She joined the party. "Everyone can see, dear, and especially I can see, how stubborn you are in your own really bullheaded way . . . Well, you were even motivated to the point of middle-aged fisticuffs. I hate to use the word 'jealous,' Dan."

"You can use it."

"Dear man. Xavier was a *visa*, that's all. You know what that means?"

Karim stood up, saying, "Thank you, thank you, I really must—thank you so much."

Time to go, time to go; he was still smiling and shaking his head, seeming to have accomplished something; waved at the door, Priscilla not accompanying him; and then he was gone. Discreet Karim, friend of the family.

Priscilla listened to his receding footsteps and then said again, "Visa. I don't need it anymore. I let the visa expire. Hey, you ought to believe me. I still like you a lot and he's just an expired . . . Dan?"

"What?"

"Pay attention." When Priscilla turned sarcastic, or turned to justifying or explaining herself, she knew she was in trouble. Her clear blue stare would have been beseeching in another woman. Sometimes the only way she could make herself clear, since words only confused matters, was by making love. "I said I still like you a lot. Believe me when I say something."

Chapter 24

If she comes back to me, I agree. If she doesn't, I also agree. I try to be a civilized individual. The smell of tennis shoes reminds me of flowers; the smell of composted weeds in the bin behind my cottage reminds me of tennis shoes. A truly civilized individual would understand that she's not coming back to me, and I do not so understand. I make do with composted flowers and old tennis shoes, exercising the part of the brain that picks out the good smells, not good sense.

Being herself kept Priscilla busy, fully occupied with the day when awake and actively realigning flesh, soul, and dream anticipation when asleep, making her way through the rhythms of the world, metabolizing herself like a healthy animal. I wanted to branch into that electricity, that directional beam; it seemed like a miracle to a person whose brain was mostly an olfactory registration device.

Life was more peaceful now. I hung on. I liked my nest, my lair, Poorman's Cottage. Like a good householder, I swept it out regularly. How noticeably convenient it was to awaken after a bad night's sleep, dreams of loss, sometimes spiteful dreams, and then to get busy distancing myself from them with a relaxing hour immersed in the newspaper and wars, fires, famines, crimes, the world's general pain. I climbed into the newspaper like a warm bath. I learned to use a better grade of coffee at breakfast—Yuban instant—because it almost tasted like good coffee. I swept the twigs, leaves, dust, and animal droppings from my front steps, catching slivers in the broom. Someday I might buy tools and wood and replace those steps myself; someday maybe. I had plans for the future. I was enjoying the San Francisco autumn, which burst upon Potrero Hill with sudden dry heat before the winter fog and shortened days came to town.

It would be wrong to complain. Clutching the coffee mug in my hands, I stare like a raccoon at the prospect of the day, and yawn like a fish, and in general lose myself in the recesses of beast mind, at one with immensity and chaos. Since the universe is crowded with the past, I am not at one with reality or myself, I'm only trying, getting along.

A kid from the Projects is playing war, crawling through the grass up the hill toward me. I go to the window, careful to show myself, taking aim with an imaginary weapon, peppering him with shots.

He rises, laughing, and spectacularly falls dead, his body jerking from the automatic fire. I applaud. He rises again and bows graciously, then trudges back to the Projects. His nightmare universe is also crowded with dreams. I put down my weapon.

I carry my cup outside; drink the last sips of Yuban Almost-Good Instant in the sunlight, blinking, violating the ophthalmologist's rule to wear sunglasses always. Nearby there is latex sex litter dripping from bushes. Unless the raccoons are taking up birth control, some of the Project kids must be inviting their girlfriends out for a stroll. But the girls don't seem to prowl; it's boys I see staring at me, sometimes their noses to my windows while I'm reading, peeing, or at the refrigerator drinking orange juice from the carton. Evidently they think I'm too dim-eyed to see out.

Little do they know, peeking at the slouched grizzled old white guy, that I take reasonable care of the machinery. It wouldn't be right to be forever young, packaged by weight training, vitamins, and plastic surgery, grinning tightly, littering up the earth. I've come to like crisped leaves, dark-edged petals, strong smells of fallen rinds, even dead raccoons on my hillside. They gradually fade into the hill, eaten inside and out by ants, rats, and squirming maggots, while the Project kids and I, too, make a wise circle around them in our roamings; we stop and stare first. I could—not a bad option—leave my body on a hillside to filter back into soil, sifting through the digestive system of other creatures. A body is only rank for a little while, until the weather and those other bodies finish working at it.

As my friends begin to die, or grow old, die a little, I am angry with them, as if the same thing isn't happening to me. I look at Alfonso, that terrific pal, the very best, and want to hit his swelling sagging belly, kick him in that drag-ass behind with heavy thighs flopping in thick pants. Retired from the police now, he thinks he has the right to a pensioner's indulgence; cops quit too young. Part-time work as a security consultant to the Pinkertons—black men didn't used to do this kind of experting—means he doesn't have to conform to weight requirements. It's not the rules that are uptight; it's Dan Kasdan, who is not fat but skinny—that's another way age takes a man. Muscle not turning to rubber; going to gristle. I have no right to resent others.

"Man, you wasn't my friend, I wouldn't want to hang with you," Alfonso said. "What happened to not giving a fuck? You used to know how. Learn some survival skill, man."

"If I'm not fun anymore—" I said.

"Okay, I'm your watchdog now, so I get to bark whenever I think of it."

He still liked to nag me about Xavier. He knew Xavier made no difference about anything important, and knew I knew it. Whatever pleasure there used to be in remembering one stupid swing of my fist had been used up.

"Hey, look at you, inspiration to a boy like me," Alfonso said. "Someday I'm gonna retire all the way, smell the bees, whatever it is you do."

"I'm not retired."

My pal the police detective and Pinkerton consultant just stared with big wet eyes. Patted his tummy. Eased himself into the too-small chair in my kitchen. "No, not retired," he said. "Just not working anymore. You nursing some kind of breakdown?"

"Eligible for Social Security, officer."

He took that in. He gave it a long think. His chest rose and fell in the too-tight shirts he wore, not because he liked tight shirts but because they just tightened up on him. My buddy the police detective emeritus was taking on the weight of an old athlete with good appetite for beer, fried potatoes, and after-shift sociability. He wasn't in a terrible hurry to compare himself favorably with his friend the divorced father in Poorman's Cottage.

"Pension time roll around, I might could finish my degree at Lincoln University, be eligible to drive a cab like the other night-school lawyers."

"Hire out as a private investigator, solo practitioner, like me."

"Maybe. But one thing I'll tell you, buddy. Not like you."

I wake and listen to the rain ticking against the window. I must be asleep, I think. No, there's a slow soaking in gusts that send scattered drops like pellets against the side of Poorman's Cottage. Just now it's coming from the east; then the wind turns, the ticking ceases, the walls yield and relax under it. Rain, wind, a steady winter downpour—the drought has stopped.

I go to the door and look out. Potrero Hill is gleaming in the dark. Reassured, I lie back down, sleep suddenly, and when I wake, wonder if I dreamed all this, which I didn't. Maybe my night prowling was not about Priscilla, about loneliness, about growing older; it was only about needing to confirm the rain ticking at my window, turning in the wind, bending the walls.

In the morning, a troop of gulls fetches in the air like infantry, ungull-like, bewildered by bayside city smells. They are sea creatures, marines, not land soldiers; normally quite good at what they do. They know most of the world is water, but adventure and hunger urge them to explore the land. Sometimes they're willing to dine on garbage deep in the city, just like human beings.

Dammit if I was going to feel sorry for gulls awking about, cawing, dropping feathers that needed a little dip in salt to feel just right. I was ready to make a treaty with nature. I wouldn't ask the gulls (or the raccoons, the Scotch broom, or the evil-eyed kids from the Projects) to feel sorry for me and I wouldn't feel sorry for them.

My present ambition: not to feel sorry for myself, either. That would complete the cycle.

In a year or two I might try myself on Xavier with the longing gaze and pretty hair; first my apology, then he might say he too was sorry; then the heart-to-heart talk. Just now the notion made my stomach churn. The urge to throw up means that fellow feeling for Xavier, even if he was jilted in his turn, isn't ripe yet. Just now I wasn't pushing for more sympathy, insight, brotherly feeling, or compassion than what came naturally to my heart. It wasn't much. Just now I still thought Xavier was a rotten asshole with hopes and dreams like every other needy creature. Zen peace of mind only took me so far. I appreciated the gulls in their swooping and scavenging.

Sometimes in winter, standing in the doorway to catch the weak sunlight, I can see the light soapy film of snow on the hills around the bay. That's about it for winter around here, although a couple of years there was actual snow on Twin Peaks, crackles of frosted water in the road that lasted an hour or two in the morning. If the town ever really froze, cars, people, and the unprepared raccoons whooping on their paws would just slide into the ocean—back into the ocean. For winter colors, about the closest I see is the dusty green of weeds, sparkles of dew pretending to be ice. That's not much winter.

Even in January, the sun barrels down on Potrero Hill. Nighttimes, there's the fog, Project kids lurking, a few whispery animals on undeveloped raw slopes. Abandoned tires do their best at the abandoned-tire task of growing mosquitoes by gathering water for the incubation season.

I like to sit outside in the sun. I prop a Goodwill kitchen chair against the warmed siding. If I can't smell the fennel from here, I trot around a little, trampling Sotch broom. When I sit long enough, I discover butterflies in the air, hummingbirds, invisible mites made visible as I wait there blinking, hands around the mug of instant. My blood pressure descends, ringing a little chime when it hits a number that ends in zero. Down the hill a way, in the shade of the next cottage, an ailanthus grows, tree of heaven. I feel my blood pressure definitely sliding, teeth recalcifying, cataracts clearing, and because it's peaceful and nice, my heart bleeds with longing and at the same time heals, seals the insult to proper thumping because that's how an optimistic metabolism works. Winter things are buzzing and blooming out here, sun nice on my neck as I turn; it's steadily rotting and garish, this untended junk garden of the good herbs and bad tires. Gradually Goodyear melts back into the sandy alluvial soil of Potrero Hill.

I pick a blackberry. It's not sweet, it's sour. That's okay, it's a blackberry and still growing. If I wait for it to sweeten, the gulls will get it. They're greedy and foolish, but they know enough to wait. I don't.

I shouldn't be looking at the sky for a carrier pigeon to bring me a message; the breed is extinct. A gull heading across the hill with wings spread and lofting might drop an invitation from Karim on my head, and why not accept it? Changing my luck would be a reasonable procedure. Karim was a faithful lover. I had tried other procedures; maybe it was time to try being an employee. Alfonso also practiced being easy and comfortable, and then he lost what mattered. Nothing can be counted on. I could start over in trouble like a kid with jolly Karim's enterprises and turn out to be a winner after all.

Let me think about it. Give me a few more years.

I bite the fennel and get the smell of licorice. I think of Jeff across town. Saturday I'll take him to the Exploratorium. Jeff, let me put my hand on your shoulder, don't be embarrassed.

I don't have to think about Priscilla, I never stop. Gulls are swooping overhead and I know they aren't vultures because vultures would circle, waiting; gulls have no real patience. As far as I'm concerned, the universe is still okay. She took my arm as if she loved me.